I0621879

ABSENCE
OF MERCY

By Joe McCoubrey

Copyright

Copyright © Joe McCoubrey 2013
ISBN: 9780957696570
Publisher: Inishfree Communications

A CIP catalogue for this book is available from the British Library.

Dedication & Thanks

To my dear sisters, Betty and Anne, and to my beautiful niece, Kellyanne, who have gone on ahead.

Thanks are also due to fellow Irish author, Brad Fleming, and to my first editor, Colin Crichton, for helping me on the path to writing.

My heartfelt appreciation goes to my editing team of Mick Keane, Brad Fleming, and Martin Graham for putting a much-needed final polish on the manuscript.

I am lucky to have four important women, and four incredibly special young men, in my life. This book is dedicated to Teresa, Brenda, Lynda and Lisa, and the next generation, Alfie, Rory, Ellis and Michael

About the Author

Joe McCoubrey is a former journalist who reported first-hand the height of the Northern Ireland "Troubles" throughout the 1970's and 1980's, firstly as a local newspaper editor, and then as a partner in an agency supplying copy to national newspapers and broadcasters. He switched careers to help start a Local Enterprise Agency, providing advice and support to budding entrepreneurs in his native town, and became its full-time CEO. He retired to concentrate on his long-time ambition to be a full-time writer. His previous novels have all been published to critical acclaim.

He lives in Downpatrick, County Down, and is proud of its historic connections to Saint Patrick, Ireland's Patron Saint.

Also available by Joe McCoubrey:
Quinn2 – No place to hide
Quinn – Thirst for Justice
Spent Force
Exposure to Truth
Absence of Rules
Someone Has To Pay
Death by Licence

Chapter 1

DAVE CARPENTER KNEW he was dying.

For the past five minutes he had tried to convince himself that he would be one of the lucky ones. He knew better than most that no two shootings were the same. Just because you get shot doesn't mean it has to be fatal.

Jeez, who am I kidding!

Carpenter slowly worked his fogged brain around to the realisation that no-one got to walk away from the effects of a .44 Magnum fired at near point blank range - okay, it was twenty yards away, but that's about the same as twenty inches for any other handgun.

Why am I even thinking like this?

As he lay on the concrete apron of a deserted airport hangar, squinting against the harsh mid-afternoon sun, he could feel the blood pooling under his back. It had been like that for some time now, though he had lost track of how long he had been stretched out, helpless and immobile.

He tried to think of Clare. He wanted his last moments to be filled with her images, but he couldn't bring a picture forward from the recesses of his mind. He knew his recall was being blocked by anger, but he couldn't fight it down.

How did the fucker get the drop on me so easily?

He remembered watching the man disappear through a door that someone had once cut crudely into the side of the deserted airport hangar. The next moment, he heard a noise behind him and there he was!

Carpenter had spun quickly, but not quickly enough. Behind the Magnum's menacing barrel, he watched the face of his killer break into a grin.

Seeing the features up close, Carpenter knew he had been right to follow his gut. When the man had earlier pulled alongside him at traffic lights in the centre of London, Carpenter sensed there was something familiar about the tossed black hair and sharp-nosed profile. He was sure it was among a number of one-dimensional images he had seen posted on the noticeboard in the agency's incident room.

Carpenter had knocked off work early to pick up flowers for his wife's birthday. He had already bought and parcelled a diamond-encrusted necklace he knew she had admired several times in the central display cabinet at the House of Fraser store. It was worth half a month's salary, but when it came to Clare, who was counting?

He had just left the florist stall and was inching his way forward to the traffic lights when the blue Mercedes stopped in the traffic flow. Carpenter had been idly glancing around at the afternoon city-centre rush of cars and pedestrians when his eyes fell on the driver, who was staring fixedly ahead, oblivious to the ebb and flow of humanity around him.

Something immediately piqued Carpenter's interest. The white snaking outline of a scar running from below the man's left ear to the corner of an upturned mouth was an absolute clincher.

When the lights turned green, Carpenter found himself shifting lanes and falling in three cars back from the Mercedes. Thirty minutes later they were on the M4 heading towards Slough, taking Carpenter farther and farther away from his home in Watford. He had convinced himself to stay with it just a while longer. He still had plenty of time to double-back, grab a shower, and take Clare to the new Italian restaurant for her birthday surprise.

As the cityscape disappeared in the rearview mirror Carpenter decided to call a halt. He had already noted the number plate of the vehicle and was just about to call in a report when the Mercedes signalled an exit from the motorway towards Maidenhead.

Carpenter followed.

Twenty minutes later on a narrow country road the Mercedes turned off into a laneway leading to a disused airfield. Carpenter maintained a safe distance and waited several minutes before entering the lane. He knew he couldn't risk going much farther; the chances of being spotted were just too great. He pulled off through an open gate into a grazing field, parked up behind a hedge, and decided to explore ahead on foot.

He grabbed a pair of Zeiss binoculars from the glove compartment, climbed out of the car, and began trudging through the heavy grass towards a rise about a hundred yards ahead. He glanced at his watch, noting that it was almost 4.00pm. He would have to abandon the pursuit soon otherwise Clare's birthday would be ruined.

At the top of the rise he got lucky. Below, less than two hundred yards from his vantage position, he could see the Mercedes in front of an old hangar. He watched the driver alight and cross to the left side of the corrugated building before disappearing through a side door,

Carpenter took off at a sprint, covering the distance in little more than thirty seconds. Not bad for a desk jockey, he thought. He had just crossed the concrete apron heading for the side of the building when he had heard the click of a weapon being cocked. He knew there was little point in trying to reach for the shoulder-holstered Glock 19. Instead, he turned calmly to stare into the eyes of a man he knew would kill him.

Realisation dawned on Carpenter as he watched the mocking grin of his assailant. It had been no chance meeting! Somehow the fucker knew who Carpenter was and had purposely drawn alongside him at the traffic lights.

He had been suckered!

Now, as he lay clinging to the last dregs of energy in his body, Carpenter cursed himself for not calling in a sit-rep. His boss, Mike Devon, would be furious at the breach in a protocol he had drilled into the team constantly in all his briefings.

"Never, ever take unnecessary risks, but above all, never, ever go it alone, without letting someone know what you're doing." He could almost hear Devon's voice, as if he were standing over him at that moment.

What would Devon have to say now? He knew for sure he would be plenty mad and would move heaven and earth to get whoever did this.

A smile crossed Carpenter's face.

Suddenly, the harsh glare of the sun shadowed over Carpenter. He forced open his eyes to look at the figure above him. The man's teeth were bared like a wild dog getting ready for a fight. Carpenter couldn't help but think that maybe the guy was pissed at the thought of his first shot not being as instantly lethal as he had intended.

The barrel of the Magnum lowered towards Carpenter's face. He didn't flinch. He'd be damned if he'd give the bastard the satisfaction of seeing fear.

Without warning, the picture of Clare filled his mind. She was in full-colour HD, smiling at him while running her fingers through her hair.

God, she is beautiful.

It was that image he took with him down the spiralling void into the total blackness beyond.

Chapter 2

ABOUT EIGHT HUNDRED crow-flying miles from where Dave Carpenter died, Mike Devon was trudging through waist-high grass in a field southeast of the Austrian city of Graz. He was in mission lockdown. No comms, no need for distractions. Just a single-minded focus on the next twelve hours or so.

Unaware of the fate that had befallen his friend and agency colleague back on a deserted airstrip in England, Devon had already trekked for four miles, mostly uphill, but showed no signs of laboured breathing. A lifetime of punishing daily exercises will do that to a man.

Especially a man whose life depended on having an edge.

A fast-fading evening sun dappled the countryside with magical shadows. Each time he crested a ridge he half expected to see Julie Andrews pirouetting through her *Sound of Music* routine.

It was that kind of scenery.

Not that Devon paid it much attention. He was here to kill a man. Nothing else mattered.

Ahead, less than a mile away, he got his first glimpse of the outline of a chalet built into a mountainside overlooking the valleys below. Nice piece of real estate if you can afford it.

But money was hardly a worry for the sole occupant of the chalet. A career as an assassin had brought him untold wealth, secreted in banks dotted across the world.

After tonight, it was money he would no longer need.

Devon shifted his rucksack and forged ahead determinedly, angling away from the west side of the house to walk in the shadows of a ravine. By the time he made his final ascent in about twenty minutes from now, he judged the entire mountainside would be cloaked in darkness.

Just as he had planned.

He had flown into Hungary the day before, grabbed a hire car at the Budapest Ferenc Liszt International Airport, and driven west to Szombathely, one of the country's oldest cities. It was slap bang on the Austrian border, less than twenty-five kilometres from his target.

He had a pre-arranged booking in one of the city's smaller hotels. Just another budget tourist. Don't get noticed. Blend in, stay off the radar.

A second hire car had been waiting for him in one of the city's multi-storey parks. He would use this for the drive to Austria and return it to the same car park. It had been acquired under false papers by one of the agency's European operatives and would remain parked up until the car hire firm filed a "lost property" report with the local police.

In the event that someone spotted the car in Austria, there was no possible chance of tracing it to Devon. By the time anyone went looking for it, he would be back in Budapest with the original hire car, and safely on a London-bound flight.

Provided everything went according to plan. You just never knew. Hope for the best, plan for the worst.

The rucksack he was carrying had been left for him in the car trunk. There was no need to check the contents. He knew what to expect.

Most of the space would be taken up by one of the agency's standard wraparounds. It was a special piece of kit, designed by Devon himself, and resembled a workman's tool belt. There was a holster for a Glock 19 with suppressor, as well as compartments for two spare 16-round mags, two flash-bang grenades, a fragmentation grenade, and a small cube of C4 explosive, with det cord and a watch-sized arming device.

There were also a number of other interesting items. There would be a Ka-Bar combat knife, a folding-stock MP5 submachine pistol, night-vision goggles, a compact heat-image intensifier, a small rubberised grappling hook trailing five metres of black nylon rope, a two-metre camouflage blanket, and field rations consisting of power bars and bottled water.

Devon doubted he would need more than two or three of these items. But it paid to err on the safe side.

This was a job either for one man or a small army. Devon was happy to fly solo.

He waited in a gully for darkness to take hold before scrambling carefully up the last crest that would afford him a view of the house below. A metre from the top he dropped on his belly and crawled to the summit.

Convention for this type of situation tended to go with a 3am entry. It was reasoned that most people, even so-called nightbirds, would be safely tucked up in bed and somewhere north of noddy-land by that ungodly hour. It didn't always work out that way, of course, but as a general rule it wasn't bad.

You could never legislate for someone suffering from a weak bladder and needing toilet trips every hour on the hour. In those situations, you just took the hand you were dealt and got on with it.

Devon bellied across the summit to a row of bushes that offered the best vantage point. He removed the night-vision goggles and began a sweep of the area below, hoping to pick up any trip wires or unusually flat pieces of lawn that might betray hidden pressure plates. Despite the magnification of the scope the detail was too fuzzy to be certain of any such impediments.

Next, he took out the heat-image intensifier, a small black box measuring six inches by four. He powered up and waited a few seconds for the screen to come alive. Satisfied he was good to go, he swept the box across the width of the house, noting the changing colours on the screen as the controls identified varying degrees of heat.

After several minutes of a slow traverse he was rewarded with a sharp red dot on the right of the screen. Body heat. The red dot remained static, depicting that his target was either sitting or lying. He continued his sweep across the rest of the house but found no other red dots.

It was as he had figured. His subject was alone.

Devon glanced at his watch. He still had four hours before his planned entry. He spread his camouflage blanket and stretched out ready to assemble his Glock and attach the wraparound belt. After that, he would settle down and grab a few hours of much needed sleep.

Experience had taught him to block out tension. There would be time to let the juices flow, time to accept the much-needed burst of adrenalin, and time to tune into the job on hand when the moment arrived to push off.

Right now, he intended to live off down-time. He strapped the Ka-Bar to his right leg and attached the suppressor to the Glock. He turned on his back and gazed for a while at the orangey glow of the Austrian sky. His eyelids immediately felt heavy.

An hour later he became aware of the throbbing sound of music pulsing from the building below. He snapped upright, grabbed the heat-intensifier, and waited for it to go through its power-up routine. The music was loud enough to be heard by neighbours up to a mile away. That is if there had been neighbours a mile away.

The man had chosen his remoteness well. If he wanted to dispense with earphones and fill the hills with the sound of music, that was his business. But for a man in his line of work it didn't make a lot of sense.

Devon swept the heat-image unit once more across the building. Satisfied there was still only a single red dot showing on the screen, he decided to bring forward his operation. The advantages offered by the sounds of a high-powered stereo system in concealing his approach were just too good to pass up.

He slung the MP5 across his shoulders, holstered the Glock, and pushed through the bushes to begin the descent to the garden behind the house. From his earlier sweep of the property he had already planned his approach down through the rockery and across the well-manicured lawn. Five minutes later he was standing against the building beside a pair of sliding patio doors.

The suppressed Glock was held firmly in his right hand as he gingerly tested the push handle on the door nearest to him. To his surprise it moved noiselessly across its rubberised runners.

He moved into the room, the Glock now held two-handed in front of his face as he swept his eyes over the dim interior. Light spilled from an adjoining room and the noise from the stereo seemed to send vibrations across the wooden flooring. He inched across the room, keeping his gaze fixed on the open doorway ahead.

Devon angled to his left to keep within the shadows on the edges of the light. When he reached the doorway, he glanced into the next room, barely able to believe what he was witnessing.

In the centre of what appeared to be a large study, a massive five-seater red-leather settee dominated the room. Sprawled across the centrepiece furniture he saw the head and shoulders of a man whose arms were thrashing the air in a manic attempt to conduct the raucous music blaring out from surround-sound speakers that threatened to shut down Devon's auditory system.

Devon was suddenly assailed by the notion that things couldn't be this easy. He had come prepared to fight a small army if need be, knowing that on most assignments Murphy's Law usually threw a spanner into even the best of pre-op preparations. He often found that shit hit the fan when you least expected it to, yet here he was being presented with a situation that even a rookie could deal with. Was he missing something?

He pushed the negative thoughts to the back of his mind. Sometimes you just get lucky. Maybe this was one of those times.

The figure on the settee was still wildly gesticulating when Devon strode across the room and pushed the suppressed Glock into the back of a balding head. The effect was dramatic.

The man jumped literally a foot in the air, lost his balance, and crashed to the floor as he tried to twist his neck towards the sudden intrusion. His eyes couldn't mask the shock and disbelief as he stared up at Devon.

Devon judged the man to be in his early fifties, probably little more than five foot seven, and with the kind of village schoolmaster face that didn't quite square with his actual profession. The baldness threw Devon. The collection of grainy photos they had of Max Steiner seemed to paint a picture different from the pathetic figure now lying in front of him.

Any wonder this man was able to blend in! He was the sort of guy you would barely give a second glance to. Devon could imagine the various wigs and disguises that allowed Steiner to move freely around Europe while he plied his deadly trade.

"On your knees, hands behind your head," Devon roared to make himself heard above the stereo blast.

As Steiner wriggled upright, Devon moved quickly around the settee and stood behind him. He turned the Glock towards the stereo system, loosed off two rounds and plunged the building into an eerie silence.

"Who are you?" Steiner croaked.

Devon pushed the weapon back against Steiner's neck. "I have a few questions. Answer them and I'll make this quick. Play the hero and...." Devon let the words trail off.

Despite the shock at seeing Steiner's less than impressive physicality up close, Devon knew he was dealing with a dangerous individual. It was estimated that Steiner was responsible for more than eighty kills over a career that had taken him into some very dark corners where he had dispatched men, women, and children at the whim of one paymaster or another. He had used handguns for up-close-and-personal kills, as well as his favoured sniper rifle for more expedient assignments. But knives, garrottes, bombs, and several varieties of hideous poisons also featured in his well-rounded CV.

When it came to killing, Max Steiner wasn't what you'd call a fussy individual.

And there was one other thing Devon knew about his man. He was a survivor - had to be to forge out such a long career in an industry where lifespans were not exactly on a par with the average citizen. There had to be a truckload of self-preservation built into Steiner's DNA, and right now Devon knew he would be delving into that particular gene pool to figure a way of extricating himself from his current predicament.

Devon moved two feet away from Steiner, keeping his Glock aimed rock-steady at the back of the man's head. His finger was still inside the trigger guard, resting on the half-inch strip of polymer that required little more than a few ounces of additional pressure to send the chambered round unerringly on its way. At the slightest movement from Steiner, Devon would not hesitate to fire.

The fact that he hadn't already done so was down to a stubborn desire to question his captive. There were things his organisation needed to know, things that Steiner might give up in a futile attempt to save his life. If not, so be it.

"I have a question for you, Herr Steiner. Who paid you to assassinate a Junior Minister of the British

Government in London last year?"

"This is absurd, there's been some mistake. I am not the man you call Steiner..."

Devon cut off the pathetic denial. "You are Max Steiner, a naturalised Austrian born of German parents. I don't doubt you barely recognise your own name, since you haven't been using it for more than twenty years. You've lived under more aliases that I've had hot dinners, but we've managed to track you down because you made one fatal mistake that a man in your line of work can't afford to make."

Steiner shifted his position to glance back at Devon. There was a look of resignation on his face, but Devon detected no fear.

"Keep your eyes straight ahead," Devon ordered.

"Okay," Steiner shrugged, "let's play your little game. What mistake did I make?"

Devon waited until Steiner twisted back to the forward position. "You chose the wrong playground when you came to London. We don't like it when psychos run loose in our capital, and we especially don't like it when they decide to murder one of our elected representatives. In short, you made the mistake of putting us on your trail."

Steiner appeared as if he were about to turn around again but thought better of it. "Ah, now I see. You are MI5 or is it MI6? You British are an arrogant lot. You think you are better than everyone else. Well, let me tell you there is more corruption on your little island than anywhere else in the world. The man I killed deserved to die. He had his grubby fingers in a lot of pies, but he pissed off some powerful people by not delivering on his promises. Believe me, the world is a better place without him."

Devon had not expected the tirade, but knew he had to keep the man talking. "And just what were the promises he failed to keep?"

There was a momentary silence before Steiner

responded. "He had been taking large bribes for years on the basis that he was in a position to shift certain energy policies in a direction that would suit my clients. When the time came to deliver, the rat reneged. He got what he deserved."

"Who were your clients?"

Steiner laughed. "Get real. You know how this works. Everything is done anonymously, Even if I wanted to, there's no way I could guess at who the paymasters were."

"Then I guess we're done here." Devon laced the comment with as much menace and finality as he could muster.

"Wait, wait," Steiner pleaded. "I have details of my payment going from one bank transfer to another. Maybe your people could track these back to the original source."

Devon knew it was a stall. His finger began a final constriction on the trigger. "I'm not buying."

"I have *one* thing you will want to hear." Steiner's announcement was delivered with the bravado of a man who believed he was holding the last ace in the pack.

Devon paused before answering. "I'm listening, but you'd better make it quick. I have to catch an early flight home, and to tell you the truth I think you're fresh out of time."

Steiner shifted uneasily. "I was contacted about taking out an assignment against British Secret Service agents. I turned it down, but others will take my place. You can't afford to risk the lives of your colleagues by not listening to what I have to say."

Devon eased back on the trigger. "Keep talking."

Steiner unlocked his hands from the back of his head. "Allow me to show you what I received. It's in my safe." Steiner pointed towards a large framed picture hanging on the opposite wall.

Devon's alert radar went into overdrive.

Commonsense told him not to proceed, but there was a niggling doubt that Steiner's claim was too outrageous not to be credible. "You had better do things in slow motion. One wrong move on your part and I'll spread the contents of your skull over this nice wooden floor. Now, get up and walk to the safe."

Steiner moved his hands down to his knees and began to rub furiously as if trying to restore circulation. Suddenly he placed both palms on the floor, using them as a lever to propel his body backwards. The speed of the attack blurred the movement of Steiner's feet, which were thrusted out and upwards in search of a disabling blow anywhere he could land them on Devon's legs.

It would have worked on most people, but Mike Devon was not most people.

Even before Steiner got to the mid-point of his attack, Devon jumped back another foot and watched as the flailing legs caught fresh air and collapsed to the floor in front of him.

Devon squeezed the trigger on his Glock.

The bullet entered the back of Steiner's right knee, exploding the patella and sending shards of bone mixed with blood into the wooden floor below. The roar of pain that followed was almost inhuman. It was a high-pitched scream mixed in with laboured gasps and shrieks that would have done a howling wolf proud.

Devon knew the sounds were an automatic reaction to an appalling injury. He had seen the effects of IRA punishment shootings first-hand from his time on the streets of Belfast. The so-called "kneecappings" dished out by paramilitary squads had left dozens of young men with permanent limps and terrible tales of the agonies they had experienced.

Steiner wrapped both hands around his thigh, just above the shattered kneecap, and rolled on the floor cursing through gritted teeth. Some observers believe it's a natural reflexive action to grab a point near an injury in order to cut off the flow of blood. Others say there's a more subconscious force at work, willing the body to block out pain signals that start automatic transmission from the brain at the first sign of trauma.

Neither works.

Devon ignored the plight of his victim and stepped forward to grab the back of Steiner's shirt at the neck, pulling the man roughly across the floor towards the wall-mounted painting. He released his grip to let Steiner continue with his wailing before tugging on the painting which swung out on a well-concealed hinge to reveal a centre-dial aluminium door.

"What's the combination?"

The response was a gargled groan.

"You have precisely three seconds to help me open this door or you lose your other kneecap."

Steiner became suddenly alert and rasped out a sequence of four numbers.

Devon attacked the dial and was rewarded with an audible click as soon as the last number was entered. He swung the door open to reveal an interior comprising two shelves crammed with bundles of money and an assortment of papers.

"What am I looking for?" Devon demanded in a voice that didn't expect any arguments.

"There's a brown envelope on the right side of the bottom shelf. You'll find what I promised inside.

Devon quickly located the envelope and moved away from the safe. He crossed to a table in the centre of the room and placed his weapon within easy reach. He kept his eyes on Steiner as he tore open the envelope.

There was a sheet of paper neatly folded inside. Devon straightened it out and began reading. He visibly blanched.

The shock of what he was reading was like a piledriver to the solar plexus. He felt as if the air was being driven from his lungs and he could feel his legs giving way under him. He stared at the words, aware that that the letters seemed to be jumping across the page. For the first time, from as far back as he could remember, Mike Devon experienced real fear.

It was the kind of fear that knotted his stomach and blanked out everything around him. He lost all sense of focus, refusing to believe what he was reading, but knowing with the cold dread of certainty that his world was about to change.

He became so engrossed in the paper gripped in trembling hands that he failed to pick up on a new presence in the room. By the time he realised he had company, he knew it was pointless to try for his weapon.

A voice slightly behind and to his right confirmed his thoughts.

"That's right. You wouldn't get near it. Step away from the table."

Chapter 3

ALAN DOYLE WAS HEADING out the door at 7.00pm when the phone trilled on the office desk. For a split second he was about to ignore it but turned back. He crossed the room and grabbed for the handset.

"What is it, Dorothy?"

The agency night-shift receptionist sounded agitated. "Alan, there's a policeman on the line who says he needs to speak urgently to someone about one of our employees. I told him you were leaving but he was very insistent."

"It's okay, Dorothy. Put him through."

Doyle waited for a second before the static disappeared. The voice that followed was strident. "Hello, this is Inspector Simon Fellowes. Who am I speaking to?"

"Look, I know you're paying for the call, but I don't have time to waste. I suggest you tell me what it is you want." Doyle was in no mood for observing the irritating protocols that policemen all too often adopted.

There was a bit of throat-clearing before the voice resumed. "I'm checking on one of your employees. Can you confirm that a Dave Carpenter works for you?"

Suddenly, Doyle was all ears. "Yes, he does. What's this is all about?"

"Can you tell me exactly what it is that Mr Carpenter does for you?"

Doyle could feel his temperature rising. "Get to the fucking point, Inspector. What's your interest in Dave Carpenter?"

"There's no need for the attitude, sir. Mr Carpenter has been involved in an incident I'm currently investigating. I have to know some details about what he does for you. And what exactly is *LonWash*

Securities?"

The alarm bells were ringing off Doyle's charts. Carpenter had only left the office a few hours ago to get ready for his wife's birthday dinner. Had he been involved in an accident?

"Inspector, before we go any further, I need to know is Carpenter alright?"

The silence was barely a fraction of a second, but it spoke volumes to Doyle. He dreaded the next words. "I'm afraid Mr Carpenter is dead."

"How?"

"I'm not yet at liberty to say, sir."

Doyle's mind raced. This was no traffic accident. Detective inspectors don't get involved in such mundane matters. "Has there been a shooting incident?"

"Why do you say that, sir?"

"Answer the fucking question, man."

"As a matter of fact, there has been what you call a shooting incident."

Doyle measured his words before speaking again. "Inspector, I want you to listen carefully. You've stumbled into something that's way beyond your theatre of responsibility. I need you to move everyone from the area of the shooting. Set up a five-hundred yard perimeter and leave everything exactly as it is until I get there."

"You don't seem to understand this is a major police investigation...."

Doyle cut in. "Shut up and listen, Inspector. I want the precise location and I want you to do exactly as I say. Make sure you are available on the ground when I arrive. Two minutes after I cut this conversation you will get confirmation from your superior officers to do exactly as I'm telling you. Are we clear?"

Momentary silence again. "This is highly irregular, I don't know what weight you imagine you carry, but if you think I'm just going to abandon a crime scene on your say-so then you've got another think coming."

"Relax, Inspector. Believe it or not, we are on the same side. Why don't you wait for that phone call I promised you? In the meantime, give me your location."

"Okay, here it is, but you better have some impressive credentials when you get here."

Doyle jotted down the details before ending the call. He cursed the absence of his boss, Mike Devon. There was no way to reach him for at least another four hours. Mission protocol dictated an absolute black-out on communications until after the job was done.

Doyle had every confidence in Devon achieving a successful outcome. He just wished he would hurry it to hell up.

Get on with it, he told himself. He knew exactly what Devon would do if he were here. The two went back a long way. They shared dangers and downtime in a history laced with its fair share of ups and downs. There was a kind of telepathy between them, the kind that can only be forged by the sheer necessity of putting their lives in the hands of each other.

Doyle shrugged aside the memories and reached for the phone. He put in a call to retired General Sir John Sandford, the political head of *LonWash Securities*, an elite anti-terrorist group answerable only to the British Prime Minister. A similar group was set up in America under the Office of the President. The name of the agency was chosen to underline the base of the company's activities in London and Washington.

Doyle knew Sir John would immediately contact the Metropolitan Police Commissioner who was all too aware of the agency's counter-terrorism powers. The call to Detective Inspector Simon Fellowes was a shoo-in to be made in less than the two minutes Doyle had promised.

He tried to push thoughts of Dave Carpenter to the back of his mind. There would be time enough later to grieve for a valued colleague and friend. Right now, he needed to put his game-cap on and get his team into action.

Doyle was already sprinting for the lift at the five-storey block on Charterhouse Street, not far from the Victoria Embankment, when the Iridium satellite phone was answered at the other end. Doyle didn't waste time on the niceties. "Alfie, we have a man down."

"Who?"

"It's Dave Carpenter."

"Holy fuck, what happened?"

"That's what we're going to find out. I need you and a small team buckled up and ready to roll in five. Get them to meet at your pad. I'm on the way there now."

Doyle cut the connection, knowing Alfie Cheadle, one of the team's top operatives, would move mountains to be ready when Doyle arrived.

He stepped out of the lift at the basement garage, and crossed to a black, window-tinted Range Rover, one of a fleet kept at the ready for *LonWash* operatives. They were a unique job-lot, customised with armour-plating, and awash with all manner of stored weaponry and sophisticated surveillance equipment.

Just as Doyle climbed behind the wheel, the lights tinkled on the dashboard telephone console. He read the receptionist's name at the bottom of the screen and tapped the answer button.

"Alan, I have Clare Carpenter on the line. She seems to be hysterical and is demanding to speak with you."

Doyle cursed inwardly. What was he going to tell her? He still needed first-hand confirmation that her husband Dave was dead. Mistakes had happened before, although he knew it was a forlorn hope in this case.

"Put her through, Dorothy."

An instant later the sounds of an anguished voice filled the car. "Alan, is that you? Something's wrong with Dave. He's late, and he's not answering his phone. Something is wrong, I just know it. He was supposed to be home hours ago for my birthday surprise, but I already knew he had booked the Italian restaurant. They rang the other day for confirmation and I've had to pretend to Dave that I knew nothing about it. So, you see, if he had been delayed, he would have phoned me, he would have let me know......."

The words tailed off. Doyle knew the woman was distraught and was talking herself up a storm to conceal what must have been a rising panic over the past few hours. He knew he couldn't feed her any nonsense. She deserved to know.

"Clare, I'm sorry but we have received some bad news. Dave has been involved in something since he left the office this afternoon. I just got the call and am on the way to the scene now."

"Oh, Alan, you have to tell me. Is Dave dead?"

Doyle sucked in some air. "I'm sorry. Clare, but we have to think the worst. I promise to call you the moment I get there. Have you someone who can stay with you until then?"

He waited for the muted screams to die down. After a few moments, a more measured voice came on the line. Clare seemed to have composed herself. "Alan, bring him home to me, one way or another."

The line went dead.

What a gutsy lady, Doyle thought.

He gunned the engine and raced the vehicle out of the basement into the early evening London traffic. Cheadle's pad was about twenty minutes away, but he intended to cover the distance in little more than half that time.

As he rounded the corner into the Avenue which housed Cheadle's apartment block, he could see the ex-soldier standing on the kerbside. Alongside Cheadle, he recognised the figures of Bob Mortimer and Bill Carlisle.

When he skidded to a stop, all three hauled at the doors and climbed in. He glanced briefly at their morose features, threw the vehicle into reverse, and executed a textbook one-eighty handbrake turn.

No words passed between the men as the Range Rover roared towards the M4 motorway.

Nightfall overtook them on the silent run across country. By the time Doyle drew up to the first of the police barricades the moon decided to darken the landscape still further by ducking behind rain-filled clouds. Everything seemed designed to match the mood of the men in the Range Rover.

Doyle flashed his badge at the uniformed policeman, ordered the removal of the outer perimeter block of two police cars parked in a V-formation, and gunned the engine towards a secondary roadblock illuminated by arced lights in the distance.

He screeched to a halt at a second, larger collection of vehicles, noting the disquieting shape of a hearse parked on a grass verge. He was out of the Rover before it was stationary and scanned the faces of more than twenty men standing about in small groups.

"I'm looking for Inspector Fellowes." His voice carried more anger in it than he intended.

A small man wearing a black belted overcoat stepped forward. Doyle put him at no more than five-seven, probably in his mid-fifties, with worry lines etched across a face that showed he was attuned to the tragedy of the circumstances in which he found himself. Doyle instantly warmed to the man.

"I'm Fellowes. You must be Mr Doyle. Please accept my sympathies for your loss."

The two briefly shook hands. Doyle introduced Cheadle, Mortimer, and Carlisle. No names. They were simply his "colleagues." Fellowes seemed to accept the lack of formality with good grace, probably knowing there was little point in announcing the roll call of a clandestine agency to the nearby throng of listeners.

Doyle gently nudged Fellowes away from the group. "Tell me what's happening here, Inspector, beginning with where the body of our colleague is."

Fellowes nodded towards a laneway entrance to his right. "About a half-mile down there. It's a disused airfield, with one car parked in front of a hangar and another in a field just inside the laneway. I pulled everyone back to here, as per your instructions, but left a man on guard to protect the crime scene."

Doyle felt a flare of rising anger. "I told you I wanted the entire scene locked down with everyone pulled back."

"Listen to me, Mr Doyle. I entirely respect who you are. I got the call from on high, just as you said I would. I've been left in no doubt as to who's in charge here, but certain protocols can't be overlooked. I couldn't take the chance that some night-time rambler might wander into the area from the opposite fields, or that some of nature's scavengers, such as foxes or rats, might want a piece of the body still lying where we found it. There's no way on earth I would....."

Doyle held up his hand to cut off Fellowes in mid-sentence. "Forgive me, Inspector. I hadn't thought that one through, and I'm grateful you did. I'm sure you can appreciate this is the one type of call-out none of us ever wants to get. If you don't mind, I would like to go take a look at what's down there."

The two held each other's gaze and the moment of tension passed. Doyle nodded at his team and made his way back to the Range Rover. As he got to the driver's door he turned back to Fellowes. "Inspector, I would be grateful if you would join us. I would value your input."

Five minutes later Doyle was staring at the body of Dave Carpenter. The face of the once jovial operative was barely recognisable behind the gaping hole above the bridge of his nose. Doyle replaced the cover sheet and turned to Fellowes. "I want the hearse brought in and the body taken back to a mortuary address in London."

Fellowes was about to respond when Doyle anticipated the policeman's misgivings. "I know your Scenes of Crime people have already completed a preliminary of the area and taken a whole bunch of photographs. There's nothing more to be learned from this precise spot. This wasn't an amateur-involved shooting, and there's no need to leave Dave lying out here all night. Tomorrow at first light we'll do a detailed search of the entire area, but for now there's not much more that can be done."

Fellowes nodded an acknowledgement before walking away and speaking into a hand-held walkie-talkie.

It reminded Doyle that he had his own call to make. And he wasn't looking forward to confirming to Clare Carpenter that she was a widow.

Chapter 4

THERE WERE TWO THINGS about the threatening voice that were immediately clear to Devon.

The instruction to stay away from his weapon was delivered with the calm assurance of a professional, someone he sensed wouldn't hesitate to fire if he made the kind of move that went against what he was ordered to do.

The second thing was equally obvious. The voice belonged to a woman.

Devon knew it could be a lethal combination.

He remained stock still and let the seconds drag out before speaking. "Couldn't help but notice the twang in your voice. I'm guessing you're a Texas girl who's a long way from home."

"Yeah, after this is over, I've got a few miles more to travel than you. It can't be more than a short-hop flight from here to London."

Despite the circumstances Devon smiled. "Touché."

A few more seconds dragged by before the woman spoke again. "I overheard enough of your discussion with our friend Steiner here to know that you're probably not my enemy, but I should warn you that the pathetic creature you just shot in the leg is the reason I'm here. Anything else, including you, is just collateral."

Devon glanced across at Steiner who was still clutching his ruptured knee as he sat up to face the new visitor to his mountain den. He held out a bloodied hand in a plea gesture to the figure behind Devon. "Thank God you're here. This man shot me for no......."

Devon watched as Steiner's chest exploded and his body catapulted against a wooden cabinet. There was a final twitch before the head slumped lifeless to the floor.

It was a classic three-round burst from a semi-automatic and Devon spun in reflex to face the shooter. The woman was dressed from head to toe in black, the neoprene suit accentuating the curves in her slim but muscle-toned body. She held an FNP-45, the Belgium-made "cocked and locked" packet of raw stopping power that has been doing the rounds of USA law enforcement agencies for a number of years.

The silver and black outline was now pointed directly at Devon.

"Damn you," Devon yelled. "I needed to question this bastard. You've stumbled into something that's none of your business, and now people could die because of your stupidity."

The woman reached her left hand up to the top of her head and yanked off the black ski mask. A jumble of red hair cascaded over her shoulders and she give an exaggerated shake of her head to force it into position. She had piercing green eyes and a tanned complexion that radiated sexuality. Devon had to force himself to remember that she had just coldly ended a life.

She glanced over at her fallen victim before turning back to Devon. "Get down off your high horse, mister. I'm betting the Texas farm that you came here to put an end to that piece of shit and now I've saved you the trouble. Why not show your appreciation by handing over that sheet of paper that seems to have gotten you in a bit of a tizzy?"

"First things first," Devon responded. "I'll see your Texas farm and raise you a row of Mayfair houses that you're CIA. If that's the case we're on the same side and you can lower your weapon."

She smiled the kind of smile that in other circumstances might have stirred a touch of carnal lust. "Okay, you win. So what alphabet agency are you from? No, don't tell me, let me guess. I'll go for MI6, the

British Secret Service. And don't tell me your name is James Bond."

Devon waited until the gun was lowered. "Sorry, you don't get to know about my employers. Let's just say I'm involved in counter-terrorism and leave it at that. I'm Mike Devon and right now I need to communicate the information on this sheet. Lives are literally at risk."

She moved across the floor, swapped the gun to her left hand and held out her right. "I'm agent Chelsea Horgan. Let me see what's on that paper while you make your call."

Devon quickly shook hands, thumped the paper on the table and sprinted across the room, shouting as he exited the kitchen door. "I have to get a sat phone from my bag."

He retraced his steps to the hillside lookout point, grabbed the rucksack and bolted back to the house, fumbling inside the satchel as he ran through the garden. By the time he reached the living room he had already retrieved the Iridium satellite phone and was punching in a speed-dial code as he tore the paper from Chelsea's hand.

As he waited on the connection to activate, he glanced again at what was written. It was a typed message, the print-out from an email with no attempt at encryption. He read it again slowly.

You have been chosen to carry out an urgent termination mission on the following people. You may select as many names as you believe you can handle within two weeks of this date, but your selection must be communicated to us within 24 hours of receipt in order that alternative arrangements can be made with some of our other assets. You will be paid one million US dollars for each name selected. Half your fee will be paid into your named account upon confirmation of your selection with the remainder paid on successful completion of your tasks. The targets you may choose from are as follows:

General Sir John Sandford
Mike Devon
Alan Doyle
Alfie Cheadle
Bob Mortimer
Bill Carlisle
Dave Carpenter

You are reminded that in accordance with our previous contracts you will not discuss the contents of this directive with any individual and that failure to complete your mission will result in serious repercussions.

It was Devon's entire frontline team, not to mention the General himself. What did it all mean? How had someone obtained information that the British Prime Minister was not even party to? Who had the juice needed to attempt such an operation?

He was pulled from his thoughts by the familiar voice of Alan Doyle in his ear. "Is that you Mike? Have you finished up in Austria?"

Devon launched in without preamble. "Listen Alan, I've stumbled across something you need to know about."

"Yes, there's something here you need to know about too, Mike."

"It will have to keep. Someone is targeting our people for assassination. You have to get them together and hold them in a secure location until I get back there."

There was a slight pause that unnerved Devon. "Jeez, Mike, you're too late. Someone has just taken out Dave Carpenter. What's going on?"

Devon felt a chill run down his spine. "Dave's

dead? What happened?"

"We're still trying to piece it together, but there's no doubt it was a professional hit. I'm still at the scene but it seems he didn't have much of a chance. I will do a full run-through at first light. Are you telling me we are all on someone's hit list?"

"Who's with you, Alan?"

"I've got Bill, Alfie and Bob here. Look, what's going on?"

Devon's voice was harsher than he meant it to be. "No time, Alan. Keep everyone together and when you finish in the morning get back to Charterhouse Street. Nobody is to leave the building and for fuck's sake watch your back. I'm going to contact the General, but I need you to arrange an escort to bring him to headquarters. Do it now"

"Will do. "We'll break into pairs. I'll send Cheadle and Mortimer there pronto."

Devon cut the connection and hit another speed-dial button, praying the old man hadn't gone out and left his phone behind. It answered on the first ring.

"This had better be good. I'm nursing a brandy and engrossed in a good book." As usual, there was warmth in the General's voice. Far from being tetchy, he had made it clear on numerous occasions that he was to be disturbed at any time, day or night, if something needed his attention.

Devon filled him in on the night's events. When he finished speaking, the General's tone changed dramatically. "We'll get the bastards who did this, Mike, and I don't care what it takes to hunt them down."

"Yes sir, but right now we need to get you to Charterhouse Street. Two of our men are on the way to you as we speak."

"Way ahead of you. I've now got a Walther in my hand instead of the brandy. I'll be waiting for your team to arrive."

The response was nothing more than Devon expected. Far from being a shrinking violet the old man had seen his fair share of combat and danger, someone you wouldn't have wanted to get on the wrong side of in his prime.

Devon tapped the end-call button and slumped down on a dining table seat. It took a few seconds for him to realise Horgan was speaking.

"Bad news? I couldn't help but notice your name on the assassination list. Who are the other names?"

He pondered for a moment about what to tell her, but decided he first needed some answers. "Let's get to that later. What are you doing here? What's the CIA's interest in Max Steiner?"

She smiled. "I'm not here. Officially I know nothing about Steiner."

"And unofficially?"

Horgan's smile disappeared. "I suppose you could say he shit in our backyard once too often. He had been on our radar for some time and last year we tried to intercept an assassination attempt he made on a New York union official."

"I take it your intercept was unsuccessful?"

Devon watched as the young woman's eyes seemed to glaze over with moisture. He waited while she regained her composure. When she spoke again there was sadness in her voice. "No, we stopped him alright, but he killed one of our agents before escaping."

"Was this someone you were close to?"

"He was my partner. We were very close. Nothing romantic, but we were a great team and he had so much to live for. He was only twenty-five when that bastard ended his life." She pointed towards Steiner. "It has taken us nine months to track him down and now we can finally close the book."

Devon rose from the table and walked across the room. A thought suddenly struck him and he spun back towards Horgan. "Where were you earlier? Were you watching me the whole time I was getting ready to make my move?"

The smile returned. "I was about to break cover when I saw you arrive at the rear of the house. I was holed up about fifty yards from where you settled in. I figured you were going to be the patient type and I confess I was thinking about having to dispose of you when the music seemed to galvanise you into action. I'm glad it did. Wouldn't have looked too good if the CIA bumped off one of our cousins."

It was Devon's turn to smile. "Don't be too sure you would have been successful..."

"Aren't you forgetting I got the drop on you?"

"That was inside the house when my mind was on other things. It would have been a whole different ball game out there in the undergrowth."

Horgan looked like she was about to continue the point-scoring but seemed to think better of it. After a short pause she walked over to Devon. "How about telling me what's going on with that list of names and what precisely were you doing here this evening?"

Devon filled her in on his mission to avenge the death of a Minister of the Crown and then quickly returned to the table to repack his rucksack. With his back to her, he continued. "As you probably gathered, I knew nothing about the existence of that list until I read it here this evening."

"So, what about the phone calls? Was the news you received about someone on the list?"

"Yes, it was a member of my team. He was gunned down in England a few hours ago. It looks like Steiner was being truthful when he told me he turned down the assignment, but someone quickly filled his shoes. Now, it was nice meeting you Agent Horgan, but I have to get back to London."

"I'm coming with you."

"What? Are you mad? This is nothing to do with the CIA. Thanks for your help, not that I needed it, but

I think it's time you headed back to Texas."

The green eyes blazed. "Don't get smug with me. If your agency has been targeted for elimination, then I can't take the chance that other intelligence agencies including ours aren't also in someone's crosshairs. Seems to me that I need to brief my people and the best way of doing that will be to accompany you back in London."

"Ain't gonna happen. This is strictly a British affair and we won't have time to hold CIA hands…"

Horgan moved across to the table and slammed her gun down on the surface. "This is not about holding hands and you know it. What if a similar list has been drawn up against members of the FBI, CIA, or Homeland Security? We can't take that chance, and neither can you. If I call this in, my boss is going to get onto his boss and somewhere down the line someone with enough clout is going to start rattling your cages. Why not save us all some time?"

Devon was about to argue but decided against it. The last thing he needed was scrutiny from Whitehall. If any calls were made from the CIA it was likely they would be routed first to MI6 who weren't exactly known as team players when it came to national security. One of the reasons Devon's agency existed was to bypass the internal squabbles, throw the rulebook out the window, and get the job done without worrying about oversight. This thing needed to be kept in-house. He would rather deal with the CIA than have MI6 gatecrash Charterhouse Street.

He turned to Horgan. "Okay, but we do it my way. First, let's clean house. I'll empty the contents of the safe and rummage about down here for anything of interest. You take upstairs."

"Am I looking for anything in particular?"

"Just grab any computer, laptop, mobile phone or other electronic device you come across. We'll take everything back to our techs in London and let them get to work on recovering any information that might help us track down these bastards."

Horgan grabbed her weapon and moved quickly towards the front hall of the building, shouting as she went. "Hope you've booked extra luggage for the plane ride."

Devon responded without lifting his head. "No need. Everything we get will be left with our people in Hungary. They will have it in an overnight diplomatic bag that will probably be waiting for us when we get back."

Chapter 5

IT TOOK LITTLE MORE THAN an hour of daylight for Alan Doyle to figure out the last period of Dave Carpenter's life. The phone call with Mike Devon had unnerved him, knowing that he needed to find quick answers otherwise his team would have to look over their shoulders for God knows how long.

Doyle began his crime scene walk-through at Carpenter's abandoned car, noting the bouquet of flowers lying across the back seat, and the opened compartment on the passenger side of the dashboard that showed his colleague had reached for the field binoculars before he exited the vehicle.

Doyle looked at the trampled-down grass and followed the wavy trail toward the crest of the field. From there, he gazed down at the abandoned blue Mercedes and the crumpled piece of tarpaulin that had been used to cover Carpenter's body. Something about the scene didn't seem right.

He scrambled out of the field onto the tarmac and began walking the length of the runway, stopping only at blackened tyre tracks about three hundred yards from the Mercedes. Satisfied he had learned all he could, he turned back to the waiting group of men standing against the hangar door.

Doyle motioned at Carlisle to meet him in the open space. As an afterthought, he called the senior policeman to join them.

"The way I see it," Doyle told them without emotion, "Carpenter followed his killer to this spot. As yet we don't know why, or if he was somehow lured here, but it seems to have been an impulse thing."

Fellowes cut in. "Forgive me, but what makes you think he was following the killer?"

"That's a no-brainer," Doyle replied. "We know that Carpenter knocked off early and was in a hurry to get home to celebrate his wife's birthday. The flowers in the back of his car confirm that he took the time to stop at the florists, not exactly an errand he would make time for if he were acting on previous information or a tip-off. Something happened after he left the florists, something to make him break his journey to go off on a wild goose chase that cost him his life."

"Could it be," Fellowes suggested, "that he was working a case on his own and decided to make a call here before heading home?"

"No. The way his car is parked in the field points to the fact that he was following the Mercedes but didn't know where he was going. When the target drove down the laneway Carpenter couldn't risk being spotted in vulnerable terrain, so he pulled over and decided to explore ahead on foot."

Doyle watched for signs of acknowledgement from the others before continuing. "I can't yet figure how the bastard got the drop on Dave. We used to rib him about being a desk jockey, but he was a highly-skilled operative with a lot of mission miles in his tank before he came to work for us. He would have taken every precaution and he had the reflexes of a cat. Something tells me he came up against a rather special type of individual, someone who is well versed in our line work. There's no doubt we are dealing with a pro of the highest order."

The others nodded in agreement and waited for Doyle to finish his briefing. "One thing that's been bothering me is why the Mercedes was abandoned. No doubt it will turn up as a stolen vehicle, and you can bet it has been wiped clean, but why leave it here? We're in the middle of nowhere, so how did the perp leave the area?"

Carlisle cut in. "Obviously, someone was waiting here for him and they made off in a second car. Perhaps that would explain why Dave was taken out. He walked into an ambush."

Doyle seemed to think about the remark for a few seconds, but when he spoke again his voice carried a new conviction. "You could be right, up to a point. There *are* tyre marks farther down the runway, but they only seem to start a few hundred yards away. I'm betting they were caused not by a vehicle but by a light aircraft of some kind. If that's the case it opens up a whole new scenario."

"How come?" The question was from Fellowes.

"Well, for a start, it would make these people heavily resourced. You don't just whistle up a Cessna at a moment's notice. My original thought was that Dave could have stumbled onto something big, like drug smuggling or gun-running or....." Doyle's voice trailed off.

"What is it?"

Doyle had been pondering about how much he needed to let the policeman know. There were a lot of negatives to telling him too much, but right now they were being outweighed by the simple fact that he needed Fellowes' help. "Dave didn't stumble onto anything. He was the intended target all along? He was manoeuvred into this chase with the express intention of taking him out?"

Fellowes eyed him with suspicion. "I sense there's something you're not telling me."

Doyle gave him an abridged version of the call from Austria. "We now know from whatever Devon stumbled across in Austria that this was an attack on *LonWash Securities*, an attack on all us?"

The remark threw a blanket of silence over the group. It was finally broken by Fellowes. "It would help to know just exactly what you guys do, and why you would be a target for professional hitmen."

Doyle draped his arm over Fellowes' shoulder and edged him away from the others. He had to decide how far he could go with divulging sensitive information. "Don't go down that road, Inspector. It's enough for you to know that we are a clandestine anti-terror group, and everything about us must remain under wraps. Do not go poking around for information, do not ask questions in the wrong places, and above all do not reveal the extent of the conversation we've just had here. If you do any of these things, you'll find yourself back directing traffic on Fulham High Road."

"Now look here...."

"Please, Inspector, I don't mean to be offensive or overly dramatic. I'm a good judge of character, and my impressions of you are that you are a highly competent police officer. You are someone I would feel comfortable working alongside and believe me I don't say that lightly. The thing is that you are now in the middle of something I would rather you were not involved in. That leaves me with two choices, either I jettison you totally, or ask for your help."

Fellowes waited a moment before responding. "As you've hinted, Mr Doyle, I'm not a fresh-faced kid who doesn't know how to tread lightly. I've already got an earful from on high, and the kind of carte blanche I've been told to give you is way beyond anything I've encountered before. You guys must be big players in the grand scheme of things, so you can take it as read that I won't be rocking any boats. Now, what can I do to help?"

It was the kind of response Doyle had hoped for and expected. He held out his hand and accepted a firm handshake. "Okay, I need to use your resources. I want every possible inch of CCTV footage examined for any signs of these two vehicles. You have the number plates and I will provide you with the route Dave Carpenter took from the moment he left our offices until he stopped at Gloria's Flowers in Kensington High Street. That's the name on the bouquet in the back seat of Dave's car and I'm betting that at some time shortly before or immediately after he made that pick-up his car will be seen in close proximity to the blue Mercedes."

Fellowes whistled lightly through his teeth. "It's just the thing I would have suggested, but there will be a lot of camera outputs to trawl through. It could take some time."

"If you need more resources, I'll see that you have them. We don't have the luxury of time so you let me know how many officers you need and they will be put at your disposal. We might get lucky with a facial image of whoever drove that Mercedes. In any event I need to know what went down in the centre of London and what took Dave off into the suburbs."

Fellowes was unequivocal. "Consider it done. Might I ask what you will be doing?"

"That's easy," Doyle replied. "I'm going to find out what kind of light aircraft was in the skies even remotely close to this location over the past twenty-four hours."

Chapter 6

THE GROUP THAT ASSEMBLED IN Charterhouse Street was a solemn bunch. The death of a colleague will do that to most people. Heads were bowed as the details of the last moments of Dave Carpenter's life were being laid bare in a round-table briefing provided by Alan Doyle.

Devon and Chelsea Horgan had grabbed an early-morning flight out of Hungary and taxied straight to the imposing five-storey building not far from one of London's landmark areas near the Houses of Parliament.

General Sir John Sandford was waiting for them as they stepped off the lift. "There's a full team briefing already underway, but first we need to talk about what Agent Horgan is doing here." The General turned and marched back to his office, leaving it clear that he meant the duo to follow him.

Devon nodded at his colleagues as he tracked the General. He could see the hurt in their eyes, the determination evident in the hard set of their faces. Someone was going to pay dearly for what happened yesterday.

Inside the General's office Devon motioned Horgan to a seat but remained standing as he addressed his boss. "As I explained in my phone call from the airport, I had no alternative but to include Agent Horgan in this. She already knows everything that's going on from our escapade in Austria and, as she so delicately put it, we would start getting a lot of unnecessary attention if we shut her out."

The General leaned forward to rest his elbows on a square foot of space on the large mahogany desk that served as his altar. The rest of the space was cluttered with files and loose papers. "Quite so, but there's one thing you should know, Agent Horgan, and that is that I don't take kindly to gatecrashers. While you are a guest here you will play by my rules."

Horgan treated him to one of her expansive smiles. "Wouldn't have it any other way, Sir John. I'm only here to protect the interests of my agency. And please call me Chelsea."

Devon could see the old man was smitten. He watched as the General relaxed in his chair, his scowl fading into the beginnings of a smile. "Very well, my dear, I mean Chelsea, you are welcome to learn what you can, but I need to brief you later about some... shall we say sensitive areas... of our operations."

"I look forward to that. May I ask that I get access to a telephone? I haven't yet briefed my people and they will be wondering what's happened to me."

The General rose from his seat. "Feel free to use this space. We are starting a meeting soon and you may join us as soon as you're finished."

It was the first time Devon could remember Sir John letting anyone use his office. Amazing what a young voluptuous woman with a winning smile can achieve!

He followed the General out of the office and across to the conference room where Alan Doyle was waiting to begin his briefing. Doyle spread a series of crime-scene photos on the table. No-one wanted to look at the close-up shots of Carpenter's bloodied body sprawled on the tarmac. The gaping hole in the centre of the dead man's forehead was particularly hard to take, even for men seasoned by violent death.

Doyle launched into a detailed summary of what was proposed for the rest of the morning. "We will let the Met police deal with the CCTV surveillance. Their Inspector Fellowes knows what's needed and I'm confident he will come through by the end of the day. At the moment it's our best lead, but not the only one. I have a two-man team down at Air Traffic Control to see if we can get a line on any light aircraft in the area around the time of the incident and forensics are trying to get a match for the bullets taken from Dave's body."

Devon rose from the table and walked across to a tea trolley. He filled a large mug with black Earl Grey and turned back to Doyle. "How confident are you with running down the aircraft?"

"My guess is that they were probably flying low, off radar, by the time they touched down at the disused airfield, but I've told our people to list every private flight within two counties. We intend to interview anyone who filed a flight plan, no matter how innocuous, within a hundred miles of the shooting location. I don't care if that means scrutinising every crop duster or air taxi in the South East of England. We will look everyone in the eye to make sure they weren't involved in this."

Alfie Cheadle cut in. "What if they didn't file a flight plan? Seems to me we're dealing with the kind of people who wouldn't make things easy for us."

It was Devon who answered. "It doesn't work like that. To get started on a flight, no matter how short, it needs to be filed. As soon as an unregistered flight is detected it would raise flags that would draw attention to it and that's something that would leave a trail for us. No, it's better to file a seemingly harmless flight and then drop below radar long enough to land at that airfield, pick up a passenger, and continue on the original course. Most times these low-flying activities are of little concern, but at some point they have to rise into scheduled flightpaths and it would make Air Traffic Control extremely nervous if they didn't know about them beforehand."

Doyle nodded in acknowledgement. "That about sums it up. My guess is that somewhere among the list of flights we'll find what we're looking for. Our only problem is that what with Flying Schools and private charters we will probably have hundreds to sift through. It might take some time."

"What about forensics on the spent casings?" The question came from Bob Mortimer.

"I won't be holding my breath on that one," Doyle answered. "The chances of matching with previous ordinance on the records of any agency are pretty remote. There are not too many pros who like to leave their signature, but we'll go through the motions on the off-chance."

"Maybe I can get our people to check their records." All eyes turned to the door where Horgan stood. Devon motioned her forward and introduced her to the team before nodding to Doyle to continue.

There was an awkward silence as Doyle stared at the redhead. Devon thought he could detect a definite blushing of the cheeks. The big man was hooked!

Doyle looked away and glanced down at his notes before eventually picking up the thread of his briefing. "Okay, next up is to trace Dave's movements for the past week or so. We know what he did yesterday, but we need to find out where he's been on his time off for the past seven to fourteen days. It could be he was simply shadowed from the office yesterday, but we need to look at the possibility that he unwittingly came into contact with his killer before then."

There was a bit of shuffling and a few murmurs before Doyle held up his hand. "I know Dave was a bit of a home-bird, but we can't take the chance that he hasn't been under surveillance for some time. Let's just track his movements and see where it takes us."

The briefing lasted another twenty minutes before the General signalled an end to the discussion. "I think we've covered enough ground for today. We seem to be chasing down all the right leads, but I don't need to remind you people that finding Carpenter's killer is just the tip of the iceberg. We need to know the bigger picture. It's paramount we find out who has targeted this agency and why. Maybe it has something to do with one of our previous missions or maybe there's a reason that's not yet obvious why someone wants us out of the way."

He paused before continuing. "One more thing. So far, we're assuming this is confined to this office, but what if there's a similar list covering our American operations?"

Devon warmed to the old man's words. Not for the first time he was grateful for the experienced insight that was nurtured by a lifetime of service in the shadows. "Agreed. We'll let them know right away."

The General acknowledged Devon's reply before moving from the table and striding towards the door. He stopped and faced the group again. "Remember we have a new rule. Starting right now we move about only in pairs. We know someone has pinned targets on all our backs, so let's not make it easy for them."

As the group dispersed, Devon made his way to Doyle. The two had been through a lot in the past ten years, including an infamous shoot-out with an IRA squad in Dublin that had cost Doyle his right arm. He now wore a prosthetic that he had learned to operate with such precision that few people could tell the difference.

Devon decided to test the waters. "You okay, buddy?"

"Yeah, why ask?"

"Nothing special. It's just that I've never before seen you so tongue-tied. Could it be because our new CIA friend is a bit of a stunner? Has Agent Horgan lasered her way through that tough exterior?"

A small reddening re-appeared on Doyle's cheeks. "Don't talk nonsense. I just wasn't expecting you to include any outsiders in our briefing."

"Especially such a good-looking outsider, eh?"

"I'm warning you, cut it out."

Devon smiled and held up his hands in mock surrender. "Let's change the subject. I need to nip home to see Emma and Michael."

"Okay, give me a minute and Cheadle and I will go along for the ride."

Devon was already fishing keys from the car-pool board. "No need for that. Keep everyone busy and I'll be back in a few hours."

Doyle bristled. "For Christ's sake, Mike, you're our team leader and if you don't follow the rules then how can you expect the rest of us to? The General is right about us moving in pairs and I don't see any way you can get out that door without me."

Devon placed his hand on Doyle's shoulder. "As usual, you're right, but hurry up. I can't wait to see my wife and son."

Chapter 7

EMMA DEVON WAS CRADLING her son in the fold of her arm as she gazed out the window waiting for a car to pull up at her Bayswater home. She hated Mike's absences, particularly when he was on an assignment that could take him away from her forever. She had known what she was getting into, but it didn't make it any easier.

She knew the importance of his work and was fully committed to the part he played in helping to keep the country safe. She also knew that without it Mike could never be fulfilled. He belonged to that breed of men who were action junkies, the type who could never be content without the adrenaline rush that the job served up with dosage levels most people wouldn't understand.

There was also the fact that she knew he did it for all the right reasons. He was a genuinely-committed patriot who never thought twice about stepping up to the plate when evil threatened the existence of those things he held dear. Mike Devon couldn't sit on the sidelines and, despite her fears, she wouldn't want him to.

There was of course another side to the man. Emma knew that beneath the tough exterior there was a tenderness and vulnerability that she adored. In his downtime he acted like a big kid, forever playing pranks like hiding the TV remote control and switching channels in the middle of her soaps. When he was around his son Michael nothing else seemed to matter, even to the extent that she sometimes had to force her way into their private little world of make-believe.

She smiled at the memories of him taking Michael onto playground rides with his six-two frame squeezed into a child's toy car on the merry-go-round, or the time he insisted on joining his son in a bouncy castle in a neighbour's back garden.

The squeal of brakes jolted her back to the present. The familiar black Range Rover pulled into the kerb and Devon bolted from the passenger seat. She noted Alan Doyle behind the wheel and another figure, obscured by the tainted glass, sitting in the rear.

She met him at the door and was almost knocked off her feet by his smothering kisses and hugs. It didn't matter to him that he had an audience in the waiting car. That was another thing she loved. He grabbed his son, kissed him on the head and started throwing him into the air, the pair giggling almost in sync.

Emma waved to Doyle and noticed the car engine had been turned off. "Is Alan not coming in? Who is that with him?"

Devon glanced behind him before stepping into the hall and closing the door. "I'll tell you all about it later. First, I want to know everything you two have been getting up to while I was away."

Emma pulled Michael from his arms and retreated into the living room. "Your son has something to show you."

Devon followed and was ordered to sit in his favourite armchair while Emma walked across to the other side of the room. She lowered Michael to the floor, planting his bare feet on the carpet and removing her hands from his armpits. "Go to daddy."

The boy took a few faltering steps and then dashed across the space.

"You're kidding, when did this happen?" Devon held out his hands as the boy collapsed into them. "I've only been away two days and I miss his first steps."

"He just decided to take off yesterday morning. I guess he thought it was time to make the move before his second birthday. Once he started, I couldn't get him to stop. We're going to have to re-arrange the furniture in here."

Devon swept the boy into the air and began spinning him. "Who's a clever boy?"

"Mike, you'll make him sick. Put him down and let him run around."

With a final twirl, Devon returned the child to the floor and for the next ten minutes he kept moving his position, urging Michael to run to him. When the boy finally sat down among his toys, Devon looked up to watch Emma staring through the window at the parked Range Rover."

"What's going on, Mike?"

He held nothing back. He had made her a promise a long time back to be completely honest when his work threatened to impinge on their lives. It was a commitment made after an attempt on Emma's life by a gunman hired by a Russian oligarch whose plot to destabilise the West had been ruined by Devon. Emma had survived, only because of the intervention of Alan Doyle.

He told her about Dave Carpenter's death and about the list he had discovered in Austria. He watched as her face blanched in shock. "My God, that's terrible. Poor Dave. Have you spoken to Clare, how is she?"

"I'm going to see her later today. Right now, I'm still trying to get my head around this."

Emma again glanced out the window. "Is that why you have minders? Are we in danger?"

Devon paused, knowing that what he had to say next would not be what Emma wanted to hear. "I won't kid you. This is a serious state of affairs and until we can get a handle on it, we can't take anything for granted. Don't worry about me, the team is covering each other's back, but I need to know that you and Michael will be safe."

"What are you getting at, Mike?"

"I want you to take Michael and visit your parents for a while..."

"No way, we're in this together. I'm not leaving

you."

He didn't expect anything less, but he needed to convince her. "Darling, I think the threat to you is minimal, but if I keep coming home the chances of being followed increase with every journey. If they can't get at me, they might try to get to me through you. I won't be able to operate effectively if I have to worry constantly about you. You'll be safe in the countryside. Nobody knows where your parents live."

He could see Emma was fighting to keep her emotions in check. "You're forgetting that I was attacked on my way to see my parents last year. I'll be just as safe here and, anyway, who knows how long this will go on for. You can't keep missing large parts of Michael's life."

Devon walked over and threw his arms around her. "That attack happened because you were followed from this house, not because they knew where you were going. We have to be sensible about this, Emma. Please look at it from my point of view. Knowing you are safe will leave me free to sort out this mess. I promise to move heaven and earth to get back to you as soon as possible."

He could feel her body tremble, but when she spoke her voice was calm. "Okay, you win, but promise me that when this is over we will take a family holiday. Let's get away for a few weeks in the sun."

"You've got a date," he said as he squeezed tighter.

Chapter 8

THREE MEN SAT AROUND A MARBLE-TOPPED table in a luxurious third-floor apartment overlooking the Bundegasse, one of the most sought-after office and shopping precincts in the Swiss capital of Bern. Below them, the pedestrianised street was quiet, save for the occasional flapping of striped canvas window shades that were a feature of the area and offered practical protection to ground-floor inhabitants from the afternoon glare of the summer sun.

The men were a formidable trio of octogenarians. They had come together as teenagers and had amassed fabulous wealth over six decades of criminal activities, which had somehow escaped the attentions of the various authorities in a host of countries where they plied their despicable trade.

Felix Hoffmeier, Jurgen Kappel and Dieter Neumann had seized their chance in the days leading up to the fall of the Third Reich. A combination of circumstances had thrown them together as members of a *Kuntschutz* unit responsible for plundering gold, silver, religious treasures, and paintings from across Nazi-occupied Europe. Hoffmeier and Kappel had accompanied lorryloads of loot to secret dumps, while Neumann was attached to the office of a General responsible for opening secret Swiss bank accounts and safety deposit centres where hoards of cash and valuables were ferreted away.

While German forces retreated on all fronts in March 1945, the trio hatched their plan. On one delivery to an underground depot just outside Munich, Hoffmeier and Kappel, who were then barely sixteen years old, extracted MP38 Schmeisser submachine guns from beneath a tarpaulin and mowed down the depot's entire guard and civilian personnel. Twenty-two bodies were later discovered among smashed crates.

That same evening Dieter Neumann calmly entered the home of General Hans von Scherrling on the pretext of needing his signature on urgent papers. What he demanded was a list of all bank accounts, signatories, and passwords. In addition, he told the General, he would need signed authorisation to access the accounts, as well as an official pass allowing him and his colleagues to take two trucks through various roadblocks and across the border into Switzerland.

The General had proved a tough nut to crack, but he finally succumbed when he watched Neumann put a gun to his wife Elsa's head and pull the trigger. Neumann had then grabbed the General's ten year-old twin sons and raised the Luger to the temple of one of them.

The General fought back tears as he scratched his pen across various documents. When he was finished, he pushed them across the top of the desk and began to rise from his seat. He never made it. Neumann fired three times into the General's body and then turned the pistol on the cowering boys.

Without a moment's hesitation he completed the slaughter of the von Scherrling family.

Within days of crossing into Switzerland the trio had raided the existing accounts and safety deposit boxes, establishing new deposits in a succession of banks under a host of aliases. They began to invest in post-war industries across Europe, building up a portfolio of ownerships in car manufacture, steelworks, and coal mining. They bought hotels, office blocks and city centre retail space in a dozen cities before they turned their attention to the lucrative markets of America and the Far East.

The scale of their acquisitions allowed them to live lifestyles that few people could imagine. They were seen at all the glamour, social and sporting events around the world. They mixed with film stars and political leaders and donated millions to various charities, not out of benevolence, but as a means to ingratiate themselves with people they considered to be fellow movers and shakers.

There was one constant in their lives. They swore a bond to each other, a bond that precluded having other people involved in their businesses. They never married, a decision made easier for Hoffmeier who preferred the company of men, although for Kappel and Neumann it was also no big deal - they enjoyed paying for their carnal pleasures with a succession of the most attractive women the escort services of Europe could unearth for them.

Over the years their appetite for ruthlessness was satisfied by the various methods they employed to keep one step ahead of their business rivals. They liked nothing better than to see men and women squirm under the hostile measures they took against a succession of companies, from large conglomerates to small family-run businesses. Ruining lives and changing the fate of whole communities were often the only stimuli for closing down job-dependent ventures.

In the early days they thought nothing of killing off rivals. They took it at its most literal meaning, salivating at the prospect of watching a person gaze into the barrel of a pistol, knowing their last moment was upon them. There was something magical about the expression of terror on the faces of their victims.

They continued these indulgences into their later years, particularly because of their ability to hire the best professionals money could buy. And that took them into a whole new chapter of their lives. At first, they had specific targets to deal with, but gradually their choices became more whimsical. Often, one or other of them took a dislike to someone they had seen on television. Once it was a politician espousing a cause they objected to, and on another occasion there was a celebrity who seemed to be attracting too much attention for his modest achievements. The world would be better off without them, it was decided.

Like everything else, they eventually became bored with that phase in their lives. They kept contact with their top assassins, using them less frequently, but on higher retainers to carry out more serious assignments. It was because of this they had agreed to meet for their monthly get-together in Bern.

"I can't believe that after ten days we only have one death to show for the collective efforts of the team." As usual, it was Hoffmeier who took the lead. He had been the brains behind their 1945 operation and since then the other two deferred to him as the leader of *Das Trio Berne*, a name they applied to themselves shortly after taking up residence in Switzerland.

"I agree it is most strange, but let's give them another few days." The squeaky voice belonged to Kappel, who had recently been dogged by ill-health and ventured out less and less from his home in Gstaad.

Neumann was less inclined to be patient. "Jurgen, we do not pay good money for these people to sit on their hands. We should be seeing better results and I for one am not prepared to accept it. I think it's time we applied sanctions."

"No, no it is much too soon."

"If I didn't know better, my friend, I'd think you are losing your marbles. Why don't you go back home to bed and I'll send you a couple of lovelies to massage your troubles away."

"You can't talk to me like that, Dieter. I'll have you know....."

"Enough!" Hoffmeier had watched the growing tension between his two friends and decided to intervene. "You are both right, of course. It is unacceptable to have this delay, but it is too early to contemplate alternative action. Perhaps it would be appropriate to wait another two days, but in the meantime, I will arrange for a strong message to be sent through the usual channels."

Kappel nodded his agreement, but Neumann leaned across the table as if to emphasise his next words. "I've always relied on your judgement, Felix, but I am concerned that our timetable is in danger of slewing out of control. We have given commitments and personal assurances that we can deliver what was asked of us. I am prepared to wait no longer than two days, but I recommend we cover our bases by hiring on additional help."

Hoffmeier held Neumann's penetrating stare. "Yes, perhaps we should think about duplicating some of the assignments. It can't do any harm."

Kappel's grey-coloured skin seemed to pale even further. "You can't possibly be contemplating setting two people against the same targets. They will end up getting in each other's way and ruining any chance of completing their missions. And besides, it might end up costing us double."

Hoffmeier smiled. Despite untold riches, it was typical of Kappel to count the pennies. "Relax my friend, we will only pay out on who makes the kill. It is up to them to sort out what happens on the ground. Besides, this is a win-win situation for us."

Kappel slumped back in his chair. "I hope our friends in London see it that way. We have become mixed up with some people who are every bit as powerful as we are. I don't doubt they also have access to certain resources and, if we fail to deliver, they might set those resources on us."

There was a momentary silence before Hoffmeier responded. "That will not be an issue. We will take the sting out of things by ensuring their primary target is disposed of as soon as possible. We will concentrate our people on this man, and then we can worry about the rest of the names on the list."

Neumann looked puzzled. "I didn't know there was

a primary target. All we received was a bunch of names of people linked with a security agency in London. What makes you think one of those names is more important than the others?"

"I happen to know that one of the men we are doing business with has a personal reason for wanting to see the demise of at least one of the targets."

Neumann banged his fist on the table. "What personal reason? I thought this was about something far greater than private vendettas. I would not have agreed to become involved if I had known this.

"Relax, Jurgen. The motives are beyond question. It is just that for one of our contacts the mission is tantamount to killing two birds with one stone, so to speak."

"How is this so?"

"Because one of the targets used to work for the British Secret Service and for some reason the man pulling the strings has something of a vendetta against that particular organisation."

The chauffeur-driven Mercedes hurtled along the Flugplatzstrasse towards the Bern-Belp airport where Felix Hoffmeier kept one of his fleet of private jets. The bodyguard in the front passenger seat had his eyes fixed firmly on the road ahead, knowing that his boss was in the kind of foul mood that didn't allow for small talk.

Hoffmeier was seething at the turn of events over the past few months, the more so because he knew he had dug a hole for himself, one that only he could sort out. For some years he had realised he could no longer rely on his wartime friends. He was sick of carrying them, fed up with all the hand-holding that was involved from those early days when he had planned the greatest heist of all time. He had handed everything to them on a plate, but now he would call in the marker.

The time had come to ditch them.

The fools believed their participation in this latest project was just another adventure, something to relieve the boredom of their pandering lifestyles. What they didn't know was that Hoffmeier had no choice but to accept the demands of a man he had believed was little more than one of his many conquests. As he stretched naked in anticipation on the bed of a Rome hotel six months ago, the awful truth was revealed to Hoffmeier.

His escort for the evening emerged from the bathroom carrying a silenced Walther PPK and threw a file onto Hoffmeier's lap. As he turned the pages, he realised that it contained the life story of *Das Trio Berne*, complete with photographs chronicling their early years as young German soldiers through to the present.

He noticed with incredulity that the file also contained photocopied sheets bearing the logo of the MFAA, the post-war investigative unit set up by the allies to recover loot stolen by the Nazis. He had always believed they had escaped the radar of the Monuments, Fine Arts and Archives Unit, but somehow they had been under investigation all this time!

As it turned out, according to the mysterious man holding a gun literally and figuratively to his head, the MFAA file had been removed and all computer records erased in the knowledge that one day the contents would prove useful to the organisation he worked for.

That day had now arrived.

Hoffmeier was given a stark choice. Expend whatever sums were necessary to carry out what was described as an *urgent task* or face the consequences of the file being handed over to the appropriate authorities.

There was one other condition. When the job was completed, he was to reveal the details of all assets held by his two compatriots. Their fortunes were effectively to be transferred to this man and the people he worked for.

Felix Hoffmeier needed little time to agree.

Chapter 9

MIKE DEVON'S INTERNAL RADAR WENT on high
alert the moment he stepped out the front door of his
house and glanced along the almost deserted street.
Nothing seemed out of the ordinary, but he recognised
the symptoms of an old familiar feeling beginning to
bubble to the surface. It was an intangible sense of
danger that had served him well down the years, and he
was not about to dismiss it now.

He glanced below as Alan Doyle fired the engine of
the Range Rover and looked impatiently towards him,
puzzled by his reluctance to bound down the steps, as
he usually did.

Devon made a pretence of fixing his collar and
buttoning his coat while his eyes roamed both ways
along the line of parked vehicles. On his second sweep
to the right he clocked a brown Ford Transit, parked
neatly about a hundred yards away and looking slightly
out of place among the Rovers and Bentleys that
dominated the tastes of the exclusive Bayswater area
residents. Devon fitted in well with the exclusive
neighbourhood, but only because his wealthy parents
had bequeathed him the house and a small fortune
when they died some four years previously.

The Transit could of course be nothing more than
a working vehicle for the many tradesmen who found
lucrative odd jobs in this part of town. But Devon was
taking no chances, particularly when his inner self was
screaming for him to go on high alert.

He turned back to the door and spoke in a raised
voice. "Don't wait up for me honey, I'll be home late."

He knew that the closed door was screened by the
outcropped porch wall and that watchers would not
know that Emma was already upstairs packing a
suitcase for the planned trip to her parents' countryside

home.

He walked casually down the steps and pulled the Rover's passenger door open. As he climbed into the seat, he noted that Doyle was already cradling his Glock G19. "What's up, Mike?"

"I think we've got company. There's a brown Transit sitting back along the road. Move off normally and take the first left into the one-way street. It's a bit cramped with parking on both sides, but it will serve our purpose."

Cheadle leaned forward from the back seat. "What have you in mind?"

Devon quickly explained what he wanted. As Doyle eased into the road and headed to the corner, Devon's hand remained on the door handle. As soon as the Rover turned out of sight, Devon depressed the lever and jumped to the pavement, slamming the door behind him and running for a ramp that led to an underground car park for residents.

It was where he kept his father's prized 1963 Austin Healey MK11, a thirty-thousand pound vintage motor that he was now about to use as a roadblock! Despite being idle for many months, the engine jumped to life on the first push of the button. Devon glanced in the rear view mirror in time to see the Transit drive by in slow pursuit of Doyle, knowing that the big fella was deliberately taking his time to negotiate the narrow street.

Devon gunned the engine, swung the Austin in a wide arc and headed up the ramp. He emerged onto the street barely two hundred yards behind the Transit. Ahead of it he could see the brake lights of the Range Rover flicker out, to be replaced by reversing lights as Doyle aimed his vehicle at his pursuers.

He pushed hard on the accelerator, closing the distance to less than twenty yards. The Transit came to a stop and for a moment Devon wondered whether it would try to ram against him in an attempt at escape.

He cared a lot about his father's Austin, but right now he was too angry to think about the consequences.

He removed a Sig Sauer P226 from a shoulder holster, threw open the door, and pointed the weapon at the Transit's driver's door. He saw Doyle and Cheadle spring from their vehicle, using the doors as shields as they too brought weapons to bear on the trapped Transit.

The seconds ticked by.

Devon noticed the window on the driver door of the Transit easing down. A voice from within broke a silence that had seemed to descend suddenly on the scene. "Hold your fire. No need for you fellers to get jittery. We're with Uncle Sam and we're only here to help."

Devon cursed inwardly at the American propensity for laidbackness. There was a lot he wanted to say but contented himself with a standard order. "Step out of the vehicle, with arms raised. Be advised that if you don't do precisely as I say we will be shipping you back to your Uncle in a box."

The doors of the vehicle opened slowly and two men climbed out, their arms stretched stiffly above their heads. Devon could see only the man on the right side, but knew his passenger was being covered by Cheadle. The driver spoke. "Is this really necessary?"

Devon ignored him. "Close the doors and assume the position against the vehicle. You guys ought to know the drill. Is there anyone else in there?"

"Just us," the driver responded as he slammed the door.

Devon could hear the other door closing and he called on the passenger to walk around the front to join his buddy. When the second figure emerged, Devon had to stifle a laugh, despite the seriousness of the situation. Both men were dressed in *Men in Black* suits, someone's nutty decision for the modern-day uniform of the CIA.

"Alan, Alfie, frisk them." Devon kept his Sig trained on their captives as Doyle and Cheadle completed an expert pat-down. It elicited two FNP-45s, and two identical black leather wallets.

Jeez, thought Devon, when these people go for conformity, they go for broke.

Doyle rummaged through the wallets. "Looks like they are who they say they are. We've got agents Sam Buchanan and Tyrell Banks, both fresh out of the Academy, judging by the nice shine on their wallets and shields."

The taller of the two men, the driver, bristled at Doyle's flippancy. He lowered his arms and turned away from the vehicle. "I don't appreciate your tone, mister. We are experienced field agents and I would expect a bit more courtesy coming from your side."

Doyle was about to respond, but Devon held up his hand and moved forward, sheathing his Sig as he approached the Transit driver. "Which one are you?"

"I'm Buchanan."

"Okay, Agent Buchanan, you can climb down of that high horse and rein in. What *we* don't appreciate is being followed by people who should have had the courtesy of letting us know they were in town. That way we could have avoided this rather silly scene in front of the good folk of London, not to mention that someone could have been seriously hurt if we had played this differently."

Buchanan shrugged his shoulders. "We were only just put on assignment this morning and were running through a familiarisation exercise before making formal contact."

Devon felt anger welling up inside. His right fist needed a minimum of backlift to deliver a stunning blow to Buchanan's midriff. The CIA man buckled, the air rushed out of his lungs, and his right knee dropped hard onto the tarmacked surface of the road. He lifted his face to stare in disbelief at Devon. He was just in time to see the fist coming in a blur towards him, but not enough time to avoid the crunching blow that sent him sprawling in agony.

The second Agent began to move towards Devon but was pinned back against the van by an arm that held his throat in a vice-like chokehold. Alan Doyle smiled behind the prosthetic into the man's face.

Devon waited until Buchanan recovered sufficiently to rise groggily to his feet. "Is that familiarisation enough for you? This little exercise of yours has put my home and my family in the glare of a spotlight. That is not something I'm prepared to tolerate. If I ever see you around here again, or if this distraction leads to something down the line that affects my family, I will come looking for you both, and next time you will stay down permanently. Are we clear?"

The glare of hostility left Buchanan's eyes. "Look, I'm sorry. We didn't realise this was your home. We picked up the tail at your office, not knowing where you were going, but we were following mission orders to shadow you guys. This assassin list has got everyone jumpy."

The mention of the list made Devon angry again. "Who told you about that? Are you working with Agent Chelsea Horgan? Is this her way of repaying the trust we placed in her?"

"I've never met Agent Horgan, and I don't know what you're talking about. All we know is that our station leader briefed us this morning that you guys were on a target list that could lead to a possible threat to our own network. Maybe there's a similar list with our names on it. You can't fault us for trying to find out."

Devon ramped down his anger a few notches. "No, I can't fault you for that, but I can fault you for the way you've gone about it. I suggest you go back to your base and await the outcome of a dialogue that needs to take place at higher levels. We have to come at this with a clear strategy that doesn't have us falling over each other. The next time I wanna see you guys is when I ask to see you. Do you copy?"

To his credit, Buchanan held out his hand. "Agreed. Like I said, I'm sorry things went down this way. As long as we're kept in the loop, we should be able to work through this to everyone's satisfaction."

Devon took the offered hand in a firm shake before turning to Doyle. "Give them back their badges and guns. We need to clear the street."

He turned back to his car, shouting over his shoulder as he walked. "Gentlemen, I won't say it's been a pleasure."

The image filtering through the Hensoldt 4x21 M1 telescopic sight began to intensify under the caress of the slightest finger-and-thumb pressure on the sensitive dial. The man whose eye was pushed against the viewfinder watched Mike Devon's face come alive in his crosshairs. The foreshortened distance appeared less than an arm's length away.

The twelve-inch length of apparatus was usually rail-mounted on a Barrett M95 sniper rifle, which at that moment was folded away in its purpose-designed box in the boot of his car. It would not be needed on this trip. The man had already decided this would be an up-close-and-personal termination.

For now, he was content to treat this outing as the last part of his surveillance phase. He had watched with amusement as the scene played out in the little side street off the Bayswater Road. He had learned much from the morning exercise.

He had been given the address late the previous evening and had parked in time to see the Ford Transit trying clumsily to blend in with the neat row of upmarket vehicles. At first, he thought he had run into one of his professional rivals, but the show of badges he had just witnessed told him that the clowns in the black suits were obviously law enforcement of some variety. Strange that everyone's wires seemed to cross in such a comical fashion – still it was entertaining, if nothing else.

What concerned him was that these people seemed to be hunting in packs. Something must have ratcheted up their nerves, probably the fact that they knew they were facing a concerted campaign against their ranks. He didn't dwell on how that could have happened. In his line of work, you played the cards as they fell.

He watched now as his mark climbed back into the vintage Austin, reversed towards the ramp turn-off and descended into the underground garage. The Range Rover followed close behind.

Five minutes later the Rover re-emerged, this time followed by a small Renault Clio, driven by a woman, no doubt the wife. Both cars proceeded slowly to the end of the street before branching off in different directions.

The man lifted a leather suitcase from the passenger well, alighted from the car, and walked confidently to the front door of Devon's house. He smiled at the faded brass Yale keyhole disc. Ten seconds later he was inside the porch with the door closed behind him.

He scanned the interior looking for a security keypad. There was none, although it came as little surprise. The absence of a CCTV system on the outside, coupled with a cheap and cheerful door lock, had already convinced him he would find little to tax his skills. He shook his head in bewilderment. So much for the great British intelligence services! They were meant to guard the nation, yet they couldn't be bothered to take the time for even the most basic security arrangements in their own homes. He detested such sloppiness.

The man was a Serbian national who left his homeland eight years ago to pursue a career he had become proficient at, during those days in his country's history where the ability to take a life had become a pastime among his contemporaries. Back then he was known as Dragan Boskovic, a name that had rarely been heard since - lost as it was behind the various passport names he had conjured up in his travels around Europe.

Boskovic surveyed the cramped interior porch area with an eye for the kind of detail an interior designer would apply. In his case, though, he was not trying to imagine a makeover. Rather the opposite. The small space was ideal for what he wanted to achieve.

He stooped to open the briefcase and extracted a cube of C-4 explosive. It was little more than a pound in weight, but he nonetheless cut it in half with a pocketknife. More than enough to do the job.

He had already spotted that a coat rail, screwed into the wall about head-height, three feet from the door, would be the ideal depository for the explosive. He began to roll the malleable compound between his palms to produce a sausage-like shape about the width of the wood which held the coat rail in place. The wood made a perfect backing to direct the charge towards the door.

He pressed the C-4 firmly into place and then extracted a small, cylindrical detonator, which he bore into the compound. Sticking out from the detonator was a wire attached to a pocket watch. This was no ordinary watch. Its innards had been removed and replaced with a small solar-powered battery that would create a sufficient energy surge to race up the wire and transform the putty-like blob into an explosive maelstrom, capable of reducing the foyer to rubble. Not to mention vaporising the poor soul who detonated it.

Boskovic removed a roll of double-sided tape from his pocket, tore off a small strip, and fixed it to the back of the watch, which he placed on the wooden floor. Next, he pulled out the watch dial and trailed a thin wire over to the door mat. He lifted the mat to one side and set the dial gingerly on the ground. Just like the rest of the watch, this was no ordinary dial. It contained a miniature blasting cap, which could be activated by the slightest pressure. He used the tape to fix it in place, before covering it with the vinyl mat. Someone standing on the mat would break the dial and complete the circuit.

He had judged the placement of the dial to take account of someone opening the door, placing their feet on the mat, and then readjusting their feet to close the door. Somewhere within those movements they would come into contact with the blasting cap.

He went back to the watch and pressed a small button on the side until a counter moved up to five seconds. That's all the time he would allow. He removed his thumb from the button and stepped away. The device was now armed.

Boskovic closed the briefcase and walked down the hall in search of a back door. Three minutes later he climbed into his car and drove away.

Chapter 10

"WE'VE NAILED THE BASTARD!" The yell which greeted Devon on his return to the office belonged to Bob Mortimer, standing with the kind of grin a Cheshire cat would have been proud of, as he pulled a picture from a wall-mounted noticeboard and waved it at the assembled room. "He's been staring down at us all this time."

Devon had just stepped out of the lift, slightly lost in thoughts about Emma having to leave town, and still smarting about the idiotic antics of the CIA Laurel and Hardy duo. He knew immediately that Mortimer's antics signalled some sort of break in the clouds.

"What have you got?"

Mortimer handed off the A4 glossy sheet, barely able to contain his excitement. "This is one Charles Nightingale, all-round scumbag, and the man who we now know murdered Dave Carpenter."

Devon glanced at the grainy features, the result of a head and shoulders shot taken with a telephoto lens that captured the subject emerging from the revolving door of a hotel entrance somewhere in Paris in 2008, according to a hand-scribbled caption. It was the full face and broad beam of a heavyweight, with dark brown hair tumbling over the ears to touch hideous sideburns that were a throwback to the seventies. A small white scar snaked from below the right eye to the corner of a bulbous upper lip. The eyes were narrow slits below bushy brows that lent an added look of darkness to a face of evil.

A general babble of conversation grew in the room as Devon studied the picture, aware that Mortimer was basking in the acclaim of his discovery. Devon held up his hand in the universal sign for quiet. "Settle down everyone. I need somebody to rewind and tell me what's been going on."

Mortimer crossed to his desk to lift a sheet of paper which he handed to Alan Doyle. "Your friend at the Metropolitan Police came through with a CCTV image outside the flower shop where Dave Carpenter stopped off. It was taken from a traffic cam and clearly shows a Mercedes drawing up alongside Dave's car. We managed to tweak the digital images enough to get a good facial which has been running through our FRS for the past hour."

"Did the Facial Recognition Software come up with Nightingale?"

Mortimer's smile grew wider. "It might do if you want to wait another few hours for it to complete the full gambit of neural network analysis and 3-D matches...."

Devon cut in on what he knew was going to be one of Mortimer's long-winded explanations. "Enough with the biometrics, just give me the shorthand version."

"Yeah, sorry Mike. The thing is that while we've been waiting on the computers doing their thing, I kept getting the feeling that I'd seen this face somewhere before. I was going through some of our scrapbooks when it hit me. It was on our rogue's gallery of most wanted."

Devon followed Mortimer's gaze back to the noticeboard, a five-foot square pegboard where more than thirty images of known international terrorists and assassins were pinned. "Good work, Bob. Now, can we dig out everything we have on Nightingale?"

"Already on it," Mortimer responded as he dropped onto his seat in front of a keyboard.

Devon turned to head for his office, shouting at Doyle to follow him. "Might be a good idea to see if our old friend, Claude, can help with this one." He was referring to Claude Bartran, the former head of France's security services *Groupe d'Intervention de la Gendarmerie Nationale*.

"How come?"

Devon pointed at the caption on the picture. "Maybe our target was in Paris in 2008 because he lives in the city. If anyone can run him down, it will be Claude."

A frown on Doyle's face showed he wasn't convinced. "That's a bit of stretch. A guy in Nightingale's profession pops up across Europe all the time. Maybe he was just in Paris for an in-and-out assignment, or maybe he was taking in the sights during a break in his murderous routine. Either way, it's a bit flimsy, not to mention the fact that old Claude has retired and probably gone to seed by now."

Devon grinned. "Don't you believe it. That old rascal will have his fingers on the pulse and can still call in more favours than just about anyone I know. Okay, I agree it's a long shot, but it beats the hell out of sitting around here. Even if Nightingale is not in France, who's to bet that Claude didn't have a thick file on him at one time or another?"

"Point taken," Doyle concurred.

Chelsea Horgan watched the commotion from General Sandford's office. Something big had broken. That much was obvious. She was itching to know what it was, but right now she was skating on thin ice, a predicament made clear by the General's withering onslaught on all things CIA.

She had made her report to Langley in an early morning call that was patched through to no less than the Deputy Director, just one of the many politically-appointed suits who rode a desk and never thought it might be a good thing all round to actually mix with the troops once in a while.

The platitudes had seemed sincere. Great job... good decision-making... the kind of initiative the CIA likes to see in its operatives. Blah! Blah! Stick with it, see what shakes from the London tree. Keep working this on your own and just holler if you need anything. Blah! Blah!

The lying toe-rag! Less than two hours later she was hauled in by the General to be told two of her colleagues were caught tailing Devon around London. The General's earlier charm had evaporated, particularly when he recounted how the episode could have put families at risk. "Not something I take kindly to, Agent Horgan. Not something I expect from someone to whom I extended every courtesy."

She could see the disappointment and anger etched in his face. And who could blame him?

She tried everything to persuade him of her innocence, even going so far as to recount the actual details of her call to Langley. "Let me put me this right. I'll talk to my DD to make sure it won't happen again..."

"If it's all the same to you, Agent Horgan, I'll do the talking from here on." The General's mood continued to darken as he reached for a desk phone, pressed a number for his switchboard, and asked to be patched directly through to the Prime Minister's personal secretary. He was put on hold for barely twenty seconds.

There was no preamble. "I need you to clear an urgent appointment with the PM this evening on a matter of national security. In the meantime, request the PM to put a call through to the White House demanding that the CIA Deputy Director of current operations in London makes himself available to take a call from me in the next ten minutes."

He returned the phone to its cradle and relaxed back in his leather chair.

Horgan couldn't hide her incredulity. "Sir, forgive me for asking, but do you really have that kind of clout?"

The General's features lightened and a smile danced across his face. "When you get to my age, Agent

Horgan, you learn that you need to take as many shortcuts as possible. I don't have the patience for diplomacy the way I used to and, truth to tell, I've learned that being an old curmudgeon gets me to where I want to go quicker than dancing around people's bruised egos. We have a situation here that demands I use the full repertoire at my disposal to protect my people. Frankly speaking, this nonsense with your agency needs to be sorted out before any more wires are crossed."

Horgan tried to pick her words carefully. "I'm truly sorry if anything I did will lead to a falling out between the CIA and any intelligence agencies based in England. In truth, I still don't understand where this operation of yours fits in with the likes of MI5 and MI6, but something tells me you guys are rather high on the totem pole and have probably been doing business with our side for some time now. I'm just a grunt on the ground that has to live with the need-to-know rules, but I would urge you to consider not freezing us out."

The General leaned forward as if to emphasise his next point. "Very commendable of you to stand up for your agency, my dear. The truth is that none of this is your fault. The UK and USA agencies have been playing these little games since I was in nappies, or diapers as you would say, but every so often we need to reset the parameters...."

The sound of the telephone interrupted the General's discourse. He lifted it off the receiver and hit the speaker button.

"General, I have CIA Deputy Director John Madison on the line."

"Patch him through."

After a few seconds, a staccato voice filled the console. "Is this General Sir John Sandford?"

"It is. Thank you for calling, Director Madison."

"We both know that I didn't have very much choice in the matter. Can't say I appreciate the way in which I was roused from my bed. Couldn't this have waited a few hours?"

Horgan squirmed at the largely one-sided conversation that followed. This old boy was quite something. She had heard of people being taken down a few pegs, but this was the mother and father of all lectures. If she was being honest, she enjoyed every bit of it. The bastard on the other end of the line had well and truly shafted her. He deserved everything he got.

"To summarise," the General intoned, "you will ensure your agents do not repeat the exercise of following my operatives. You will also ensure you do not go digging into any matters concerning this investigation unless you have my express permission to do so. In short, Director Madison, you will stand down your people until I am ready to make use of your resources."

"Are you seriously suggesting that we sit on our thumbs and then jump to it whenever you decide you might need us?"

The General winked across the table at Horgan before responding. "Couldn't have put it better myself. Besides, I've decided to allow your Agent Horgan to piggyback our operation for a while. She has struck us as a very capable and dependable ally who will be able to look after your interests and report regularly to your Station Head in London. Do you have any problems with that?"

"Where is Agent Horgan now?"

The General glanced at Horgan and held a finger up to his lips. "Right now, she's sitting in on a briefing with our full team."

There was a momentary pause before Madison responded. "Agent Horgan is not familiar with our London operations. In normal circumstances she would have already returned to Washington. I must insist on one of our senior London agents joining up with you instead of Horgan."

"This is not open for discussion, Director. Agent Horgan stumbled into this and we're happy to keep her on board. I could, of course, make this official by going up your chain of command."

"There's no need for any more phone calls, General. However, I want it clearly understood that if American interests start to surface in this investigation, then all bets are off. I can be just as much of a playground bully as you when it comes to protecting my people."

The General laughed. "Good for you, Madison. I wouldn't have it any other way. Now, I think I'll let you get back to your missed sleep. It was good talking with you."

Horgan watched him hit the off button. "Did you mean what you said about me sticking with your operation?"

"Yes. I allowed you to listen into that conversation so that you understand the ground rules. Are they acceptable to you?"

"Affirmative, sir."

Devon and Doyle were deep in conversation when Horgan stepped out of the General's office and moved towards them.

"That old codger Claude is still trying to take the Parimutuel to the cleaners with his daily tilt at the horses. He swears that if he had saved his bets all these years, he would already be a multi-millionaire." Devon was referring to the former French intelligence officer's love of gambling, though in fact he knew Bartran wagered only modest amounts.

"Can he help us with running down Nightingale?" Doyle asked.

"What do you think? Says he'll be glad of something to do. He's intending to pay a call to the GIGN offices and will let us know what he finds.

Knowing Claude, he'll probably camp out there until something shakes loose."

Devon became aware of Horgan's presence and turned to face her. "I see the General has been making it clear what we think of the CIA."

She smiled at him. "That's quite a boss you have there. He has spelled out how things are to go from here on in. He has also agreed that I will be sticking with you guys for a while."

Devon frowned. "I want you to know that I advised differently. Seems to me that the CIA has become a distraction we don't need just now...."

She held up her hand to stop him in mid-sentence. "No need to go any further. The General has already read the riot act, and one riot act per day is enough for any gal. I wanna help, but only as part of your team. Anything I report back to my station will only be by your say so."

"Fair enough. I've already briefly introduced you to Doyle here. You will be working closely with him. Alan, why don't you bring Chelsea up to date on where we are with our friend in France?"

Devon turned and marched down the hall, knowing that Doyle's face was starting to redden again as he ushered Horgan to his office.

Chapter 11

IT HAD BEEN A LONG DAY for General Sandford. The loss of one of his men burrowed deep into his soul. He felt Dave Carpenter's death as keenly as if it were his own son. He had always been like that. From the moment he took command of his first regiment in those almost-forgotten army days and continuing into his work with various strands of the security services, he was fiercely protective of the men under his charge.

Yes, he rode them hard. He demanded a relentless regime of training and retraining and insisted on old-school discipline. It was done to keep them at their peak, to provide them with the skills needed to survive in a murky world. In return, he offered them total support, both in their professional and private lives. It was the kind of leadership that bred fierce loyalty and mutual trust.

It was why he now sat facing Mike Devon outlining his plans to spend money. A lot of money. He had prevaricated too long on giving the green light for a shopping list he had drawn up months ago. He would wait no longer.

Devon looked on bemused as the General made a succession of telephone calls, the first of which would set *LonWash Securities* back a cool ten million. It was the latest in the range of Dassault Falcon executive jets, a luxury 10-seater that could set his team down anywhere in Europe or the Americas without the frustrating booking and boarding delays experienced with commercial airlines.

Sandford made clear to Devon that the Dassault 2000Ex was not intended for cushy junkets. It was for mission-critical flights that would provide the unit with a distinctive edge. Powered by two Pratt and Whitney Canada engines, the jet was capable of 0.8 mach speed that would shave crucial hours off the time needed to get where they wanted to go. It also came with an Iridium ST3100 Aircell unit, which provided instant access to satellite communications.

Devon was impressed, but he had one query. "How do we deal with the logistics of getting available pilots, not to mention storage and maintenance?"

Sandford smiled. "Already taken care of. Three months ago, I hired two experienced pilots, highly rated by all accounts. They have been on a small retainer to keep them available until now. They don't know it yet, but they start with us full-time tomorrow."

"So, this was not a spur of the moment thing?"

The General looked rueful. "It was something I should have done long before now. To tell the truth, I'm not sure why I've waited. It's not as if we can't afford it, and the events of the last few days have convinced me we are dealing with an imperative to move this organisation up a few notches. I made a sizeable deposit to secure the option to buy and, as you've just heard in my call to a very grateful broker, the final payment will be transferred later today."

Devon was about to speak when the General raised his hand. "Before you ask, the jet will be delivered to a rented hangar at the Trafalgar Flying Club's private airfield near Stansted. We already have our own maintenance crew itching to start work. It will give them something else to do besides running constant checks on our Bell 407 helicopter."

The wide-eyed stare from Devon was just what Sandford expected. "Oh, didn't I tell you? It arrived yesterday after I'd haggled a good bit of change from two million. We already have a helipad on the roof, so we will be good to go from this evening."

"Sir, you're telling me we now have a jet *and* a helicopter?"

"Yes. The helicopter will be more practical and efficient for moving around the UK. It can be whistled up and on the helipad within ten minutes. All the licences and permits are being rushed through the Civil Aviation Authority, which will list us as a priority one carrier. I've had it on my mind since that cross-country chase to safeguard your wife last year."

Devon frowned as he remembered how Alan Doyle had pursued a hitman assigned to kill Emma Devon and her son. After a frantic two-hour dash, Doyle had just managed to intercept the assassin before he ran Emma off the road. In the end she had swerved and crashed down an embankment but had survived thanks to Doyle's intervention.

Sandford snapped him away from the memory. "Next item of business is to beef up our personnel. By my reckoning we need at least four new recruits. Our resources are being stretched to the limit and we need to ensure we have the capability to match whatever is being thrown at us, not just with this current crisis, but for everything that lies ahead. I'll leave that to you and Doyle to decide."

It was music to Devon's ears. "We have a standby list of potential new operatives. Alan has narrowed it down from a trawl he did six months ago among his old Special Forces buddies. I dare say we can match you for getting things sorted pretty quickly."

"Good," the General responded as he shuffled papers on the desk. "I'm also pressing ahead with the conversion of the top floor into sleeping quarters for all staff. The showers and toilets were completed last month, but I intend to accelerate the creation of a dozen rooms, each holding beds for at least three people. I have builders coming in to work around the clock until they are finished."

"Why the panic now, if you don't mind me saying?"

The General rose and paced the office. "There was always a certain logic to having live-in quarters for staff pulling long shifts or being needed for standby. I have to admit though that with this hit-list I'd be happier if everyone is confined to barracks, so to speak, until this blows over."

Devon was unequivocal in his agreement. "It will make things a lot easier for us, but what about those people with families? We can't risk leaving them exposed. These assassins might use the families as bait."

"I think I've got that one covered. I'm arranging a two-week holiday charter to Spain for the families. Everyone will be shipped out for a bit of sunshine to leave us free to find these bastards. Our finance boffin, John Avery, will be going around today to make arrangements. I want this completed within forty-eight hours, by which time all essential staff will gather up what they need and report back here to their new temporary address."

Devon sat in silence for a few moments before responding. "You seem to have thought of everything. Might I ask where all the money is coming from?"

Sandford laughed. "Least of my worries, dear boy. What with the profits coming in from our legitimate Government-sponsored private security contracts, not to mention the funds we've managed to liberate from the scum we have to deal with, we are what the city would call cash rich. We are a private enterprise and, as such, we don't have to worry about oversight. An organisation like this is expected to have all the corporate frills, so why not start acting like we belong among the high-fliers, no pun intended. Don't know about you, but I rather enjoy a spending spree from time to time."

He was still smiling when he returned to his seat. "Now, I have a meeting to attend with the Prime Minister. I want you to accompany me as part of our new security arrangements. That way, I can brief you on the way back to my club where I intend to spend the night. A lot is riding on how the PM reacts to what's going on."

"Suits great," Devon told him. "I'll take Alfie Cheadle with me. He lives alone, so after we drop you off, we'll swing by his house to pick up his belongings, and then head over to mine to grab a few clean shirts, among other things. As you know, Emma's gone to her parents so Cheadle and I will be the first house guests of *Hotel LonWash*. We'll make arrangements for the others to filter in when the renovations are completed."

The General's meeting with the Prime Minister couldn't have gone better. He had arrived at the back entrance to Downing Street determined not to accept anything less than full control over the activities of all covert agencies until this crisis had passed. The PM had to be made to understand that the attack on *LonWash Securities* went to the very heart of the country's ability to successfully combat terrorism.

It was one of the reasons why the General had bypassed his usual briefing with the PM's top aide, Sir Norman Melrose. Although Downing Street had made it clear the door was always open to Sandford, it had become custom and practice over the years for Sandford to feed everything through Melrose. Apart from the PM, Melrose was the only Government official to know the true nature of *LonWash Securities*, and the intelligence work they carried out on behalf of the country.

The General regretted leaving Melrose out of the loop. The aide was a staunch ally of the organisation and had proved his worth on countless occasions by helping divert attention from its operations and following through on whatever he was asked to do. The General would make it up to him.

Right now, he needed to look the PM in the eye. He wanted to see for himself if the man blinked at any of his requests.

The General's reasoning for taking control had a solid foundation. He was a member of the Government's crisis COBRA committee, and it was known he had the ear of the PM when it came to dishing out advice on security matters. This had provided him with the ideal shield for *LonWash Securities*, an organisation the heads of other agencies believed had benefitted greatly not only from the General's vast experiences, but also because of the inside track he had cultivated with the PM.

There were times when MI5 and MI6 had cut across *LonWash* operations but saw them as little more than the blundering intrusions of a private sector firm, albeit one that seemed to have a lot of political clout. Sure, there were jurisdictional arguments, but these were usually resolved through the interventions of the General, a man they admired and respected for his services to his country, even if he had swopped his uniform to build what appeared to be a nice little nest-egg business.

What they couldn't know was that the General was still serving his country, perhaps more diligently than any of them. All the private contracts and apparent lavishness of *LonWash* was designed for one purpose only. They were a camouflage for the true nature of the organisation, the development of a covert team that offered lethal responses to the actions of terrorists.

They didn't build cases, they closed them. They didn't believe in giving an enemy of the State his day in court. Instead, they offered only a one-way ticket to obscurity.

In the ten-years since he had established *LonWash*, the General had managed to keep these activities hidden from view. But now someone, somewhere, knew all about them. Unless the person could be found, there was no telling where this would lead.

He needed to convince the PM to agree to give him

a certain carte blanche.

As it turned out, he needn't have worried. He had rarely seen the PM in such a foul mood. As he eased back into the rear seat of the armoured Range Rover on the return journey from Downing Street, Sandford could still remember the parting words. "I don't care what it takes, or what it costs, you find these people and put them out of business. If anyone stands in your way or feels you don't have the authority to do what you need to do, you have them call me. Until further notice, you are top of the tree of every police force, security agency, coastguard, customs, or whatever organisation your investigation cuts across."

After relaying the main bullet points to Devon, who was behind the wheel, the General's mind whirred with a succession of thoughts and ideas about how to proceed. He needed time to think this through. He was determined to prepare a strategy that would galvanise the vast resources that had just been placed at his disposal.

He was glad of his decision to head to his club, knowing that for most of the evening and into the early hours of the morning he would make use of one the club's private suites to meet with people who didn't usually like to have their feathers ruffled by interference from outsiders.

Chapter 12

THE ASSASSIN SAT IN HIS CAR just a block away from the world-famous Harrods department store in the heart of Knightsbridge. He had parked up more than an hour ago, with a clear line of sight to the imposing five-storey Georgian building, one of many on a street that housed some of London's most exclusive offices and private members' clubs.

Only a small, polished brass plaque - fixed into place at the top of three steps leading from the pavement - announced this as the home of *The Shannon Club*.

The uniformed attendant standing guard under an expansive gold-braid awning was a clearer indication that there was something special about the otherwise unadorned building.

The Club was founded in 1820 by a group of the city's leading financiers. It was strictly a gentleman's club, which was proud of its boast that in almost two hundred years no female had stepped foot inside its hallowed precincts. Over the years the bankers and investment brokers had allowed their ranks to be swelled by industrialists, retired Army personnel – provided they were at or above the rank of General – and by politicians, but only if they had held office as a Minister of the Crown.

Applications to join the Club were unheard of. Potential members had to be put forward in the strictest confidence, without their prior knowledge. Existing members voted by using small black or white balls, which were deposited in a locked box in the grand hallway on the second floor. If the box contained even one black ball at the appointed time of opening, the individual would be turned down and his name prohibited from being put forward again for a period of at least five years.

It was an antiquated organisation that had clung to its traditions despite the march of modernisation in the outside world. To General Sandford it was an anachronism, but one that served his purpose well. He used it as a retreat, making use of its luxurious lounges, its five-star cuisine, and its total assurance of discretion. It also had an upper floor of bedrooms that matched the finest of London's hotels and were at the disposal of members who needed to stop over for the night, or who had become too intoxicated to make their way home.

At fifty-thou a year, membership of *The Shannon Club* didn't come cheap, but as many of its patrons often observed: "If you need to ask how much, you most likely can't afford it."

The assassin knew the history of the place. He had read about it during his research on General Sandford's movements. He knew his target visited here often and had determined this would be the best spot to carry out his assignment. He had waited here patiently for each of the past three evenings and had snorted with derision every time someone entered the building. The decadence of the place made him want to throw up.

The lights of a vehicle entering the street caused him to jump in his seat.

The General watched as Devon eased the Range Rover against the pavement directly outside the Club. In the passenger seat Alfie Cheadle was already reaching for the door handle.

"Don't bother, I can take it from here," the General commanded.

"I'll walk you to the door..."

"That's not necessary."

Cheadle swivelled to face the General. "Sir, our orders are to stay with you and, with respect, it was you who issued those orders to the whole group. None of us are to be alone over the next few weeks."

"I know what I said, Alfie, but believe me this is one of the safest places in London. Besides, no one knows that I'm a member here. I intend to stay the night. You can pick me up at 8am. Now gentlemen, I will bid you goodnight. Go home and get some sleep."

The General pushed open the door and stepped onto the pavement. He noticed the doorman stiffen and reach for a wall-mounted keypad. It was a regular occurrence. His job was to ensure that by the time a member reached the top step the number sequence would be completed, and the automatic door would spring open. It would not do to keep a member waiting.

On this particular evening, however, the new arrival would not reach the top step.

The assassin waited until the Range Rover passed his position. The tinted windows meant he couldn't see into the interior, but it had the look of a Government-issue vehicle, and that was good enough for him to swing into action. When it slowed and pulled to the kerbside, his reactions were immediate. He grabbed a Mini Uzi submachine pistol from where it was lying under a blanket on the passenger seat, thumbed the safety switch to off, and climbed out of his car.

He transferred the pistol to his right hand, which he held down by his side as he crossed the road. He was less than fifty yards from the Range Rover when the rear door opened.

He tensed as he continued his walk. If the person who alighted was not his target, he would simply mount the pavement and walk away in the opposite direction. If it was his target, he was a dead man walking.

He recognised the familiar shock of white hair and the side profile of his target as the man slammed the door behind him and began to walk toward the steps leading to *The Shannon Club*. There was now less than twenty yards between them. He hoisted the Uzi and pointed it at the receding back of General Sandford.

"For fuck's sake, what are you doing?" Devon yelled at the General, but by that time the rear door was slamming shut.

Devon had already unbuckled his seat belt and pushed open his door to block the General's path. As he rose to his feet, he became aware of a shadow approaching the car from the rear. He didn't wait to look. The hairs rising on the back of his neck was all the warning he needed.

Devon dived low, aiming for the General's knees in a classic rugby tackle. Even as the old man's legs give way and he started to topple on top of Devon, the sound of automatic gunfire filled the quiet street with a deafening and foreboding echo.

The General's body seemed to spasm as he collapsed on Devon, who rolled over him and screamed back at the car's interior.

"Alfie, danger, danger on your nine."

It was a superfluous warning. Cheadle had detected the movement through the car's side mirror and was scrambling across the car to dive out the open driver's door when the shots rang out.

Glock in hand, Cheadle threw his arm across the roof of the vehicle and began firing at the gunman whose response was to shift the Uzi in the direction of the new menace. He squeezed out a long burst, which forced Cheadle to duck behind the Rover's armoured exterior.

By this time Devon had his Sig Sauer P226 unholstered. He rolled out from the rear of the vehicle, taking less than a millisecond to acquire his target. The figure was about ten feet away, turning the Uzi away from Cheadle's position to point directly at him.

Devon didn't give him a chance to depress the trigger again. The Sig spat out four quick 9mm rounds, all aimed at the gunman's head. Devon watched as the figure was thrown backwards to crash heavily onto the tarmacked road.

Devon jumped to his feet, raced past the vehicle, and sprinted towards the spreadeagled figure. He kicked the Uzi away from the outstretched hand and stared down at a mangled face. His rounds had all found their target. For good measure he added a fifth, drilled directly into the dead man's forehead.

He rushed back to the Rover, dreading what he would find. Cheadle was bent over the General, and there was a large pool of blood spreading out from below the prostrate figure.

Devon tried to walk forward, but his legs refused to budge. It was as if they were paralysed by shock. He would never forgive himself for not protecting the one man he admired above all others.

And then he heard the faintest of moans.

Chapter 13

THE SOUNDS OF EARLY MORNING rush-hour traffic drifted up from the streets to the New York penthouse apartment where Carl Stratton was hunched over a laptop reading the encrypted email that had pinged him awake.

Despite the brief contents expressing apology for failure, Stratton smiled at what he was reading. While he had slept, one of the assassins commissioned by *Das Trio Berne*, the bungling triumvirate led by Felix Hoffmeier, had made an attempt on the life of General Sandford. The General was currently in an intensive care unit at the Princess Grace Hospital in London's Marylebone district, but his chances of survival were not known.

Alive or dead, it didn't matter to Stratton. The fact that an attempt had been made, and that the old bastard had been put out of commission, would serve its purpose just as well.

For the time being, at least.

Stratton took stock of what had been achieved by Hoffmeier's hired guns. One man dead, another in hospital, and no news on any of the other targets. To top matters, the assassin who had tried to snuff out General Sandford had been killed at the scene. No wonder Hoffmeier's email was full of apologies and promises to do better. In any other circumstances Stratton would hop on a plane and pay a final visit to the former Nazi murderer.

Instead he continued to smile.

As he reread the email message, he noted one other interesting piece of information. The CIA had somehow gotten involved. It was a lot sooner than he expected, but it might just help things along.

When he had first confronted Hoffmeier in his hotel room several weeks ago, Stratton had held out little hope of any meaningful culling of the *LonWash Securities* top team. What he had needed was a patsy to throw a spanner into the works, although he had hoped things would have progressed a lot further by now.

It was time to nudge them along.

He spent the next hour working on a new email mandate, but this time it would not go to Hoffmeier. In an important break from protocol, Stratton decided to make direct contact with the list of assassins, a list he had insisted on receiving as part of Hoffmeier's original instructions.

There was nothing direct, however, about the way in which the emails would eventually end up in the inboxes of the recipients. Stratton was a computer genius, well-versed in the methodologies of piggybacking servers and bouncing the message across several continents in an untraceable trail of confusion.

Anyone trying to backtrack would simply run into a spaghetti configuration of red-herring codes. There was simply no way of breaking through.

Unless the original sender wanted you to.

The challenge for Stratton was to lay a few crumbs, an IP address fragment here, a longer-than-usual server bounce there. Done in such a way that it would appear to an expert to be the result of carelessness or amateurishness on the part of the sender.

Satisfied he had ticked all the right boxes, Stratton hit the send button and eased back in his chair. His grin had just got wider.

He loved manipulating people. It was what he had done for the past twenty years, mostly spent standing in the shadows while his various bank accounts grew to obscene amounts, money that he needed to fulfil a lifetime ambition.

Find a weakness and you can make most people do just about anything. That's what he had done with

Hoffmeier and his two cronies, Jurgen Kappel and Dieter Neumann. In many ways he admired how as young men they had seized the opportunity to rise from obscurity to the heights of power, crushing minions with a ruthlessness similar to what he himself had demonstrated on many occasions. In another era he might have enjoyed working alongside them, but their time had been and gone.

He had stumbled across their exploits quite by chance when he hacked into the computers of the Monuments, Fine Arts and Archives Programme on behalf of a client who wanted to trace a priceless artefact believed stolen by the Nazis in Paris in 1942. He was fascinated by a number of post-war investigations that kept throwing up the names of *Das Trio Berne and* became convinced that these men had pulled off one of the greatest financial coups of the twentieth century.

He had quickly downloaded whatever information he could find about them before computer-scrubbing all mention of them from official MFAAP records. In less than six months he had compiled a detailed dossier of their financial activities over almost half a century, in the knowledge that the opportunity would arise to bend them to his will.

He had done much the same thing with a prominent politician whose proclivity for young boys was brought to his attention more than a decade earlier. Stratton had bided his time, spending considerable sums in gathering evidence, including videos, to ensure his target was snared. He pounced at just the right moment, shortly after the man was appointed to one of the top positions in the Government of the United Kingdom.

Like *Das Trio Berne*, the disgraced politician had become little more than a jigsaw piece in Stratton's master plan to bring that same Government to its knees.

Container ship captain Charlie Wilson enjoyed a grandstand view of the Felixstowe port from his bridge high on the superstructure's quarterdeck. He shifted his gaze from the windows to the clipboard held by one of the Revenue and Custom officers who had completed their inspection of the belongings of those crew members disembarking from the vessel for shore leave.

Security of the containers was handled by a shipping agency via secure computer tracking software which was shared with the Custom authorities. Any tampering with the sealed locks would immediately blip an alarm.

Wilson's own distinctive bright red laptop was flashing pages from the software tracing system, with a corner of the screen showing a GPS fix on his ship's current location within European shipping lanes. He wouldn't go anywhere without it.

"Just sign here, Charlie," the Customs man requested.

Wilson scrawled his signature across the clipboard sheet before bending to power off his laptop. He folded down the screen, removed the power lead, and stuffed the machine into a shoulder carry bag. "I'll be taking this with me as well."

The Customs man nodded in acknowledgement. "Okay, you're good to go. See you next trip."

Wilson walked from the bridge, crossed a passageway, and disappeared into a lift which took him down four levels to the gangplank walkway. He emerged onto the quayside and climbed aboard a shuttlebus waiting to take the crew to the train station almost a mile away. It would take less than two hours for Wilson to reach his destination.

Inside his small London apartment, he removed the laptop from its bag, hit the power button, and waited for it to go through its start-up routine. When the desktop finally settled, he simultaneously pressed four buttons on the keypad and watched as the console sprang open to reveal its inner workings.

He leaned in to stare at two battery compartments, each about the size of a standard iPhone, and each with identical manufacture markings denoting the battery's structure and content.

Only one, however, was actually a battery.

Wilson used his thumb and forefinger to lift the left side component from its housing. There were no wires connecting it to any other part of the machine and it came free easily under the slightest of pressures.

He pushed down on the corner of the keyboard panel to snap it back into place and reached across his desk to grab a brown padded envelope. He inserted the false battery into the envelope, sealed it, and shoved it into his coat pocket.

Outside on the pavement he hailed a taxi for the cross-city trip to Charing Cross Station where he made his way to a bank of lockers. He fished in his pocket for the key to his designated locker, withdrew the brown envelope, and pushed it into the two-by-two compartment.

It was a journey he had made with anger and trepidation every month for the past year. He didn't question what was in the strange battery-shaped packages. The man who had been waiting for him with a silenced pistol inside his apartment had made it clear his life would be forfeit if he tampered with the packages in any way. As an added incentive, he pushed across two recent photographs of Wilson's grown-up daughter. They were taken with a telephoto lens aimed through the kitchen window of her home.

Wilson had been estranged from his family for more than fifteen years, but his devotion to daughter Rebecca was stronger than ever. On many occasions he had driven by that same house hoping to catch a glimpse of her. He would do anything rather than let harm befall her.

Satisfied that Wilson would do what he was told, the intruder produced a bright red laptop which he cable-linked to Wilson's dilapidated old machine. It took him less than ten minutes to copy-and-clone the contents of Wilson's hard drive.

He then showed the old sea captain the coded sequence for unlocking the body of the custom-made machine, pointing out the empty housing for a spare battery. He explained that each time Wilson's ship docked at one of its regular ports of call in the Bahamas he would be given a battery to be placed inside the laptop.

After going through the rest of the instructions the man stood up to leave. "One more thing. Always make sure the laptop is powered up when the Customs people are aboard. That way they won't have reason to suspect the machine is not what it's supposed to be. You will become familiar to them for carrying your laptop on and off the ship."

"What if one of them decides to open the inner casing structure?"

The man smiled. "Even if they feel inclined to do so, all they will discover will be a double-battery mechanism, a not uncommon sight in certain bulk-manufactured models."

When the stranger eventually left, Wilson knew that his uncluttered life had changed forever. He slumped into his favourite old sofa chair and felt real fear for the first time.

As he wept, he could not know that he had joined a list of five other people who also now owned a bright red laptop.

He was also unaware that outside on his porch, Carl Stratton was smiling at the ease with which he had added one more puppet to his lethal sideshow.

Chapter 14

DEVON KNEW THERE WAS NOTHING to be gained by continuing to pace up and down the hospital corridors. It had been a long night. The General had survived a five-hour emergency operation, after which the surgeon had put his chances at "slightly better than evens." Despite a few scares caused by the occasional ear-splitting bleep from the bank of monitors surrounding his bed, the old boy was still fighting from somewhere inside an induced coma.

One of the assassin's bullets had nicked his heart. A centimetre lower and it would have been curtains. As it was, the delicate repair work was not guaranteed to compensate for the massive shock and trauma to the system. The next forty-eight hours would tell the medical team if their efforts were to be rewarded.

Devon needed to get back to his team. He had provided Doyle with updates during the night, knowing that everyone at headquarters was staring at the phones and refusing to grab some sleep. It was time to leave the General to his personal life-struggle and get back in the fight.

It was time to get on the front foot and end this war on his organisation. Once and for all.

He nodded at Alfie Cheadle - who had remained at his side throughout the night - and barged his way out through the hospital entrance, oblivious to the irate stares of a few people who were forced to stand aside to let him through the large swinging doors.

Cheadle took the wheel of the Range Rover and eased into the Marylebone traffic. At the first set of traffic lights he moved to the outside lane and looked across at Devon. "Now would be a good time for you to grab a change of clothes before we head back to the office."

Devon was about to argue but thought better of it. His home was less than five minutes away. "Good idea. Might even treat myself to a quick shower."

Both men jumped from the car when it stopped alongside the kerb outside Devon's house. Cheadle pulled his Glock from the holster and held it down by his side as he scanned the road.

Devon bounded up the steps, fished his bunch of keys from a coat pocket, and inserted one into the door's faded brass holder. As a matter of habit, he made a quarter turn anticlockwise, before returning to the twelve o'clock position. He was about to turn the key in the opposite direction when he noticed that a small green light was not pulsing as it should be in a dust-covered glass shield high up in the door frame.

Despite the outward appearances, the decrepit-looking Yale lock was in fact a state-of-the-art security mechanism that reacted to a pre-coded sequence. The absence of a green light told Devon that someone had tampered with the lock since he last left the house.

He removed the key and walked back towards the car. "Get in and drive around the corner to the underground garage. I've had an unwanted visitor. Let's see if he's still there or if he's left something for me."

Three minutes later they were standing outside a private door connecting his house to the car park. This time a green light blinked when Devon repeated the opening sequence. "We're clear."

He pushed the door fully open to reveal a small porch leading to the kitchen at the rear of the premises. He motioned for Cheadle to go right and moved forward to the left, holding his Sig in a two-handed sweep. There was an eerie silence, broken only by the squeal of his rubber-soled boots as he edged up the parquet floor.

He paused in the hallway to glance through an open door leading to the front living room. Satisfied the room was empty he turned his attention to the front door.

He spotted the moulded block of C-4 almost instantly, letting his eyes trace the wiring down from the coat rail and across the floor to disappear under the porch mat.

He whistled for Cheadle to join him but warned him to stay back while he knelt to gingerly lift the mat. "Just as I thought, a pressure-pad ignition. Simple, but highly effective."

Devon pulled the wires from the disc pad and then rose to yank the other ends from the C-4.

Cheadle winced. "Jeez, Mike, you don't believe in subtlety, do you?"

"It's okay, Alfie. Once the pressure pad was disarmed the rest was pretty useless. When you've been around these things as long as I have, you get to know when to jump in and when to run."

"Mike, this is all getting pretty fucked up in a hurry. What do we do now?"

"Don't know about you, but I think I'll take that shower now."

The office was frantic with activity by the time Devon and Cheadle dumped their change-of-clothes holdalls on the floor inside the conference room.

As usual, Doyle brought calm to the proceedings. "Listen up, people. We need to bring Mike up to speed with what we've got so far." He waited until the general buzz quietened down before continuing. "We tracked last night's gunman down to a hotel near St. Pancras train station. Good job for us that he was still carrying his room key. I sent a team there in the wee small hours and discovered the room was booked by one Alexei Baronova, who checked in three nights ago. We accessed his room safe and found three passports, all in different names."

Doyle leaned forward and picked up the passports from the conference table. "We ran the photos from these through the usual software systems and almost immediately got a hit with an Interpol mugshot. Seems he's wanted in about a dozen countries."

Devon crossed the room to take the passports from Doyle's hand. "This is great work team."

"Wait, there's more, a lot more. We retrieved a laptop from under the bed and got it back here fast to the techie boys. They're boasting it took them less than a minute to get past the password protection..."

"Actually, it was about forty seconds." The interruption came from Tim Halloran, head of the *LonWash* computer surveillance team.

Doyle exaggerated a bow of courtesy towards Halloran. "Okay, it's your show. Tell us what you found."

Halloran lifted two pieces of paper and waved one in Devon's direction. "This is a print-out of an email that matches exactly the one you discovered in Austria. Quite obviously it's a group message, but just as before it's heavily encrypted with no chance of breaking down either where it came from or where it went, apart from the two recipients we already know about."

"So, what's the other piece of paper about?" Devon asked.

"This," said Halloran triumphantly, "is the breakthrough we've been waiting for. It's a second email which arrived less than an hour ago while we were still searching through the laptop's deleted message trail. I think it's best if I showed it on the big screen."

He hit a few buttons on an iPad linked to a projector. An image flashed immediately on a white screen fixed to the wall at the head of the room.

Devon could hardly believe what he was reading.

Message Title: Final Warning

From: Me
To: Alexei Baronova
Copy: Max Steiner, Charles Nightingale, Dragan Boskovic, Martin Greene, Jeff Millar.

All but one of you has so far failed to carry out the missions that were contracted to you. You were made aware that failure to do so would result in the ultimate sanction. Any contract remaining unfulfilled at midnight on August 6 will leave me with no choice but to invoke the terms of our agreement. There is no hiding place. You will know by now that my reach is without boundaries.

EXECUTE OR BE EXECUTED!

Devon read the message several times before taking a seat. "Is this what I think it is?"

Doyle jumped in. "There can be little doubt that we now have our list of assassins. Whoever has been sending these messages appears to have made a crucial error in his encryption techniques. It's like the old saying about giving people enough rope and they'll hang themselves."

Halloran coughed slightly to get attention. "Actually, this is not the kind of mistake an expert techno-geek would make. I don't doubt the authenticity of the email. It follows the previous techniques, although at a guess I would say it originated from a different source server and displays the characteristics of a different hand on the keystrokes."

"Explain," Devon said brusquely.

"Apart from the obvious mistake of forgetting to hide the names of all the recipients, the message is also showing IP address fragments which might lead us back to the source, if we get lucky. This kind of sloppy work was certainly not apparent in the first email we recovered. It's just not the sort of thing a trained operative would overlook."

Devon lifted the copies of both sheets of paper, not quite sure what he was looking for. "So, have we a hoax second email, or are we just looking a gift horse in the mouth?"

"Like I said," Halloran continued, "there are too many similarities between the two to dismiss the conclusion that the names on the list are who they appear to be. I would like to do a lot more work on trying to track the other proxy server fragments that we've detected. That should tell us a lot more about what's going on here."

Devon thought about this for a few seconds. "Could it be simply a case that two different people in whatever organisation has targeted us were responsible for each sending out a message, but the second person was not as technically gifted as the first?"

Halloran shook his head. "Don't think so. The second message still displays a high level of expertise. The knowledge of hacking into random servers and laying a ghost trail around the world is not something anyone can just pick up. If it wasn't for the obvious mistakes, I would have a healthy respect for both senders."

Devon rose and walked away from the table. "Okay, we're going round in circles here. Let's go with what we have." He turned to Doyle. "Alan, put everything we've got on tracking down all available information on the four names who are still living. By sometime this evening I want us ready to go on the offensive. We're going to need four different teams, so I suggest you hurry up about bringing in those extra pairs of hands you've been promising us."

He continued his walk to the door, before stopping to look at Halloran. "I hope I don't need to tell you that we need your team to bring us back answers on those computer fragments that seem to hold an important key. We need those answers yesterday."

"Consider it done," Halloran said as he brushed hurriedly past Devon.

The noise in the room grew as Devon stepped out into the corridor. He was aware of a rustle behind him and turned to face Doyle.

"Aren't you staying to help out, Mike."

"Nah, I've got a few things to do. I'll join you later."

Cloistered in his office, Devon leaned back in his chair and rubbed the fingers of both hands against his temple. Despite his earlier flippancy about taking a shower after discovering the bomb at his home, his morale was at the lowest point he could remember.

What if Emma had returned to the house unannounced? He couldn't shake the image of her cradling his son and opening the front door to step into the killing zone that had been created inside his porch. How could he live with something like that?

The simple answer was that he couldn't. Not for the first time his job had put his family in harm's way. This time, however, he knew he needed to do something about it. At forty-one he was not the young gung-ho trailblazer he once was. This was a game for younger men. For younger, single men, he corrected himself.

He had done his bit. It was time to move aside. It was time to be the husband and father he had promised himself he would be. He was a moderately wealthy man, thanks to a sizeable inheritance from his parents, and could chose to live whatever way he wanted.

Sure, he would miss the action and the adrenaline. He had known nothing else since he was a teenager drafted into MI6, now known as the Secret Intelligence Service, and sent on his first undercover mission to America. He had chased terrorists all around the world before signing up to General Sandford's new off-the-books agency. The surroundings might have changed, but the job hadn't.

He had lost count of the men he had had to kill in a twenty-two year career spent protecting his country from all manner of global threats. Twenty-two years! That's more than anyone had a right to expect.

And then he considered the fate of the General. Would a younger Devon have reacted differently and kept the old man out of harm's way? He was pretty sure he knew the answer to that one.

As he continued to think through his circumstances, he became more convinced about what he would do when this current crisis ended.

A knock on the door dragged him from his reverie. He looked up as Doyle stepped into the room, closing the door behind him. "What's up, Mike?"

"Just thinking a few things through."

Doyle crossed the room, lifted a chair and straddled across it in front of Devon's desk. "Don't try to kid a kidder. We've been around too many blocks together for me not to realise something other than these agency attacks is bothering you. I saw that look in your eyes when you left the briefing."

Devon was about to argue, but realised the man sitting opposite was probably the only true friend he had managed to hold onto for more than five minutes. Doyle was, of course much more than that. Devon doubted if he could have continued pushing his limits had it not been for the presence of the likeable and lethal ex Special Air Services sergeant. They had shared many a scrape, saved each other's hide in a dozen fucked-up scenarios, and developed a bond that few men get to experience.

Devon decided to tell all, including his decision to leave the agency.

When he had finished, Doyle frowned. "Let's get one thing straight. The General would be dead by now if it had not been for your quick thinking. Stop trying to second-guess yourself that ten years ago you could have shaved a second or two off your reaction time. That's a mind-game for idiots. The fact is the General has a good chance to pull through because it was you who was there. Who's to say any of the rest of us would have been able to do anything differently?"

Devon was about to cut in but was stopped by Doyle's upstretched palm. "And another thing. It was your instincts that got Emma and young Michael out of harm's way. It has been those instincts that have made this agency what it is. Without you, we would be nothing."

"Am I not entitled to a normal family life?"

"C'mon, Mike. We don't do normal around here. Give Emma some credit. She knew what she signed up for when she said *I do* to that ugly mug of yours. I agree we need to do more to protect our people. We need to make sure that nothing can touch our private lives and those of the other people who work here. Let's clear up this mess first and then sit down to overhaul the way we do things. If you still feel the same way, I'll back you one hundred percent in whatever decision you take."

Devon forced a smile. "Is that the pep talk finished for the day?"

"Yeah, how'd I do?"

This time there was nothing forced about Devon's smile. "I wouldn't make a career out of it if I was you, but for an old Army grunt you do show a surprising sensitivity now and then."

"And fuck you too!"

The two men burst out laughing. The mood had lightened considerably, but both knew they would be returning to the subject in the not too distant future.

Chapter 15

CHARLES NIGHTINGALE SLAMMED the hotel telephone receiver back onto its cradle and cursed about having to check out of the penthouse suite at such short notice. He had insisted on having his bill ready and a taxi waiting outside the door in five minutes. There was not a second to lose.

He finished cramming the last of his clothes into a suitcase, ignoring his usual fastidious packing habits. When it came to his weapon, however, he took extra care to ensure a round was chambered and ready to go. He might have need of it before this night was over.

"Fuck, fuck!" The cursing erupted at regular intervals as he stared again at the email blinking at him from the opened laptop on the dressing table. How could someone have been so careless as to include his name on a list that was now accessible on a half dozen machines?

Nightingale prided himself on being a careful individual. He had a healthy respect for intelligence agencies around the world. These people were not exactly dummies when it came to using the vast array of sophisticated spyware at their fingertips. Why make their job any easier?

And yet this latest email, with an open list of names, including his own, was now bouncing around cyberspace and multiplying by compounding factors the chances of somebody, somewhere zeroing in on him.

It was time to cut and run.

Just an hour earlier Nightingale had been congratulating himself on a job well done. He had checked his Swiss bank account to confirm the addition of one million euros, the promised payment for his elimination of one of the names on the *LonWash*

Securities contract.

Nightingale got lucky when he picked the name of Dave Carpenter from the list. At the time he didn't know his chosen target was not an active operative. That much was clear from the ease with which he had lured his subject to the deserted airfield and dispensed with him at no loss of sweat.

His decision to prearrange a private charter flight to pick him up from the airfield was a masterstroke. After killing Carpenter all he had to do was make a quick call to a pilot he had used on many occasions and who was on standby less than fifteen minutes away. Had Carpenter refused to take the bait, the call would have been cancelled until another day.

But Nightingale was born lucky. It had always been like that, although he tended to agree with the South African golfer, Gary Player, who said, "the more I practise, the luckier I get."

Meticulous planning, that's what it was all about. The Carpenter job was a model of precision. Locate the target, devise a plan, and execute. Job done. Home and clear, and on his way to Paris in less than a day.

But now this!

Nightingale knew the chances of his name being discovered had now risen a hundredfold. His photo would be dredged up from some intelligence directory or another and circulated to co-operating agencies across Europe. If someone tied in the private charter to Paris, his time in the French capital was extremely limited.

He decided to take a taxi across the city to a hire-car agency where he would use one of his fake identities to grab a set of good wheels and hightail his way east towards Germany or Italy. He would work out his final destination as he drove through the night.

Thirty minutes after leaving the hotel he was settled behind the wheel of a Mercedes, careful to observe the speed limits as he passed the Charles de

Gaulle Airport on his way to Saint-Soupplets, an obvious gateway to Berlin.

For the first time that evening he dropped his shoulders and relaxed.

Claude Bartran also considered himself a lucky individual. As the former head of France's premier security service, he had recognised on many occasions the need for a bit of good fortune when it came to protecting himself and his country.

What else could he call it when he happened to drive up to the fifth hotel on his itinerary for visits, and there fleeing from the lobby was the man he had come to track down?

Bartran had spent the past two days meticulously going over everything he could find on his files about Nightingale, and had surmised that the best way to start a hunt for the man wanted by his old friend Mike Devon was to show a mugshot around the ten best hotels Paris had to offer. If he drew a blank with the upmarket places to stay, he would simply start into another list comprising some of the city's less ostentatious flea joints. After that, he would circulate the photo to all his old law enforcement contacts.

For now, Bartran was prepared to be patient. No need yet to raise a general alarm that might spook Nightingale and send him deeper undercover.

Retirement had provided Bartran with a lot of time on his hands. He could afford to be patient, despite the obvious urgency in tracking down the assassin. He would give it forty-eight hours before sparking an all-out manhunt.

And here he was. Less than six hours into his allocated time for sweeping the top hotels, he's watching his quarry walk down the steps of *La Parisienne*, a five-star mecca for those who can afford the cost and convenience of laying down their heads less than a stone's throw from the Champs-Élysées.

Bartran knew a fugitive in a hurry when he saw one. He had chased enough men and women to recognise the awkwardness of their movements, the familiar dip of the shoulders, and the furtive glances as they hurried along. People who were trying hard to blend in, but by their very actions stood out like sore thumbs.

He didn't need to glance at the mugshot lying on his passenger seat. The image was burned into his brain. There was no doubt that the man he was watching from his car, parked across from the hotel entrance, was Charles Nightingale.

A master of counter-surveillance techniques, Bartran kept his little Renault a safe distance from the taxi as it shouldered its way through the notorious traffic build-ups for which Paris was noted. Ten minutes later the taxi pulled into a Hertz hire compound.

Bartran knew he had to act quickly. If Nightingale was intent on leaving Paris by road, there was little chance of pursuing him over long distances in his 1200cc runaround. He swung the Renault off the main driveway and headed to the rear of the large office complex.

It took a minute of pounding on a large rear door for someone to respond. Bartran produced his security credentials, which were still active despite his retirement, and ordered to be taken to the manager.

By the time Charles Nightingale completed the rental paperwork and climbed into the Mercedes, Bartran had fixed a magnetic GPS locator to the inside of the car trunk before it was driven to the reception area pick-up point.

Chapter 16

TIM HALLORAN LOVED MESSING ABOUT with the inner secrets of computers. Even allowing for his obvious exaggerations, it was hard to argue with his standing boast that given enough time he could discover what someone had for breakfast, just by taking a look at their hard drive.

He had proved it over and over again, starting with his work as a troubleshooter for some of London's major banking institutions, and continuing into his early career as a leading cyber security expert with GCHQ, the Government Communications Headquarters based at Cheltenham, northwest of London. It was here that Halloran blossomed, rewriting existing data capture techniques and devising new SIGINT software that became the benchmark for signals intelligence-gathering throughout Europe.

His boast was that everyone who switched on a device, be it computer, tablet, or smartphone, for the purposes of getting online, was opening a door to *his* world and in doing so ran the risk of him watching what they were up to. The layers of cryptanalytic spyware, which he had continually updated, had reached levels of intrusion that even he himself had found disconcerting at times.

Halloran had already left the organisation when whistleblower Edward Snowden went public with his claim that GCHQ was acting outside its remit by amassing all UK online and telephone data through a programme known as *Tempora*. The Great British public had gone apeshit at the thought of this unwarranted intrusion into their private lives, little knowing that *Tempora* was perhaps the least invasive of the many programmes Halloran and his erstwhile colleagues had dreamt up and implemented.

Lured to *LonWash Securities* by General Sandford's promise of a higher salary and an unlimited budget, Halloran had continued to tap into these programmes, refining them to new standards that had yet to be reached by GCHQ.

He was enjoying life in the private sector, but right now he was feeling cheated.

He had tackled with relish the confiscated laptop belonging to the assassin, Alexei Baronova, believing that its trail of emails would offer a cyber-hunt challenge worthy of his skills. He had set aside six hours for the task.

It took him less than an hour.

He grabbed his papers and went in search of Devon, finding him as usual in the middle of his team, issuing orders and looking like someone who wanted to be out of the office and into the field.

Devon looked up. "Tell me you've got something."

Halloran knew better than to start explaining his morning's algorithmic exploits. Better to just wade in with the bottom-line information. "I can tell you the server address where the second email originated from. I think we've found the sender, or at least someone who ought to know what's going on."

Devon looked like someone had just told him his lottery ticket had come up. He beamed a wide grin at Halloran. "Great work, Tim. Who did you find hiding under the stone?"

"The IP address is registered to one Felix Hoffmeier at an office in Vienna. My guys are currently putting together a dossier on him, but what we know so far is that he is some kind of billionaire industrialist. He's involved in a myriad of businesses across the world and is known as something of a philanthropist when it comes to charities and good causes. To all intents and purposes he's a model citizen."

Devon smirked. "I'll bet when your people start peeling back the layers, they'll find Herr Hoffmeier's skeletons. Keep them at it, Tim."

Halloran nodded in acknowledgement. "There's one more thing. I know you don't want to hear the techie stuff, but the bottom line is that this was too easy. As I mentioned at the earlier briefing, the encryption levels were a hotchpotch of brilliance mixed with stupidity. For someone who clearly didn't want to be found, they left a trail of crumbs that a child could follow."

Devon patted him on the shoulder. "Don't do yourself down. These things might come easy to you, but not everyone can operate at the levels you do."

"No, Mike, believe me this is not something I can take credit for. This just doesn't smell right."

"Okay, Tim, let's cut to the chase. What's your gut telling you?"

Halloran held Devon's gaze. "It looks to me like someone not only wanted us to find the email sender, but also the recipients. I can tell precisely where these emails were accessed from."

"What? Are you serious?"

Halloran smiled. "Yes, three of the emails were opened right here in London. The fourth was opened at an address in Paris."

The room was still buzzing five minutes after Halloran left. Devon had to admit that he didn't have a clue about the significance of his tech chief's statement, but that would have to wait for another day. Halloran and his team would work non-stop to find out what they could about this Hoffmeier character and would launch immediate SIGINT surveillance on everything going into and out of the offices in Vienna.

He had no doubt that he would know all he needed to know within the next thirty-six hours. After that, he intended to have a less than friendly chat with Herr Hoffmeier.

Right now, his sole concentration was on four assassins who were still at large, and seemingly intent on killing his people. That simply wasn't going to happen.

He banged the table for attention. "We need four separate teams for overlapping missions. Here's how it's going to play out. Cheadle is with me and Alan will pair up with Agent Horgan."

He paused to watch Doyle and Horgan exchange swift glances. There's definitely a spark there, he thought.

He turned his attention to two men seated at the end of the conference table. Terry Hunt and Jim Cross had been brought in less than an hour ago and introduced to the group as new members of the team. Former SAS buddies of Doyle, he didn't doubt their expertise and had no qualms about throwing them in at the deep end.

"Hunt you're with Bob Mortimer and Cross goes with Bill Carlisle. I'll assign targets in a moment, but there's one thing I want to stress. We go in hard and fast. I don't care about messy. We haven't time to mount surveillance-and-follow procedures. We find these people, we take them out. Nothing else matters."

No-one spoke, so Devon continued. "We can assume at least three of the targets are still in the UK, probably within the Greater London area. They have still not fulfilled their contracts and, judging by the emails they received, they will be getting jittery about hurrying things along. We've got to flush them out."

Doyle interrupted to announce to the group that dossiers on the three men had been completed and that a general alert was going out to all agencies. "Their photographs have been circulated to MI5 and the Metropolitan Police, but now we've also got a starting point from the work of our techies, who were able to pinpoint locations where the second emails were opened. It they're smart they will have already moved on, but you just never know."

Devon walked to the whiteboard at the head of the room and began scrawling the names of the four targets. Then he added an arrow alongside each and wrote in the names of his team. He turned back to the group. "That's how our assignments are going to go down. Any questions?"

Doyle nodded. "I see you've selected Charles Nightingale for yourself. We know he's fled to Paris, but is it a good idea for you to be out of the country at this time?"

"This one's personal. I owe him for Dave Carpenter, and I want to look him in the eye when he realises he made the biggest and last mistake of his life the day he came after one of us."

"I'd sure like to be there when you catch up with the bastard."

Devon glanced at his sidekick, realising for the first time that this was the kind of mission he usually wouldn't contemplate without his right-hand man. "I know how you feel, Alan, but you're needed here. We can't afford to leave any of our targets running free for a day longer than is necessary."

Doyle hid his disappointment with a smile. "Could be you want to take the out-of-country assignment just to try out the new Dassault jet?"

"Yeah," Devon replied, "and I can't wait to see old Claude's face when I roll into Paris in that."

Chapter 17

AT THAT PRECISE MOMENT Claude Bartran was more than a hundred miles from Paris. He glanced down at the GPS tracking screen and estimated he had already lost about twenty miles on the high-performance Mercedes being driven by the assassin Nightingale.

Until ten minutes ago he had not been concerned about the growing gap between the two cars. But something had suddenly clicked in his mind.

It was the realisation that if Nightingale abandoned the hire car, he would not arrive at the location in time to be able to pick up a trail.

Bartran cursed at his own complacency. How could be have been so stupid?

The pursuit had already taken him past the city of Reims in the Ardennes, and as they headed towards the France-Germany border just outside Saarbrucken, Bartran realised the route ahead offered too many chances for the assassin to disappear off the radar.

Once inside Germany, the main autobahn linking Mainz, Frankfurt, Leipzig, and Berlin, was awash with opportunities to grab trains, buses, or planes to just about anywhere in Europe. By the time Bartran reached the abandoned vehicle, Nightingale could have disappeared.

What then would he tell Devon? Why hadn't he called for back-up? Had retirement dulled his senses so much?

It was time to eat humble pie.

Bartran reached for his satellite phone, lying among the usual pile of horseracing magazines and daily papers on the passenger seat. He held it on top of the steering wheel and switched his gaze frantically between the console and the road ahead as he thumped a single speed-dial number that was burned into his brain.

It took only a few seconds for the static to clear. A familiar voice echoed. "Claude, tell me some good news."

"Mike, *mon ami*, I have the mixture of good and bad. I have located the rat Nightingale, but I fear I might be in danger of losing him. I am an old fool. I think I have chewed off more than I can bite, *n'est-ce pas*?"

"Close enough, Claude. Over here we go with biting off more than we can chew. You'd better tell me what's going on."

Bartran outlined the events of the past few hours and finished by explaining his fears that he had fallen dangerously behind in his pursuit of Nightingale. He glanced at a road sign coming up on his left and called out his latest position. "Our friend will now be close to the German border. He could stop there and use the airport or train station at Saarbrucken."

There was a moment's silence before he heard Devon's response. "Here's what we're going to do. I have contacts in the BND. We will send them a picture of Nightingale and ask them to despatch people to each of the major stops where there is an airport or train station between Saarbrucken and Berlin."

Bartran was aware of the BND, Germany's Federal Intelligence Service, which operated under the exasperating longhand title of *Bundesnachrichtendienst*. He had worked closely with them on many occasions, often marvelling at their speed and efficiency when it came to dealing with terrorist threats. "Let's hope they can get their people in place quick enough to spot our friend should he choose to leave his vehicle."

"It's the best we can do for now. Keep on the trail and let me know if there's any deviation from this route, or if the vehicle becomes stationary for more than a few minutes. Maintain your current speed, don't try to push it, and for God's sake don't attempt to tackle this on your own if Nightingale happens to stop somewhere. This is one sick individual, Claude. He won't hesitate to start a killing spree if he thinks he's being cornered."

Bartran shrugged. "I think I'm beginning to learn the limitations of my old age. I will not risk this mission any more than I have already."

"Nonsense, you old goat! If it weren't for you, we wouldn't have a lead to follow. Just sit tight. I'm coming to join you."

Bartran smiled at the way Devon always seemed to put a positive spin on things. "You are a true friend, Mike, but I fear I have already wasted too much time on bringing you up to speed. Even you could not make it here on time unless you have somehow sprouted wings."

There was the sound of a chuckle from Bartran's earpiece. "Funny you should say that, Claude. I'll explain when I get there but suffice to say I will be touching down in Frankfurt in less than an hour. In the meantime, keep calling me with updates."

Charles Nightingale shifted uncomfortably in his seat, trying to ease the stiffness brought on by more than four hours of driving. He reckoned he still had at least an hour of travel time to Mainz, the Rhineland capital city he knew well from previous visits.

The earlier tension had left his body. Satisfied he wasn't being followed, he had spent the last few hours working through a strategy for disappearing from the European scene, at least for a few years. He had enough funds to live comfortably anywhere in the world. Right now, his preference was America.

He would stop at a hotel in Mainz, register under one of his aliases, and then leave immediately. He would grab a taxi to the central train station, and head for Frankfurt. From there, he would take the first available flight to the USA.

By the time anyone found the hire car, he would have already blended into life in Boston, Chicago, or New York. It was just a matter of which city popped up first on the Frankfurt flight schedules.

He smiled. Chalk up another successful operation to the master craftsman.

Chapter 18

DEVON SETTLED INTO THE LUXURY seating of the Dassault 2000EX and gazed out at the greyish-blue blur of the North Sea, looking strangely static from a view thirty-thousand feet away. His thoughts, however, were elsewhere.

Before he had received the update from Paris, he had intended to visit General Sandford at the hospital. He had to settle for a quick phone call to the surgeon in charge. The news was positive. The medical team had eased the General out of his induced coma over the previous two hours and were encouraged by the progress he was making.

The surgeon warned they still faced a crucial few days, but the General's chances of survival had been upgraded dramatically.

Devon sighed with relief, realising once again just how much the old man had come to mean to him. The thought of losing him was not one he wanted to dwell on. At least now he could turn his full attention back to the mission in hand.

The total flight time of less than eighty minutes would put him on the ground in Frankfurt a few hours sooner than he could have managed by having to go through the check-in and waiting times of commercial airlines.

Plus, his arrangement with the BND came with a nice bonus. There would be no customs inspections, meaning he was able to carry his own weapons. He had agreed to a demand from his German anti-terrorist hosts that these would be solely for his own protection. The intention, they told him, was to take Nightingale alive, if possible, and to follow proper arrest procedures.

Devon's intentions differed somewhat. If he caught

up with Nightingale, he would not be allowed to live. He knew there would be a massive fall-out from breaking his word, but right now all he cared about was hoping he wasn't already too late.

The information from Bartran's vehicle tracking system, one that Devon's team had presented to the Frenchman several years before, had already been relayed back to the *LonWash* offices where the satellite software was scanned and shared on a computer screen fixed to a console in the passenger cabin of the jet. Devon was now watching the blinking position of Nightingale's Mercedes tracking its way across an enhanced map of Europe.

It was still moving and still keeping to the main route into Mainz. So far so good.

Alfie Cheadle fidgeted in the seat opposite him. "This is the way to travel. Have you worked out what we're going to do when we reach Frankfurt?"

Devon frowned. "Excuse the expression, but it looks like a case of flying by the seat of our pants. We will be met on arrival by a BND agent who has transport to take us down the autobahn towards Mainz. I want to close the gap on Nightingale so that we can react quickly to any deviations he makes. Instead of staring at a blip on a computer screen, we need to get eyeballs on that car as soon as possible."

"A lot can happen before we get there."

"Tell me something I don't know," Devon responded good-naturedly. "To be fair to the BND boys they have already put a dozen cars unto the roads converging from various locations to try to pick up the trail. They have the car registration number and I'm hoping to hear soon that someone has moved into position behind it."

Cheadle thought for a moment. "By my reckoning, if Nightingale keeps going at his current speed, he will reach Mainz before we do. Instead of striking out to intercept him, we might have to play catch-up in the opposite direction. It all depends on whether or not he stops anywhere."

"That's why we have to be prepared for all eventualities. My big worry is that he stops somewhere soon and allows Bartran to close in. That old fool's just liable to rush in and get his head blown off."

The Hilton Mainz Hotel was ablaze with lights as Nightingale swung into its generous car park and found a vacant space alongside a tall perimeter wall. He killed the engine, climbed out, and stood for a moment to take in the surroundings. Raindrops glistened as they speared down from a dark sky, heavy with the threat of an impending deluge. He blinked them away and continued his sweep of the area, confident there were no signs of a tail. He reached into the back seat to retrieve his suitcase and marched confidently to the ornate entrance.

Five minutes later he was in his room, having left a fake passport as part of the mandatory registration checks carried out in hotels across Europe. He would not need it again. There were plenty where that came from.

He had presented a credit card for pre-verification of payment for a 6-day stay and asked not to be disturbed the following morning. It was not unusual for guests to have a sleep-in on their first night, usually because of fatigue brought on by long journeys. By the time hotel staff discovered he had done a runner he would be on the other side of the world.

He worked efficiently, dumping the contents of the suitcase on top of the bed. Folded up in one corner was a small holdall, which was all he would need for the few belongings he intended to take with him as cabin luggage. He pushed a number of items to one side, discarding the usual detritus of the traveller. A paperback thriller, maps of Paris, a spare pair of Nike trainers, dirty socks, two pairs of used underwear, and a t-shirt that still had coffee stains from a trip to a cafeteria the previous night.

He opened a small packet and removed one of his favourite Cuban Bolivar cigars, which he tucked into the breast pocket of his jacket, together with a long, slim silver lighter. He would have one last satisfying smoke before entering the airport on the last leg of his journey.

He crammed the rubbish into a plastic carry bag, retrieved from a small bin placed beneath a dressing table. Reluctantly, he lifted the Magnum and a spare box of cartridges and shoved them into the bag, knowing he could not take the items through airport security. It was like saying goodbye to an old friend, but he smiled at the thought of how easy it would be to acquire a new model in America.

He packed the holdall with a smattering of essential items, which included a change of clothes and a small zipped bag of shaving accoutrements. Then he hoisted the holdall over his shoulder, grabbed the plastic bag, and exited the room. He was good to go.

He stepped out of the elevator into a busy foyer and strode to the front door. Just another guest heading out for a night on the town.

He walked to the rear of the building, looking for the hotel service area. A row of industrial bins lined one side of a fenced enclosure, which had an opened gate flapping in the strengthening wind. He marched inside, lifted the lid of the nearest bin, and flung the plastic bag among the littered contents. Returning to the front of the hotel he stood waiting under the entrance awning for a taxi. When one pulled up, he climbed in, and settled back for what he was sure would be his last journey in Europe.

Claude Bartran didn't believe in déjà vu. Yet here he

was in another hotel car park, watching the same man stride from the entrance into a car, albeit this time as a passenger. Twice in the space of six hours, he mused. What were the chances of that?

Thirty minutes earlier, Claude had contemplated giving up the chase. He was bone-weary, feeling every day of his seventy years, knowing he had little left in the tank. Then he noticed the light on his tracker was no longer moving. Nightingale had stopped, probably to switch transport and disappear into the ether.

A burst of adrenaline flooded his system and his right foot seemed to take on a life of its own. It pushed the accelerator all the way to the floor, with such intensity it threatened to burst through the aluminium and fibreglass footwell. What followed was one of the most hair-raising drives of Claude's life as he hurtled the little Renault at speeds it was never intended to safely cope with.

He tracked the static light straight into the Hilton Mainz Hotel and had just completed one circuit of the car park when he spotted Nightingale walking towards a taxi.

Bartran breathed a sigh of relief.

He kept the Renault three cars back from the taxi, thankful the rain showers had now turned into a full-blown downpour that made it impossible for Nightingale to pick up a tail. Just as he tracked it into the central train station entrance his satellite phone vibrated noisily on the passenger seat.

He grabbed it, knowing already who the caller was.

"Claude, what's happening? We've noticed the Mercedes is now stationery. Where are you?"

"Mike, I have him in sight. He stopped at a hotel, no doubt to throw us off the scent, but he is now pulling into the Mainz train station in a taxi."

"Great work, Claude. Now we have to figure his next move."

"*Mon ami,* it is not the science of rockets. He has

to continue eastwards. My guess is either Frankfurt or Berlin. That is obvious, *n'est ce pas*?"

There was a short silence before Devon spoke again. "Claude, you have to listen to what I'm about to tell you. I agree with your logic, but you are to break off the pursuit. We will be at Frankfurt long before the next train from Mainz makes a stop there. We can pick him up without too much bother, but we don't need him spooked before he walks him into our arms."

"Ah, you think old Claude will make a blunder. Maybe my teeth are too old, but I was running counter-surveillance before you were in nappies. The day I can't complete a simple assignment like this is the day I will put a gun in my mouth. Do not worry about me. What if we're wrong and he does not go east? What if he simply exits the station and grabs another taxi somewhere else? Would you not look foolish pacing up and down the platforms at Frankfurt while our friend gets a free run?

"Point taken. I just worry about you, you old coot."

"*Très bien*, we are agreed. I will follow this snake and keep you posted. Now, I must go and do my duty."

Chapter 19

THERE WERE usually only three ways for this kind of situation to develop. As he stood on a deserted platform five at Frankfurt, Devon ran through the main scenarios, ignoring the umpteen other ways things could go pear-shaped. Dealing with cock-ups is best done if and when they arise.

Best case planning was for Nightingale to walk straight into the heavy, covert police cordon. Public access to platform five was shut down while BND officers, in the guise of porters, travellers, and canoodling couples, attempted to present a scene of normality to the passengers stepping down from the Mainz Express. In an ideal world, the anti-terrorist operatives would simply box in their target and take him to the ground with a minimum of fuss.

Worst case was Nightingale spotting the trap, grabbing a hostage, and trying to shoot his way to safety. Worst case was to be avoided at all costs.

Somewhere in between lay the third option. Maybe Nightingale would remain aboard and ride the Express all the way to Berlin. In that eventuality, the police would swarm the compartments and attempt to take him in transit.

Whatever way it played out, Devon was convinced of one thing. The assassin would not allow himself to be taken without a fight.

And that would suit Devon just fine.

No further messages had been received from Claude Bartran. That could only mean that Nightingale had boarded the Express and was on his way. Any deviation and old Claude would have been on the sat-phone immediately, unless of course he had been rendered immobile.

Devon didn't want to go there.

He had resisted several urges to ring Claude but held back. The last thing he wanted was to compromise his friend by drawing attention to him at an inopportune time. Despite his misgivings about Claude not being at operational peak he trusted the old boy's experiences and instincts.

What was really occupying Devon's thoughts was how he could dispose of Nightingale before BND slapped on a pair of handcuffs. The capture of Nightingale was not enough to assuage the desire for vengeance. The assassin had to pay for the slaying of Dave Carpenter, and wallowing in a German prison was not Devon's idea of payment.

One way or another it would end here.

The squeal of breaks and the hammering of wheels on the track cross-ties stirred him from his reverie. The Mainz Express was slowing for its approach to platform five.

Busy train stations the world over share cacophonous characteristics. The metallic clangs of carriages, being coupled or uncoupled, mingle with the thrum of idling engines across a dozen platforms to compete with the incessant shunting of baggage trolleys in a symphony of noise that breaches even the most liberal of decibel codes. To complete the mix, all that's needed is to throw in the constant grating of tannoy announcements and the steady babble of humanity shouting farewells to departing loved ones.

A train station is not the place to be for those of a sensitive auditory disposition.

When Charles Nightingale stepped onto platform five something was missing. In fact, quite a lot was missing. No carriages were being coupled or uncoupled. No engines were idling on nearby platforms. No baggage trolleys were being pushed up and down the concrete walkways. The grey tannoy speakers were strangely mute. Oddest of all, was the complete absence of voices, save for those of the handful of people who exited the carriage with him.

He quickly shifted his gaze to the people already waiting on the platform. There was no interaction between them, no-one spoke or gesticulated to each other. To a man, and one woman, they all stood staring at the roof of the train. It was unnatural. Then he noticed their bearing. Shoulders back, feet apart, two with their right hands buried beneath their coats. Nightingale had learned through experience to spot law enforcement a mile away.

He had also learned to never look for a silver lining. Forget coincidences; don't assume they're after someone else. Take whatever has been thrown at you and get on with it.

He kept within a small cluster of people as he watched passengers disgorge from the compartments ahead of him. His window of opportunity wasn't going to get any better than it was right now.

He flung his holdall onto the platform and delved into his jacket pocket. What he wouldn't give for his Magnum 44! His hand folded around a cigarette lighter, which he withdrew in a show of defiance. It was nothing more than a prop, but at a distance he might fool the bastards into believing it was something that carried a higher degree of lethality. It was now all about bluff and confidence.

He reached forward and threw his left arm around the neck of a young woman, holding her in a vice-like grip while he pressed the half-covered lighter into her right ear.

"Back off, back off!" he screamed.

One of the umpteen ways for things to go pear-shaped had just kicked in. Devon watched the scene unfold but couldn't make out the weapon held by Nightingale. It looked to be some sort of small, custom-made, single-shot device, the kind of porcelain mechanism that is often smuggled through security checkpoints. He just couldn't be sure. For now, at least, Nightingale was calling the shots.

Devon glanced at Cheadle as pandemonium descended on platform five. BND officers shrugged off their various attempts at blending in and withdrew a succession of firearms. The familiar slide-racking of Heckler and Koch MP5s mixed with the screams of passengers, many of whom bolted from the scene to collide with the policemen who were trying to take up kneeling positions.

The small knot of people, who were immediately behind Nightingale when he first grabbed the woman, began to thin out, but Devon spotted a familiar face.

Bartran had held his position and was now inching forward towards the assassin. The slightest noise, or shadow passing behind, would alert Nightingale who would have no hesitation in gunning down any threat.

Devon did the only thing he could think of. He fired his Sig into the air and yelled. "Give it up, Nightingale. There's no need for anyone to die here." He then placed his gun on the ground, held up his arms in surrender, and walked forward.

"Don't take a step closer," Nightingale ordered.

Devon ignored him. "I'm surprised you don't recognise me. I was one of the names on your list. Pity we didn't get the chance to meet earlier, but being the cowardly rat you are, you chose an easy target at that deserted airfield in England."

Recognition washed over Nightingale's face. "You! Is this what this is all about? I can't believe you chased me all this way because of a paper-pusher. Yeah, he was an easy mark, just like you're going to be when........."

The distraction provided by Devon had given Bartran

the opening he needed. He had withdrawn a large penknife the moment Nightingale grabbed the woman but was certain he could not close the gap before being discovered.

Staying on the assassin's blind side, he shunted forward, thankful for the soft rubber soles of his Hush Puppy shoes. They were worn down so much they resembled discarded house slippers, the only footwear that seemed to give him relief these days from his fallen arches.

As he moved behind Nightingale, he judged the difference in height to be almost a foot. That suited Bartran fine. He stooped slightly to provide launch impetus and threw himself upwards, aiming the four-inch blade at a point in the nape of Nightingale's neck.

He drove the blade into the cervical spine, pushing upwards into the brain. It was a copybook killing technique, one he had learned in hand-to-hand combat exercises, and had passed on to other raw recruits. Slicing the spinal cord away from its attachment to the brain was a guarantee of immediate paralysis and instant death, particularly effective for ensuring that fingers wrapped around a weapon would immediately open in the absence of a motor neuron signal to do otherwise.

Nightingale followed the training manual hypothesis. His arms flopped to the side of his body, which folded like a puppet that just had its strings sheared. He made no noise as he crumpled to the ground, dead before the head bounced off the concrete walkway.

The Chief Director of the BND couldn't make his mind up about throwing Devon, Cheadle and Bartran in jail or tossing them the keys of the city of Frankfurt. As he paced up and down his office on the top floor of one of the organisation's regional headquarters in Frankfurt's

Elbestrasse district he switched frequently from what was clearly an angry rant to a more conciliatory tone, which came complete with a smile.

He didn't seem to notice that sometimes he spoke in English and at other times reverted to German. It was difficult for the three men to follow precisely what was being said, so they did the only thing they could. They sat back and listened and pretended to be engrossed in every word.

They caught snatches of a rant about being unprofessional and uncooperative. There was even mention of serious breaches of protocol. An official inquiry would have to be held, paperwork would grow into a mountain, and endless debriefings would have to take place over the course of the next few weeks.

All of which had the potential to tie Devon down at a time when he could least afford to be diverted.

If the Director persisted on going down this road Devon knew he would have to play some ace cards. He was not averse to coming up with a tirade of his own, maybe throw in the threat to Britain's national security if he was not back on his plane within the next few hours. He could even threaten to have the Prime Minister speak directly with the German Chancellor. Such a move was highly unlikely in the absence of an input from General Sandford, but he was confident he could summon up enough bluster to convince the BDN man otherwise.

He was getting ready to launch his verbal onslaught when the Director suddenly stopped pacing and walked directly across the room to stand in front of Bartran. He stretched out his arm to offer a handshake. "Monsieur Bartran, you have my gratitude for your swift reactions. I cannot think of the consequences if this terrorist had used his hostage to earn a safe passage away from the train station, or worse still, if the hostage had been killed during any attempt to stop the man from leaving. We would have been highly embarrassed, not to mention being left facing some serious scrutiny of how we handled this situation. As it is, we have successfully saved an innocent woman and killed a man who could have been plotting a terrorist attack on our capital."

Devon saw an opportunity to wrap things up. "Herr Director, might I suggest you use to your advantage the fact that Nightingale was a known international assassin, responsible for the deaths, among others, of high-ranking politicians. Who is to say he was not in the country to kill one of your Government ministers? We have a lengthy dossier on him and will be happy to message this to you as soon as we return to London. As far as anybody is concerned, we were never here. This was a slick BND-only operation for which you are to be congratulated, and I will see to it that our people in Whitehall dispatch a message of thanks to your Chancellor."

The BND man thought for a moment before reaching a decision. "Yes, I think it best if you leave now. What you suggest is a better way for dealing with the paperwork."

Devon, Cheadle and Bartran stood on the pavement waiting for an official BND car to take them back to the airport. Bartran looked decidedly uneasy, shifting constantly from one foot to the other.

"Claude, what's up?" Devon said.

"You are not angry with me for killing Nightingale? I know this was personal for you, perhaps even more than you let on."

"No, my friend, I feel like a great weight has been lifted from my shoulders. I wanted to kill this man so badly it was all-consuming, but watching you plunge that knife into his brain was one of the most satisfying sights I have seen for a long time. I'm just glad I was there to witness it."

Bartran smiled. "Then I too am happy.

The two men bumped shoulders in a gesture of

celebration before Devon looked down quizzically at the little Frenchman. "By the way, where did the knife come from? I've never known you to use a blade."

"I must confess I bought it only recently to help me eat my apples. I do not trust my new dentures, so I must cut things up into small pieces to help with my chewing."

Devon burst out laughing. "Thank heavens for false teeth."

Chapter 20

THE FLIGHT BACK to London proved to be a restless one for Devon. Despite needing some shuteye, he couldn't make himself comfortable in the luxurious leather-upholstered armchair, constantly shifting his weight before giving up and rising to reach for a whiskey decanter nestled in a small shelf unit that masqueraded as a minibar. He poured generous three-finger measures into two crystal glasses and handed one to Cheadle, who seemed engrossed in some iPad war game, judging by the animated figures dancing across the screen.

Devon chucked down the contents of his glass in one swallow and reached again for the decanter.

"What's up, Boss?" Cheadle had been aware of Devon's growing restlessness, but until now had pretended not to notice.

Devon slumped back into his seat, staring at his glass as if looking for answers. "Sorry, Alfie, but something's screwy about what's been happening over the past week. I know this sounds like an old record, but I can't help feeling we're being suckered into something that's really got fuck all to do with a bunch of assassins."

"If you ask me," Cheadle responded, "I think we're doing the right thing by putting everything on hold while we eliminate the threat to our personnel. We've already lost one good man and I know you're not about to let that happen again. If I were you, Boss, I'd stick with the mission. Let's wipe these bastards out before we even think about putting up the business-as-usual signs."

"That's it! Devon yelled.

Cheadle jumped in his seat. "What? What did I say?"

"I think you've just hit the nail on the head. How could I be so stupid? That's what this is about. We've stopped doing our usual business, and that's exactly what someone wants us to do."

"I'm not following you," Cheadle said.

"Think about it, Alfie. What do we normally do? We're constantly surveilling and monitoring threats to national security. We're like leaches sucking intelligence from just about every source that's available and when we see something that doesn't look right we chase it down. Our whole reason for existence is to kick down doors, bang heads together, and do what the mainstream security agencies can't do. We're not hamstrung by protocols, laws, or procedures. We don't go begging for warrants to tap phones, plant bugs, hack personal computers or corporate servers. We break into safes and bank vaults purely to satisfy ourselves that there's a reason for every financial or trade transaction that might affect this country."

Devon slammed his empty whiskey glass back on its shelf. "When we want answers, we usually get them, if only because the people we interrogate know we won't hesitate to pull the trigger of the gun aimed at their head. We're good at what we do, mostly because we're unrelenting. We don't stop, we're at it twenty-four seven. We pride ourselves on having more patience and stamina than the people we're after and, thanks to the General, our resources continually grow to keep us ahead of the opposition."

"Wow! Cheadle stared open-mouthed. That's quite a speech. So, what's changed? What am I missing here?"

"Don't you see?" Devon replied with a touch of exasperation. "For people who don't stop in pursuit of averting security threats, we've suddenly ground to a halt. We've put everything on hold to go chasing after a bunch of assassins. All our usual counter-intelligence surveillance work has been virtually switched off and redirected towards finding these targets, which I may add have been fairly easy to find, thanks to some inept exchanges of emails. Now, what does that tell you?"

Cheadle pursed his lips to make a soft whistle. "Are you saying that someone wanted us to switch off to deflect us from uncovering something else? Jeez, Mike, it would have to be something big to hire so many top guns just to act as a diversion."

"That's exactly what I'm saying. Best-case scenario would have been the assassins wiping us out completely, but someone thought up a contingency plan to make sure of the next best thing, and that was us taking our eyes off the bigger picture. We've been chasing trees without realising we've become lost in a forest. Something's going down and that something requires us to be well and truly out of the way. Christ, how have I been so stupid! It's been bothering me that whoever hired these people knew who we were, almost as if they requested a print-out from the personnel department. So much for being a highly covert operation!"

"Are you saying we've got a mole?" Cheadle asked with some trepidation.

Devon shook his head. "No, I'd bet my life on everyone inside *LonWash*. The General's vetting would have seen to that, but someone, somewhere got hold of the names of our operatives and we need to find whoever it is."

"Where do we start?"

"We don't need to worry ourselves on that score. There's one more thing I'd bet my life on, and that's the fact that the General will track him or her down as soon as he climbs out of that hospital bed."

Cheadle laughed drily. "Yeah, I wouldn't wanna be someone the General's chasing after."

Devon turned to look out the window at the familiar London landscape as the Dassault crossed the Thames on a south-east heading to the Trafalgar Flying

Club's main runway. It angered him that someone sold out his agency, but it bothered him more that whoever had bought the information seemed to know an awful lot about the importance of neutralising the agency. That kind of knowledge was available to only a select few involved in the intelligence field.

He decided to push the thought to the back of his mind. Right now, all he wanted was some downtime with his family.

Chapter 21

CARL STRATTON never had a problem with leaving things behind. He didn't attach sentimentality to anything, least of all to an apartment that had been his home for the past ten years. He pulled the door behind him for the last time and walked to a single elevator at the end of a short hallway. He didn't look back. He never did with anything.

It was time to leave New York to start the final phase of his operation in London. A week from now he would fulfil a lifelong ambition. It mattered little that he would probably die doing it. He was prepared to make the ultimate sacrifice.

Stratton's career was an odd mixture of experiences. Born in France to an English father and an Algerian mother he majored in politics at Cambridge University before being recruited to the British Intelligence Service, becoming one of the famed *Licensed to Kill* MI6 operatives, popularised by the keystrokes of James Bond author Ian Fleming. In truth, Fleming had only scratched the surface in revealing the murky depths to which men like Stratton sunk to carry out their duties on behalf of Queen and country.

Sure, there were lots of killings, most of which could be written off as little more than meeting fire with fire. There was something almost clean and wholesome about dispensing with threats to the nation by men, and women who didn't deserve to live. Somehow, it was acceptable justification, all packaged up and tied in neat little ribbons and filed away on a top shelf somewhere in the cellars of Vauxhall Cross.

The reality was much different. The destabilising of national governments, support for genocidal factions in far-flung corners of the world, and the manipulation of stock markets, all went into the blender that became the world of Carl Stratton. Where a gun was not effective he used a bomb, and when more subtle methods were called for he had no hesitation in throwing a mark from the top of a twenty-storey building. Results were all that mattered.

To his employers, Stratton was almost indispensable. What they didn't know was that his insatiable drive to succeed was fuelled by a dangerous passion.

Stratton was a radicalised Muslim. He got that from his mother who taught him everything about the one true religion. It began at an early age, without the knowledge of his father, and always with the aim of teaching him how to live a double life. He began slowly to realise that he was being groomed for something important, something that would require a dedication and discipline few men possessed. He must never reveal his true calling. He must demonstrate extreme patience in the certainty that it would lead to an ultimate goal. He had a purpose in life – one that Allah would reveal to him when the time was right.

His mother, Almeira, was a remarkable woman. In her early days she was a member of a dedicated and active guerrilla fighter group operating out of the Béchar region of Algeria. She fought in the Algerian War of Independence in 1954, losing her left leg to a bomb that detonated prematurely outside a French army compound on the outskirts of Algiers. In a strange twist of fate, she was mistaken by the French for an innocent passer-by and airlifted for hospital treatment to Paris where she later met and married Stratton's father.

She settled into a normal family life, but never forgot her roots. She continued secretly to promote her ideals among like-minded French citizens and helped raise funds for the Islamic Salvation Front during the 1991 Algerian Civil War. She died from a heart attack two days after her sixty-fifth birthday in 1999, an event that triggered her son's determination to seek his true destiny.

A year after his mother's death, Stratton turned forty, an age considered to the watershed for active MI6 operatives. He didn't waste a second. He informed his boss he had no desire to take on lighter work, or to become involved as an instructor, and left the building with empty platitudes ringing in his ears.

Bolstered by a secret stash of funds left to him by his mother, he became involved in various lucrative business ventures, many of which were helped by the underhand lessons he had learned as a spymaster. He also used his mother's old contact book to enlist the support of a number of Middle-Eastern oil tycoons, only too willing to help fund any campaign to establish the supremacy of the Muslim faith.

He decided at an early stage that his ultimate goal would be the destruction of what he saw as British interference in Islamic affairs. To achieve this, he intended to blow up the Houses of Parliament, a notion that would have been laughed at as utterly ridiculous in his days as an agent, but one he knew could be made a reality by the use of a new breed of super explosives. He had first come across *Malponium 23*, a liquid variant of PBX explosives, when he was engaged in an MI6 operation against dissident Russians in Chechnya. He had tracked down a young scientist to a remote farm near Grozny and was amazed to discover what had been achieved by combining traditional bomb-making ingredients, such as Torpex, Tritonal and Amatol in a new process that produced results to match those of the destructive power of a nuclear payload.

What struck Stratton as incredible was that the equivalent energy output of a five-kiloton nuclear device could be replicated by using only a fraction of its size and weight, and with no telltale signatures which could be picked up by terrestrial or orbital satellite surveillance.

He spared the scientist's life, arranged for him to be spirited out of the country, and set him up at a holiday home in the Bahamas. He put him to work, making a new batch of *Malponium 23*, which was later transferred into small, specialised containers made to look like batteries for laptop computers.

The next problem for Stratton was how to transport the explosive to Britain. His knowledge of the country's intelligence-gathering methods and operations provided him with a vital edge in being able to operate under their radar. In truth, he believed it would be no great challenge to defeat them.

At first, he thought of simply mass-producing a new range of laptops and shipping them, complete with their lethal battery units, to a bonafide electronics wholesaler in London. He knew from experience that MI6 would have no reason to question what appeared to be a perfectly legitimate import trade transaction involving everyday goods. Yes, they might ask for a Customs report on the goods, but would accept at face value whatever turned up in a routine inspection. All that a Customs official would see was the normal inner workings of a laptop, complete with two replica batteries.

He established a small manufacturing plant in Nassau, secured the services of an established distributor, and lowered the price range well below the High Street offerings of leading brands. Just one more manufacturer flooding the market with cheap foreign goods.

The initial plan was to prepare a special order of twenty machines, complete with the *Malponium 23* payload, for delivery to a small shop he had opened as a front on London's Woodburn Road, near Euston train station. It was run by an unsuspecting woman who had replied to a job advertisement placed by a recruitment company, which continued to deal with the business paperwork on behalf of a shell company.

It was all done with Stratton's usual penchant for patience. Don't draw attention by rushing into completing the little tasks. Establish a presence, get known by the local populace, and don't offer an excuse for the authorities to question the legitimacy of a new activity. Take time to build a cover, blend in, and wait for the opportunity.

But then something happened that made Stratton rethink his strategy. The high-ranking politician he had ensnared because of his fondness for little boys had tipped him off about a secretive counter-terrorism outfit that seemed to be operating with a special mandate from the Government, and which was achieving results far beyond those being recorded by the official agencies.

It was a game-changer, not least because Stratton didn't like dealing with the unknown. Having covered all the bases as far as MI6 was concerned, here was an X-factor capable of throwing a spanner into the works.

He hated off-the-books operations. Having been involved with them on too many occasions, he understood how they worked. No chain of command, no rules, no interference. Cut corners, get the job done, and forget the niceties.

Whoever they were, they needed to be dealt with.

Stratton started digging up everything he could about *LonWash Securities*. The first report he received told him all he needed to know. One name jumped off the page.

Mike Devon.

One of the new breed. A younger version of himself. They had never worked together, but he had heard about Devon's exploits shortly before marching through the Vauxhall Cross revolving door to be deposited on Civvy Street.

So, what had taken Devon through that same door to a new career? Was a chance to be independent too good to pass up? What kind of operation was he heading up? What kind of resources did he have at his disposal? What were his parameters? Who had he recruited?

As the answers came together, Stratton decided on the simplest method for dealing with *LonWash Securities*. Divert their attention away from their normal duties. Send them off on a wild goose chase. Give them something to deal with outside their comfort zone.

Put a price on their heads and watch them chase shadows.

It had taken three years for Stratton to put together the components of his London operation. Three years was nothing to a patient man.

Everything was in place, but he needed a hook. There had to be more to it than simply being responsible for a blockbuster event. He needed a sign from Allah that this was what he had been singled out to do. He wanted to leave a legacy that would change the world for Muslims.

The rise of *Islamic State* provided him with an answer.

Formed as a Jihadist militant group, the IS began a sweep across Iraq and Syria in a campaign of unprecedented terror, which convinced Stratton that here at last was a unifying force with the potential to create a new order. Influenced by the Wahhabi movement's roots in the Sunni religion, IS demonstrated a capability to unite the Muslim world in a way never before achieved.

They grabbed the attention of America and its western allies with a series of brutal genocides, including the slaughter of children, and announced their intention to establish a modern Caliphate, a state ruled by a single political and religious leader. The West had heard it all before, but when Islamic State began the public beheading of captured American and British nationals, a sombre mood of realism descended on Washington and London.

Looking on from the sidelines, Stratton saw a golden opportunity. If Islamic State were to fulfil its potential it needed to demonstrate its capabilities outside the Middle East. His planned attack on London would now be carried out under the IS badge.

Finally, Allah had shown him a way.

First, he had to deal with *LonWash Securities*. They were too much of an unknown quantity to ignore. He realised quickly that he needed a change in approach for transporting his explosive-filled laptops. Instead of making a single delivery – something that could be stumbled on by Mike Devon's new agency - he had decided to move the false battery components through a number of couriers, all of whom, like the captain of the container ship operating out of the Bahamas, were coerced into carrying out his wishes.

He now had twenty-four battery units stockpiled in a safe location in the centre of London. Enough to make three lethal packages, each comprising eight units, and each capable of demolishing buildings within a two-hundred yard radius.

The three would be delivered to separate targets in London, using different methods for getting them on site, and ensuring each operation was independent of the other. It would be a failsafe *Blitzkrieg*, the kind of sudden attack that could not be countered.

The main target was the Houses of Parliament. The removal of one of the world's landmark sites would be the icing on the cake. The guaranteed death of many thousands of people, including perhaps hundreds of politicians, would reverberate for decades.

Carl Stratton smiled as the Virgin Atlantic Boeing 787 left the runway at John F Kennedy International Airport and climbed to its cruising altitude of thirty-five thousand feet. In a little over seven hours from now he would touch down at London Heathrow to begin the final phase of his masterplan.

Chapter 22

THE SUN THREW shadows across the garden of the country house in Basildon, Essex. Less than an hour's drive from central London, the scene could well have been on another planet. Clean, scented air and the chirping of a dozen species of small birds was a world away from the pollution and clamour of a city locked in some sort of crazy fast-forward mode.

Devon sat at a patio table, his hand wrapped around a coffee mug, and watched as his son scampered excitedly across the manicured lawn in pursuit of a butterfly, which steadfastly refused the child's earnest pleas to fly into his cupped hands. Every so often the boy stumbled, rose to his feet in a fit of giggles, and continued the chase. It was a priceless scene, one that Devon didn't mind admitting he could observe for hours.

He turned at the sound of the patio doors opening and watched as his wife crossed to the table. He knew she had only just climbed from her bed, yet her hair was immaculately groomed, and there was a hint of make-up on her cheeks. The sunlight hit her face, adding to the radiance of her complexion. It was another scene he could relish for hours.

"Someone got up early," Emma teased, as she ran her fingers through his hair.

"Thought you deserved a lie-in. Besides, it's about time I took my early-morning turn with young Michael. I can't believe how he continues to grow. Must be all this country air."

Emma pulled up a seat and looked anxiously at her husband. "Did you sleep alright? You tossed and turned a lot during the night."

"Never better. I admit the past week has been stressful but seeing you and Michael was just what I needed. We still have a lot to do to wrap up this mess, but I'm hoping things can get back to normal within a few days."

Emma leaned forward. "Can you tell me what's going on?"

Devon didn't hesitate. He had never kept things from his wife, and he wasn't about to start now. "We tracked down Dave Carpenter's killer and, thanks to Claude Bartran, he won't be killing anyone else."

"Claude! How did he become involved?"

"Long story short, he did all the donkey work in finding him. By the way, he sends his regards and insists we take up his offer to spend some time at his holiday home in Brittany. I assured him we would."

"What now?"

"For starters, I intend to visit Clare Carpenter. She deserves to hear about this first-hand. I don't know if it will help, but I made a promise to let her know about any developments."

"Trust me," Emma said, "it will help knowing that her husband's killer has been brought to justice."

Devon nodded. "My next port of call will be to visit General Sandford. They tell me he is sitting up in bed and ordering the nursing staff around. It will be good to have him back on board, particularly with a lot of loose ends still to be tied up."

"What kind of loose ends?"

"Alan Doyle and the team are chasing down leads on the three remaining assassins. The last I heard they were in pursuit of a target heading towards Scotland, would you believe? For now, I will let them get on with it. There are other things that need to be done."

Emma frowned. "I get a sense there is more to this than you are letting on."

"No, darling. I just need to find the man who paid for these assassins. Maybe then I can figure out the motive. Right now, I can't help thinking we're dealing with a lot of smoke and mirrors. There's got to be more to this than some personal vendetta."

Emma smiled and reached out to clasp her husband's hand. "You'll work it out, you always do. When are you heading back to London?"

Devon stood and walked towards the garden, shouting over his shoulder. "I thought tomorrow would be time enough. What about a picnic this afternoon?"

Alan Doyle was out of his comfort zone. A long way out. The brash ex-soldier didn't usually waste too much time caring what people thought about him. His hard-drinking, womanising days might have disappeared in the rear-view mirror many birthdays ago, but he still retained a certain aloofness and, yes, even disdain, for the fairer sex. He didn't need women in his life. They weren't worth the trouble.

So, why had he taken extra care with his grooming this morning? How come he felt like a schoolkid waiting to pluck up the courage to ask the girl next door for a first date?

The answer sat beside him, their knees occasionally touching, and her perfume doing strange things to his inner workings. Agent Chelsea Horgan was stirring Doyle in a way he hadn't felt in a very long time.

He needed to get real. Why would a stunning young woman be interested in a one-arm tosser like him? His repertoire that barely extended beyond a detailed knowledge of rugby teams, the inner workings of a car engine, and the films of John Wayne. Yeah, that would make for some sparkling conversation with a young lady, who was probably an avid book reader, frequently attended the opera, and could write a thesis on world politics.

Talk about a non-starter!

He chased the nonsense thoughts from his head and continued to stare at the countryside as it flashed past the windows of the London to Edinburgh train. Two hours earlier, they had tracked one of the assassins, Martin Greene, to a small hotel in London's Hounslow district. According to staff, he had just booked out after asking for information about trains to Scotland from King's Cross Station.

By the time Doyle and Horgan had arrived at the station, one of the regular services had just left. They decided to take the next train on the hour-by-hour schedule, hoping to pick up Greene's trail from Waverly Station in Edinburgh. *The LonWash* techies, with their usual efficiency, had come up with photos of their suspect, which they would show around the taxi ranks. The might get lucky. For now, it was all they could do.

"Hello, is there anyone at home?"

Doyle turned to face Horgan. "Sorry, I was a million miles away."

"I was asking you about Mike Devon. You two seem to be awfully close. What's he like to work for?"

Doyle was usually reticent about engaging in chit-chat, but he found himself talking freely. "Mike's one of the good guys. I owe him a lot. In fact, I owe him everything."

"Let me guess," Horgan interrupted, "he once saved your life and now you feel you owe him something?"

"It's not like that at all. Yeah, he did save my bacon on more than once occasion, but the truth is he pulled me out of the neck of a bottle and helped put me back on track at a time when I was at a low point. If he hadn't looked me up when he did, I doubt I could have survived another year."

The smile drained from Horgan's face. "Look, I'm sorry about being frivolous. Care to tell me about it?"

It was the first time Doyle had ever spoken about his earlier life to a stranger. Somehow, it felt right. He told Horgan about the time he spent with Devon on an undercover mission in Northern Ireland, one that had ended in a bloody gun battle in which he had lost his right arm and led to his discharge on medical grounds. "I didn't deal well with it. I wallowed in self-pity, hit the drink pretty hard, and kept a loaded pistol by the bed while I worked up the courage to end it. Don't remember much about it other than the days and nights blurred together and there didn't seem any reason to go out other than to the nearest off-licence."

Horgan sat listening, reluctant to say anything that would stop Doyle talking.

"Anyway, Mike tracked me down, gave me a bit of a lecture, and made me get my ass in gear. He spent a few weeks at my home, weaned me off the bottle, put me through a crash course to restore my fitness, and then offered me a job with *LonWash Securities*. I've a lot to thank him for."

"Wow," Horgan exclaimed, "I didn't see that coming. I didn't mean to pry, but I'm real glad you told me. From where I'm sitting, I see a two-way street. I'm betting you did a lot for him as well. If you ask me, Mike Devon is a pretty lucky guy to have you as a friend."

Doyle felt himself blush. He rose quickly. "I need to use the head, sorry, toilet," he blurted as he stepped into the aisle and walked towards the rear of the compartment.

He was back in less than twenty seconds.

"That was quick."

"You're never going to believe who I just saw through the door into the next carriage!"

Chapter 23

"MARTIN GREENE! Wonder why he didn't catch the earlier train? Boy, this is gonna save us a lot of legwork."

"Yeah," Doyle agreed. "Who knows what happened. Maybe the taxi driver stretched the fare by taking him on the tourist trail or could be he's just a thicko who couldn't find his way around a whorehouse with a fistful of cash."

Horgan smiled. "A rather colourful analogy, if you don't mind my saying."

"Sorry, just a product of spending too much time around a barracks room."

"So, how do you wanna play this?"

"We take him here and now. I'm not gonna risk losing him among the crowds at the next station. We go in hard and fast and put the bastard down before he knows what hit him."

Horgan raised her eyebrows. "You mean we just mosey on in there and clobber him as we walk past? Think it'll be that easy?"

"Nothing's ever easy, but we'll have the element of surprise on our side. We'll just be an ordinary couple walking between carriages, with nothing to arouse his suspicion until we're on top of him."

Horgan shook her head. "You're not thinking this through, Alan. Don't forget, yours is one of the names on Greene's hit list. Maybe you were even his main target. In any case there's a chance he has seen a file on you, probably studied your mugshot, and burned those craggy features into his brain. This thing could turn real messy if he jumps up and starts shooting the moment we enter that carriage."

"You got a better idea?"

"Sure do. I'll go in alone."

"What! Are you mad? There's no way I'm letting you tackle this guy on your own. I take it you read the same paperwork that I did? He's a sixteen-stone six-footer who's probably had combat training, which means he probably knows how to use his fists as well as a selection of guns and knives, and that makes him one extremely dangerous individual. And no probably about it."

Horgan reached over to place her hand across the back of Doyle's balled-up fist. "Look, I have done this before, you know. When it comes to training, I wasn't exactly manicuring my nails for twelve intensive weeks at Maryland. His height won't matter when he's sitting cramped behind a fixed table, and as far as his bulk is concerned, I intend to use it against him."

Doyle let her hand stay where it was. It felt good. Was he letting his feelings for her cloud his judgement? He held eye contact for a few seconds before speaking. "Okay, tell me what you propose to do."

Horgan stepped through the compartment door, pushing it shut as she pretended to stare ahead. Her peripheral vision picked up Greene exactly where Doyle said he would be, on her nine o'clock, three cubicles up the left hand side. He was facing her, his arms resting on an empty table. No laptop, no mobile, no newspaper, no distractions.

There were five other people in the carriage. Two on the left behind Greene, three on the right. Four men and one woman, all sitting at different tables, one sleeping and four staring out the windows. Bored commuters, doing what they could to pass the time.

Horgan started walking. Not too slow, not too fast. She paused at Greene's table, mentally shifting her feet to where she wanted them to be. Not too close, not too far.

She switched on her best Texas drawl. "Scuse me,

Sir, do y'all know what time the buffet car opens?"

Greene glanced up, looking totally disinterested, his eyebrows cinching in a clear signal that he didn't welcome the interruption. "Don't know anything about British Rail's catering arrangements. Don't know, and don't care. I like to mind my own business."

As a brush-off it was as good as she'd ever got. She pretended to not notice the rudeness, lifting her arm to point to the rear of the coach. "Does that sign say the buffet car is in the next compartment?"

Greene turned to follow her outstretched arm. His head almost completed a half-swivel before an alarm signal flared in his eyes. It was something he had been taught never to do. Disengage from the actions of others, ignore leading gestures, focus on facial expressions, watch for danger signals. He had just broken the rules, and now something inside was telling him he had been suckered.

An instinct for self-preservation forced him to turn back quickly, his right hand disappearing inside his jacket to fumble for the pistol grip jutting out from the shoulder holster. In any other circumstance it would have been an impressive blur of reflex speed.

But not this time.

Horgan had already shifted her weight to the right, her foot planted to provide the springboard she needed. She hoisted her left leg, bent at the knee, and snapped it forward in a vicious kick aimed directly at the side of Greene's head. It connected with a satisfying crunch.

As the opening blow in a fight it was a pretty telling one. It wasn't too shabby as a closing blow either.

Greene's head was pushed violently sidewards by the impact and follow-through of Horgan's size five boot. The hard bone just above his right ear made a sickening hollow sound as it bounced off the aluminium window guard. Greene's eyes flared momentarily in shock before he slumped unconscious across the table.

The other passengers rose to their feet, fearful of the short-lived commotion, leaving one man still snoring gently in his seat, oblivious to the takedown of one of the world's most dangerous assassins.

The door behind Horgan hissed open and she turned to watch Doyle sprint across to the table. "Are you alright?" He shouted into her ear, unaware he had grabbed her in a bearhug and was squeezing tightly.

"I will be, just as soon as you let me breathe."

He let go and looked sheepishly at her. "Sorry. That was magnificent. Remind me not to get in a fight with you."

She punched his arm playfully. "I'm not so sure. That was a fairly good grapple you had going there. Don't think I'd mind doing nine or ten rounds with you."

"Dammit, Chelsea," Doyle said with a grin. He reached out both arms and pulled her towards him. And then he kissed her. Hard.

Devon was walking towards his car, preparing for a sombre drive back to London. He hated leaving Emma and Michael, but he needed to get his team back together again as quick as possible. The sound of his sat-phone stopped him just as he was climbing into the driver's seat. He looked at the display and punched the receive button.

"Mike, it's Alan. Thought you could do with a sit-rep."

Devon's mood lightened at the sound of his friend's voice. "You do know that your name comes up on my screen before I answer?"

"With your fading eyesight I don't like to take any chances."

"Okay, wiseass, what've you got?"

Doyle told him of the capture of the assassin

Martin Greene. "To be honest, we weren't quite sure what to do with him afterwards. Chelsea wouldn't let me put a bullet in his brain. Said it didn't square with her about shooting an unconscious prisoner, so we used our security credentials at the train station and whistled up an ambulance. The local police even provided us with an escort to the nearest hospital."

"So where are you now?"

"Here's the rub. Our friend up and died on us before we reached our destination. Guess Chelsea's Kung-Fu kick caused more internal damage than we thought. Good riddance I say. Anyway, we've checked into a small hotel for the night. Figured we'd travel back to London first thing in the morning."

Devon burst out laughing. "Oh, you did, did you? Don't think I didn't notice the cosy Chelsea-this and Chelsea-that thing going on. You two seem to be hitting if off, but if you think we're going to foot the bill for a night of hanky-panky you've got another think coming."

"C'mon, Mike, it's not like that. It's just that we've been on the go all day and both of us are dog tired. Give a guy a break here."

"Listen to me, Doyle. I've been round too many corners with you not to recognise feigned indignation when I hear it. The last thing on your mind is sleep unless it happens to be in the arms of a pretty redheaded CIA agent. Sorry to do this on you, old buddy, but I need you back in London ASAP."

Devon told him about the murder of Charles Nightingale before adding: "There's something else I need to go over with the whole team. Even though this is a secure transmission I don't want to go into it right now. Suffice to say, we need to take an urgent shift in direction."

Doyle recognised the change of tone and his response to an emergency was typically brief. "I'm on my   way."

Chapter 24

WHEN IT COMES TO putting price tags on luxury properties no city does it better than London. Los Angeles has its Beverly Hills, Paris has its Avenue Montaigne, and Berlin boasts the Zehlendorf district, all of which lag some distance behind the clamour for the London hotspots of Mayfair or Belgravia, or for that matter anything with more than ten bedrooms and carrying a NW1 postcode. It was at the latter's tree-lined area that Carl Stratton gazed as his chauffeur-driven Daimler hung a right into Prince Albert Road and slowed at the gated entrance of a mansion overlooking Regent's Park.

It had been some years since he'd last visited. The property held no sentimental attachment for him. It was bought using one of his aliases as nothing more than a sound investment. There was also the bonus that it offered seclusion and anonymity less than an hour's drive from Heathrow Airport, and would prove a useful bolthole that he figured might come in handy one day. This was a neighbourhood with no neighbours, just other residents, equally cocooned, minding their own businesses, oblivious and uncaring about whoever else happened to share this particular few square miles of real estate.

The chauffeur pressed a remote control button on the dashboard and waited as a single iron-constructed gate retreated on its runners to disappear behind a ten-foot-high perimeter wall. By the time the Daimler reached the front porch of an imposing four-storey structure, the gate had returned to its locked position, to all intents and purposes sealing off the property from the outside world.

Manfred, the chauffeur, killed the engine, climbed out of the car, and hurried to the rear to retrieve a large suitcase from the spacious trunk. He didn't bother with opening the door for his passenger. He wasn't that kind of a chauffeur.

Stratton stood on the porch, stretched his back, and waited for Manfred to open the large mahogany door. He used the few seconds to take a cursory glance at the security systems, which included burglar-alarm wires neatly tacked against window frames, and four swivel-mounted CCTV cameras covering this side of the house. He knew there were twice as many covering the sides and rear of the building, plus at least a dozen under-soil pressure plates buried strategically around the gardens. He couldn't conceive a situation that would require their use, but in his line of work he had always operated on the principle of leaving nothing to chance.

Both men entered the house, shutting the door firmly behind them, before reaching out and grasping each other in a warm embrace. "It has been too long, Manfred. It is good to see you looking so fit and well. I take it all the arrangements are in place?"

Manfred stood back from the embrace and burst out laughing. "Carl, I swear you are the only man I know who has so little time for chit-chat and so much time for business. In case you're interested, I have fully recovered from my little heart scare, my arthritis is getting worse, and I think I've developed gout in my feet. The rest you know about."

It was Stratton's turn to laugh. "You know me too well, old friend. Now that I've got the health story, I warn you not to start a conversation about the English weather. That would be too much. Come, show me what you've been up to."

As they walked across a large foyer leading to a hallway that ran to the rear of the house, Stratton thought about the journey he had travelled with this man. Manfred Stelling was an East German border guard back in the day when The Wall played a large part in his life as a British Secret Service agent. He had managed to convince Stelling to take bribes in exchange for looking the other way at his sentry station in a remotely-wooded area on the edge of the city.

For more than a year Stratton had enlisted Manfred's help to transfer important East German scientists to the West, always at great personal risk, and always with just the smallest window of opportunity, when vital seconds were all that stood between them and discovery by other guards.

Manfred was the only son of an elderly couple who had both perished attempting a crossing. Under pressure from an escape organisation, fearful that the infant boy would cry out at a crucial moment, they had left him with a family friend. He was brought up under a different name and the connection to his parents was never made. By the time he was fifteen he had already grown over six feet tall and was earmarked for military service. When he learned about the fate of his parents from his surrogate mother, he became determined to help others. His meeting with Stratton six years later provided the answer.

On a snowswept November night in 1985 Stratton was making his way towards Manfred's lookout tower when he was bathed in light from a search beam operated by a two-man mobile patrol hidden in a small copse. Stratton, and a young woman he was guiding to safety, could do nothing but throw their hands in the air and await their fate. Out of nowhere, Manfred Stelling unleashed a burst from his Karabiner S semi-automatic carbine, killing the two sentries and shredding the searchlight. He had watched the commotion from his tower, threw down a rope ladder, and sprinted to help his benefactor.

There was nothing left to do but for Stelling to accompany Stratton and the woman back to the West. They climbed the ladder, hauled it up and threw it over the other side, just as two vehicles screeched to a halt beside the dead guards.

Stratton never told his bosses about Stelling. He established him in a safe house in West Berlin and provided him with funds until the chance arose to secure a false passport and transfer him to England. Soon afterwards, Manfred was ensconced in the house at Prince Regent Road, becoming its full-time caretaker. Over the years he carried out numerous other jobs for Stratton, jobs that were usually outside England, and which usually required the use of deadly force.

It was hard to believe, Stratton reflected, that they had been together for almost thirty years. He watched now as Manfred opened a door into a room that resembled a public library and was just as big. Floor-to-ceiling bookcases covered two walls and three two-seater settees were arranged around an open fireplace. In the corner farthest from the door sat a Victorian mahogany desk, positioned to catch the sunlight from the shuttered windows, but also close to a built-in bar area that wouldn't have looked out of place in the best of hotels.

Stratton ignored the mustiness of the room and watched as Manfred walked behind the desk, stopping to touch a concealed switch. A portion of the tiled floor began to slide back in the centre of the room to reveal concrete steps leading to a basement area. Sensor lights kicked in as Stratton began a descent to a room that measured about the same size as a double garage.

Benches ran around the outer walls and a sturdy worktable occupied the centre of the room. One wall was covered with an assortment of weaponry, hung neatly on nails, above an array of drawers that Stratton knew contained thousands of rounds of ammunition of varying calibres.

Three packages stood on the table. They were standard brown cardboard boxes, each measuring a foot square by nine inches deep. Pieces of coloured wires and scraps of duct tape were strewn around them, as were a variety of small hand tools, a set of work gloves and two overalls. On the bench immediately to the right of the table sat what looked like several uniforms, neatly folded into plastic wrappers, the top one clearly displaying the logo of a well-known parcel delivery service.

Stratton walked across to peer inside the open boxes. "You have done everything according to the instructions?"

"Yes," Manfred replied. "Each battery pack has been wedged carefully into place using cotton wool strips, and the wiring was attached at the precise points indicated on your drawings. All that is required is for the wiring to be attached to the detonation units, which are still sealed and kept in a separate location." He nodded at the bottom drawer in one of the units behind him.

Stratton slapped him on the back. "Excellent, Manfred! The detonators are uniquely-sophisticated miniature transceivers that operate by remote control. It will need nothing more than for me to hit pre-dial numbers on my cellphone to complete the circuit."

Manfred looked puzzled. "Just one question. Why did you decide at the last minute to change the payload? Originally, your instructions were for each box to contain eight batteries, but now you have switched to ten units in two boxes and just four units in the other box."

"I thought you would be curious about that," Stratton told him. "I have decided to leave nothing to chance, so the small package will be for a diversionary target. I want to direct all attention away from our primary targets, which will receive the full brunt of our attack. With the beefed-up payloads the carnage will be incalculable. London, and the world, will never forget what we are about to inflict on them."

He patted the top of one of the boxes. "Tell me

about the other arrangements."

Manfred cleared his throat as if to underline the importance of the report he was about to deliver. "We bought the Thames river cruise boat. The owner was at first reluctant to sell, but when we offered twice the value, he quickly caved in. The boat was removed from service to carry out the alterations you requested, but it is now back to ferrying sightseers and partygoers four times a day."

"No problems with the licence?"

"No, the river authorities were happy to transfer this to the new owners, and they accepted our plans to remove it for a few days for an overhaul and safety checks. We rehired the boat skipper at twice his previous salary and things are business as usual."

Stratton beamed. "Excellent! What about the other matter?"

"A parcel delivery van and a small Renault Clio back-up car have been obtained and are parked in a secure garage. They are brand-new vehicles, but every day I visit them to make sure they are starting and turning over properly. There is no risk of engine failure."

"Smart work," Stratton interrupted, "but there is no need to visit again until we are ready to go."

"When will that be?"

"Three days from now. First, there are a few loose ends we must tie up"

Chapter 25

WHEN TWENTY PEOPLE occupy a room designed for less than half that number, a few basic chemical reactions will occur. Ambient temperature is forced up at a dramatic rate by the combined effects of body heat emissions, while oxygen levels will dip alarmingly, particularly where the room is located in the building's innards, with no fresh air available through open windows. Mix in a factor for body odours, which help to further foul the atmosphere, and the chances of triggering nausea and unconsciousness increase exponentially.

Strangely, after more than thirty minutes, none of the room's occupants looked uncomfortable, nor expressed any desire to leave.

It was not as if Mike Devon was any great shakes at oratory, although he was holding his audience spellbound by a passion and anger they had seldom seen before.

As his eyes darted around his agency's full complement of field agents, computer whizkids, crime techies and support staff, Devon's gaze seemed to emit a personal challenge to each of them.

He had spent those thirty minutes recapping his conversation with Cheadle and affirming his belief that the agency had been targeted by assassins in order to deflect them from mainstream operations. "Starting now," he told them, "we go back to basics. We recalibrate all our surveillance systems to their usual settings. We start with the assumption that the country is facing a terror threat bigger and more frightening that anything we've yet encountered. We gather in and disseminate every scrap of information we can find, and we leave nothing – I mean nothing - to chance. Don't overlook anything, assume that even the tiniest kink in behaviour might reveal something, and chase down the flimsiest of leads in the hope we get a handle on what is lurking out there."

He paused to compose himself. "Understand this. We will probably have to take risks, we will certainly push ourselves beyond our usual protocols, and if that means we become exposed to our other intelligence agency brothers and sisters, then that's a call I'm prepared to make right here and now."

A babble of voices erupted in the room, and Devon signalled for silence. "I know this goes against the grain of our usual protectionist principles, but I've no doubt this situation is so serious we simply cannot take the time to skirt around things. We go at this full tilt, and if it turns out to be our last operation, so be it. At least by then we will all know that we did what we could to avert what appears to be a lethal attack on the very fabric of everything we hold dear."

Silence descended on the room. Predictably, it was Doyle who broke the spell. "We're all with you, Mike, but so that we're clear about things, are we dropping pursuit of the remaining two assassins?"

The answer was unequivocal. "Yes, I don't want to hear them mentioned again. If they come at us, we'll deal with it, but for now we've lost enough time and energy worrying about them. There's a bigger picture that needs our undivided attention."

Computer surveillance team leader Tim Halloran leaned back in his seat. "What about this lead we had on the server registered to a Felix Hoffmeier in Vienna? Surely we can't just let that drop?"

Devon paused before answering. "Thanks for bringing that up, Tim. Part of me says it could be just another red herring, but there's also a part that says we need to check it out. I think I can spare someone to pay a visit and rattle Herr Hoffmeier's cage." He looked at Alfie Cheadle. "Think you're up to it?"

Cheadle beamed. "Just tell me what you want me

to do."

"My office later. For now, let's get back on track."

A pronounced cough diverted Devon's attention to the rear of the room where Chelsea Horgan was sheepishly holding up her hand.

"You have something to add, Agent Horgan?"

She stood up to make herself seen. "Just before we started into this meeting, I got a call from our London station chief to tell us that one of the assassins, Jeff Millar, was flagged on a flight to New York this morning. Because he was an American, I recognised from the list, I had already passed on his details in the hope something like this might happen. I had forgotten to mention it previously to you."

"Don't apologise," Devon told her. "What's happening about picking him up when he lands?"

"The CIA's NY office has alerted the FBI who are standing by to take him into custody on a number of outstanding federal warrants, including his suspected involvement in the assassination of a Senator in Chicago two years ago. The flight is due at JFK within the next hour."

Devon smiled for the first time that morning. "Excellent! So, who does that leave us with?"

Doyle chipped in. "The last name on the list is Dragan Boskovic. He checked out of a bedsit yesterday morning but has disappeared into thin air. We don't have a clue as to his present whereabouts."

"Okay, what I said before still goes. We forget him. I'm afraid we have a long stretch ahead of us, so let's break and get at it." Devon was about to leave the room when he suddenly remembered something. "Oh, one last thing. You'll be pleased to know that the General is considered fit enough to be allowed out of bed for a few hours, and I'm told he has been spending the morning using up his full month's allocation of mobile phone minutes. I'm heading over there now to see him."

174

Chapter 26

GENERAL SIR JOHN Sandford was at that moment sitting stiffly in a bedside armchair, draped in a pink blanket thrown over his knees, and hooked up to an IV drip that made it difficult to use his left arm. The early-morning dosage of painkillers was beginning to wear off, but he was determined to put through one last call before the arrival of his visitor. After that, he would reluctantly climb back between the sheets for the four or five hours of midday recuperative sleep prescribed by the consultant physician.

His final call went through to the Prime Minister's private number in Downing Street. It was perhaps the most difficult one he'd ever had to make. But things needed sorted, and for ten minutes he discussed a range of options before hitting the red off button and pushing his shoulders wearily into the back of the chair.

He lifted his eyes at the sound of footsteps on the tiled floor and raised his head as his oldest friend, Sir Norman Melrose, his direct liaison link to the PM, advanced to the foot of the bed.

"Norm, sorry about the early morning call. I appreciate you coming in at short notice." He motioned to a visitor's chair and waited for Melrose to sit down. "I needed to talk to you urgently about what has been happening over the past few days. There have been some significant developments"

Melrose didn't attempt to hide his agitation. "Johnny, this is lunacy! You know, I haven't quite forgiven you for going behind my back to the PM to get a carte blanche for your operation, but putting that aside, you need to take a back seat. You're just not up to dealing with things until you've had a chance to fully recover. For that reason I've arranged with the PM for the reins to be handed over entirely to MI6. Your agency is being stood down until further notice."

Sandford's eyes narrowed and a frown creased his features. "Unfortunately, Norm, I know it would suit your purposes to have me out of the picture. I admit I'm not able to function on all cylinders but lying in that God-forsaken bed has at least provided me with the time I needed to take stock. I can see clearly now what I should have realised a week ago, but maybe I just didn't want to believe that a man in whom I have placed my entire trust has stabbed me in the back."

"I'm afraid I'm not quite following you, old boy....."

Sandford slammed his right palm down onto the wooden armrest. "Don't make this any harder than it needs to be. I know it was *you* who sold out the names of my people, and what's more I know, or at least I can guess, at what was used to lever the information from you."

"This is preposterous! Have you taken leave of your senses?" Sir Norman rose and glared down at the General's frail figure. "I'm not listening to any more of this hogwash."

"Sit down!" The command in the General's voice left no room for doubting his visitor would do otherwise. "I have a number of things to say, and you would do well to listen carefully. It's no exaggeration to tell you that your entire future, including how much time you will spend in prison, rests entirely on my being satisfied about your full co-operation and utmost honesty from this point forward."

Melrose slumped into his chair, but there was still some fight left in him. "This is absolutely unbelievable. I don't know what kind of delirium has been induced by the drugs they're giving you here, but it's obvious they are the cause of your incredible fantasy."

"Enough!" The General barked. "Let me take this from the top. I don't mind telling you that I had almost driven myself crazy trying to work out the traitor in our mist. Then last night it struck me that it really couldn't have been anyone else. You alone have had unbridled access to my operation, a price I was willing to pay in order to keep the PM happy that he had oversight on what we do and who works for us. It didn't appear to me to be too great a sacrifice to let a man I have known and trusted for many years to be the one acting as the buffer between *LonWash* and Downing Street."

"John, you've got this all wrong...."

The General ignored him and kept talking. "When I finished crossing off all the names and was left with yours, I kept looking for an excuse, something that would absolve you. Maybe, you were just the victim of loose talk, or maybe you were careless with a memo, or email, or some such correspondence. I know you didn't do it for money because you've already got more than a single person should ever need. I know you didn't do it for some kind of ideology, or because you want to reshape the world. Frankly, you've always been too selfish and insular to stick your neck out that far."

Sandford was struggling for breath, but he was determined to finish. "In the end it could only come down to one thing. You were compromised, probably because of your known affinity for sex with young boys. There have always been whispers around Westminster, but most of your peers turned a blind eye, probably in the hope that you could keep a lid on it, or at least be ultra-discreet in pursuing your sordid pleasures. I'm betting someone caught you literally with your pants down and used this to get you to betray everything I believed you held dear."

The General was winging it. He didn't know, nor could he prove, anything he had been saying for the past five minutes. He *had* narrowed a small list of suspects down to Melrose, but everything he had was based on conjecture, supposition, and guesswork. He knew, however, that if he confronted Melrose with the right mixture of confidence and bluff, he would discover how close to the mark he was.

If there was one thing Sandford had learned over the years, it was an ability to read people. He knew all the tells, the often tiniest signals emitted by people who were being evasive or who were simply downright liars. The furrowing of brows, the dilation of pupils, the appearance of red marks on the ears or neck, the swelling of the larynx, and the involuntarily, almost imperceptible, small muscle spasms and shakes that affect hands and feet movements.

Sir John was trained to read all the signs. And he didn't like what he was reading off the man sitting opposite. "My God, Norm, it's all true, isn't it?"

Melrose bent forward and lifted both hands to cradle his head. His voice was little more than a whisper. "Believe me, Johnny, I didn't want for anything like this to happen. I couldn't see a way out. I thought it was just the usual things you cloak-and-dagger boys get up to. I thought all he wanted was to understand how your agency worked. If I had known he had intended to target your people I would never have gone through with it.

"Don't dare try to exculpate yourself from this!" The General was shaking with rage. "Your protestations are embarrassing and, quite frankly, insulting. I have a man dead because of what you've done. My entire team and their families have been exposed to the most grievous perils because you sold out!"

"What could I have done?"

"You should have come to me. I would have helped. Now, I'm afraid you're beyond all help."

Devon stopped at his home to grab a quick shower, scrape off two days of facial growth, and change his clothes. The house was empty without Emma and young Michael, but he hoped it wouldn't be for much longer. Something told him this operation was in the end zone, and as he closed the door behind him, he was in a much cheerier mood than he knew he had a right to be.

When he walked into Sandford's private hospital ward his mood changed alarmingly. He recognised Sir Norman Melrose immediately, although the figure slumped in the chair bore little resemblance to the normally-effusive man who was noted for his loud, almost brash, voice and bombastic manner.

His first thought was that there was bad news about the General, who looked tired and drained and wore an expression of deep sadness as he turned to greet him with barely a flicker of his eyes. But then he detected a tension in the air, the kind of silence that took awkwardness to a whole new meaning. Something had passed between these two men, and whatever it was appeared to have changed the dynamics of their relationship.

The General nodded across at Melrose. "I have found our mole. This is the piece of garbage who sold out our agency."

"What?" Without realising it, Devon had already crossed the room and was lifting Melrose out of his chair. His hands were encircled tightly on the Downing Street aide's neck."

"Stop, Mike. We need him alive to...."

Devon turned to see Sandford stumble out of the chair and fall across the bed. He let go of Melrose and raced around to his boss. He gently lifted the old man and cradled him in his left arm as he reached out to press a nurse station call button on the panel above the bed.

The General squeezed Devon's arm. "Take this man into custody and sweat him for everything he knows. Get him in front of a sketch artist and make sure he co-operates fully."

"Don't worry, Sir, he will, but right now you need to take it easy."

Sandford ignored him. "I spoke this morning with the PM who knows all about this. He has instructed you to continue in my absence, but he wants you to link up with MI6. This thing is too big for us to go it alone. Give them what you have but be careful to protect the ethos of *LonWash*. The PM has agreed to lift the terror threat to its highest level and has promised you all the resources you need. There is to be a meeting of the COBRA security committee at noon today. You will attend in my absence...." The General's voice began to fade, and his eyes fluttered closed.

Just then, two nurses and a doctor ran into the room and pushed Devon aside. They laid Sandford carefully across the bed and hooked him up to a battery of monitors. The doctor turned to Devon. "Don't worry, he's just exhausted. If you really want to help him, please stay away for a few days to let him fully recover."

Devon nodded and reached out to grab Melrose by the collar of his jacket. "On your feet. We have a lot to talk about."

He frogmarched his prisoner out of the room, turning back to glance briefly at the pulses of light that were creating steady peaks on one of the General's monitors.

Chapter 27

THE MARCH OF technology has propelled sketch artistry to dizzying heights in less than a decade. Enhanced computer software is producing 3D high-definition, photo-quality e-Fits that are now replacing the old pencil outlines, at least in the eyes of the public, as one of the most valuable tools in the armoury of law enforcement. But lurking behind these dramatic images can still be found the skill of the individual artist - men and women whose craft continues to be relied on by the new generation of programmers.

Malcolm Thompson was one of those artists who found it easy to make the transition from paper to screen. Leave him alone in front of a computer and he could produce amazing results by marching a mouse in and out of the sidescreen toolbox as he methodically constructed all manner of human faces. However, Thompson never started anything without first grabbing a sketch pad and his little box of carbon crayons and pencils.

A large block of paper was resting on his knee as he sat across from Sir Norman Melrose, ready to begin his latest assignment in a small office on the third floor of the *LonWash Securities* building. The crayons and pencils remained on the desk in front of him. Thompson needed to establish a general baseline before continuing.

He had learned long ago never to rush a subject into trying to conjure up facial images. What was needed was a patient approach. He preferred always to get a general description of the subject, concentrating on ethnicity, height, general build, age range, and impressions of fitness and health. Answers to those questions provided him with a general outline of a face that was either gaunt or plump, lined with age or worry, or perhaps showing signs of energy and vitality.

Now came the building blocks, the time to add detail. Thompson started with the hair. Short? Long? Wavy? Curly? Flecked with colour? Above or below the ear? Spiky? Styled to the left or right? The gentle questions kept flowing.

What about the eyes? Did they seem large or small? Were they dark- or light-coloured? Were they framed by heavy eyebrows? Did they appear narrow, or did they sparkle with moisture?

As he moved down the face, the questions developed the same pattern as Thompson teased out every memory of facial construction. Nose, lips, cheeks, chin. Finally, he looked to factor in details of any distinguishing features, such as scars, pock marks, birth spots, blemishes of any kind. Was the subject clean-shaven or did he have a stubble? Was he wearing glasses or earrings? The last question always made Thompson chuckle, remembering as he did the old days when ear, nose and lip piercings seemed to be the exclusive domain of females.

It was only when Thompson had completed his checklist of questions that he reached across to grab a pencil and begin massaging it lightly across the page. He worked in silence for twenty minutes, pausing only to swap pencils, or lift a crayon, or use his finger to smudge across the lines he had created. Finally, he stood up and walked away from Melrose to sit behind another desk. He fired up a laptop and began frantically moving a wireless mouse across a large plastic mat. He found it too cumbersome to use the small rectangular finger-activated trackpad on the laptop console.

After thirty minutes he leaned back on his seat and gestured for Melrose to join him. He used his left leg to hook a seat close to the corner of the desk, waited for Melrose to sit, and swivelled the monitor in his direction.

"Is that the man we're looking for?"

Melrose was astounded. The image staring at him from the screen was unquestionably the man who had held him at gunpoint in the London hotel room. "It's amazing. Yes, that is just like him, only he had more flecks of grey hair above his ears, and I don't think his nose was as big as that."

Thompson made the alterations, updated the file-save function, and clicked on the printer icon. He selected an initial run of fifty A4 colour prints, rising to lift the first sheet as it was deposited in the collection drawer. Before leaving the room, he nodded at a security guard who crossed to the desk and motioned for Melrose to follow him. He was being returned to a holding cell in the basement.

Thompson took the lift to the second floor and strode down the corridor to Alan Doyle's office, waving the sheet as he pushed through the door. "Hot off the presses!" he said, with more than a hint of pride.

Doyle studied the image for a few seconds, before glancing back to Thompson. "Pass these around to every member of the team but hold off on general circulation until we hear back from Mike."

"Where he is?"

"It seems," Doyle smiled, "that our illustrious leader has been summoned to a rather high level meeting of suits. Talk about a fish out of water! Forward this to his phone in case he wants to use it."

Cabinet Office Briefing Room A, which provides the initials for one of the British Government's emergency committees, COBRA, is not a particularly auspicious room. Housed in the first floor of a suite of offices at Whitehall, the forty-foot long room is largely unfurnished, save for a large conference table that runs down the middle and has a seating capacity for up to twenty-four attendees. The floor is covered by a rough hemp carpet that matches the bland chocolate colour of wood panelled walls, into which are recessed a ribbon of small lights running around the perimeter, about four feet below the high ceiling.

If it were not for the other wall adornments, a visitor would have been forgiven for thinking they had stepped back in time to the Victorian age of the room's original construction. A bank of computer screens, which provided live video feeds and satellite imagery, completely covered one wall, and small pop-up monitors ran down the centre of the conference table. The twenty-first century had well and truly arrived at Whitehall.

The Government has a number of emergency committees that deal with how it will react to crisis situations, such as extreme weather, fuel shortages, health pandemics, attacks on the nation's financial systems, and public disorder. Each of these committees has use of its own briefing room, but the most important by far is the one that meets in Room A and is tasked with monitoring and reacting to all manner of terror threats. Today, as usual, the committee was chaired by the Prime Minister.

The buzz of conversation ceased the moment he strode into the room and walked to the head of the table. He nodded at his two most senior Cabinet colleagues, the Home Secretary and Foreign Secretary, and then swept an acknowledgement around the table at representatives of the military, at the heads of MI5 and MI6, at the Metropolitan Police Commissioner, at the two most senior officers of Scotland Yard's Anti-Terrorism Unit, and then at the bureau chiefs for the Maritime and Coastguard Agency and the Revenue and Customs Smuggling Division. Finally, his gaze fell on Mike Devon.

"Ladies and Gentlemen," he announced, "we have a new face in our midst today. Allow me to introduce Mr Devon, who is here on behalf of General Sir John

Sandford. Most of you will know that four days ago Sir John was the target of an assassination attempt, an attempt that has largely to do with why this meeting has been called. I gather Sir John is making a splendid recovery and we send our best wishes. In his absence Mr Devon has been cleared to act on his behalf and to relay any information the General might be able to help us with."

He smiled briefly at Devon. "I think it would be best if our guest filled us in with everything he knows."

It was the moment Devon had been dreading. He had had less than an hour to concoct a plausible account as to why a private security firm such as *LonWash* should command the attention of COBRA and spark the lifting of the nation's security threat to its highest level. Uppermost in his mind was the General's admonition to protect the ethos of the agency at all costs.

He cleared his throat and began speaking. "I work for Sir John's company. We have security contracts across the world, dealing mainly with private enterprises, although occasionally we work with other governments on sensitive internal issues, usually involving investigations of their own law enforcement agencies. These latter contracts are all notified to and cleared by the Foreign Office."

The Prime Minister interrupted. "Mr Devon, we are all aware of the extensive portfolio of Sir John's work. Indeed, it is one of the reasons he is such a respected and trusted member of this committee. There is no need for you to set a background for us, just bring us up to speed on the events of the past week."

Devon was grateful for the intervention, knowing the PM was as anxious as he not to let the spotlight shine too brightly on the activities of *LonWash*. "Thank you, Sir. Five days ago, one of our operatives was shot dead here in London and this was followed closely by the attack on Sir John. We uncovered an assassination list containing the names of all our senior personnel, and at first we believed we were being targeted by some individual or group that may have been disgruntled by some of our past operations. However, we now believe that the attacks were designed to divert our attention away from a potential terrorist threat to this country."

There was a gentle murmur of voices, broken by the strident voice of Peter Ramsden, the head of MI6. "Why would someone attach any importance to your agency in the protection of our nation?"

Devon had already rehearsed his answer. "I agree, Sir. The idea would otherwise be preposterous, but we believe it's possible that we previously encountered these individuals who might have been fearful of us raising a flag if we spotted anything unusual that connected to them. There is also the fact that it would have been anticipated that Sir John would have asked MI5 and MI6 to help him track down the assassins, thereby also distracting resources away from their usual activities. I understand Sir John was in the process of doing just than when he was gunned down."

"Yes," Ramsden acknowledged, "I was due to meet with him the following morning."

Devon continued. "Our enquiries over the past few days have led us to believe the assassination list is nothing more than a smokescreen. There's no doubting the veracity of the list, or the very great trouble and expense that someone has taken to activate it, but, in our opinion, it is still nevertheless a smokescreen."

Ramsden interrupted again. "I'm guessing your hypothesis is that only something noticeably big would warrant such an elaborate, pre-planned attack on your people. But why should this involve the country? Could this be nothing more than a pre-emptive strike on your organisation by someone you've rubbed the wrong way"

"You said it yourself, Sir," Devon retorted. "We're just not big enough or important enough for that degree of investment. Why hire a whole army of assassins and provide them with only a small window within which to complete their tasks? In any other circumstances it would be seen as rank amateurism, if it not were for the effort that was clearly expended in putting all this together."

"It still seems a bit flimsy." The voice belonged to Matthew Harding, the renowned Scotland Yard terrorist hunter. "I mean, we're preparing to move to a state of high alert based on a lot of supposition."

The response came from the PM. "The answer comes in two parts. First, General Sandford is adamant that a clear danger exists. We all know the General's track record for accurate assessment of situations such as this, and if he believes we are in danger of imminent attack, I for one will not be taking any bets against his being wrong."

He paused as if to choose his next words carefully. "I am sorry to say that the second, most compelling reason for concern is that we learned this morning that Sir Norman Melrose has been implicated in whatever has been going on."

There were audible gasps as delegates looked at each other in bewilderment. The PM waited for the noise to settle. "All we know so far is that Sir Norman appears to have been coerced into supplying the list of names to the assassins. At present he is helping to put together a photofit of the man who inveigled him into this plot, but I'm arranging for him to be transferred to Scotland Yard this afternoon." He looked directly at Matthew Harding. "I expect you to uncover every detail of his involvement. In the meantime, let's take stock of where we go from here."

The next two hours proved fascinating for Devon. It was an opportunity for him to witness first-hand how the combined wheels of civil governance worked. And he was mightily impressed. These people left nothing to chance, taking their discussion from conjecture on the nature of the threat, to specific ways and means of countering all eventualities. Nothing was ruled out, although uppermost among their concerns were the possibilities of potential high-level, political assassinations, and the use of conventional or chemical explosions.

The time was divided between detecting the threat and nipping it in the bud, and the steps that needed to be taken to prevent large-scale casualties in the event that their detection efforts failed. It was determined that GCHQ, the Government Communication Headquarters at Cheltenham, would take the lead in trawling back through its cyber-surveillance work of the past week in the hope of picking up something that might have been overlooked. Air and freight manifests of the past seven days would also undergo a thorough recheck, as would passenger arrivals in all major airports. Every known terrorist suspect or supporter would be rounded up and interrogated, and every police informant would be activated to look out for and report suspicious activity. The logistics that were about to be employed were mind-boggling.

It was agreed that security would be stepped up across the capital, necessitating the use of extra plainclothed and uniformed officers to work alongside civilian guards at airports, train stations, ferry terminals, the docklands, and yacht marinas. Department stores, along with public facilities such as museums and tourist centres, would be ordered to introduce bag checks. Finally, it was agreed that emergency vehicle stop-and-search powers would be activated.

The citizens of London were about to face delays in just about every aspect of their daily lives.

Chapter 28

DEVON WALKED THROUGH the revolving door and stepped onto the pavement outside the Whitehall office block, grateful for the blast of cold air that helped to clear his lungs. He was about to hail a taxi when he heard a voice behind him. He turned to see MI6 Chief, Peter Ramsden, walk in his direction.

"A moment of your time, Mr Devon, if you don't mind."

Devon tried to get a read of the man's face but couldn't detect any animosity. "What can I do for you, Sir?"

"Let's drop the formalities, shall we? Just call me Peter. That was a pretty impressive performance you gave in there, but don't think I was fooled for one minute by the way you downplayed the role of *LonWash Securities.* I know you boys swim in bigger rivers than you would like the rest of us to know about. I need you to cut the crap and tell me exactly what's going on here."

Devon was taken aback. He had no way of knowing how much Sir John had worked with this man, or how much he had taken him into his confidence. One thing was for sure, and that was that he was not going to allow himself to be tripped up. "I'm not quite following you."

Ramsden laid his arm gently on Devon's shoulder. "Let's grab a coffee," he offered, pointing at a small cafeteria at the corner of the street. "If it makes you feel any better, I'll do the talking."

Five minutes later they were seated at a window overlooking one of London's busiest thoroughfares. Ramsden waited for Devon to take his first swallow of Cappuccino. "I know your organisation is rather more than a private security company. I am aware that Sir

John has the ear of the PM and has been involved in things that, shall we say, would normally be under the purview of my own organisation, and others I won't even mention."

Ramsden paused to take a sip of his coffee. "I don't need you to confirm or deny anything. Good God, man, give me some credit for occupying the position I currently hold. Do you really think your agency has been operating unnoticed, or that I wouldn't know about some of your more high-profile engagements, which I have to say have led to some spectacular successes? Yes, I know more about you than you would imagine."

Devon slammed his cup onto the saucer and stood up. "I'm not listening to any more of this. I've got nothing to say, so if you don't mind, I'll leave now."

Ramsden smiled. "Relax, Mike. I'm not here for a pissing contest. The old General has always played square with me. He has been good at keeping me in the loop and making sure I was never embarrassed by having to explain things after the horse had bolted, so to speak. I'm grateful for the number of times he gave me a heads-up on some pretty nasty situations, and even on occasions allowed us to take public credit for things that were resolved entirely by your agency. Unfortunately, he is now out of the picture, temporarily I hope, but I need to know that in his absence I can trust you to do the same as he would."

For once, Devon was lost for words. He slid back into his chair, unsure about how to proceed. He decided for the moment to stick with his script. "I have no way of confirming what was discussed between you and the General. I'm just a foot-soldier who carries out orders and keeps his mouth shut. I think I've already proven by my attendance today that we will co-operate fully with all agencies, and that we have nothing to hide. Anything else you think might is going on will have to be taken up with the General."

The smile left Ramsden's face and for the first time he looked genuinely agitated. "Get down of that high horse! Don't play smug with me, boy. I know all about you. Hell, you used to be one of us. I know your record, which is pretty damned impressive by the way, and which is why the General headhunted you for his organisation. I'm not looking to rock any boats here, but you should know that neither am I prepared for any lone-wolf actions, or for your people to be getting in our way. We are now all agreed that we are facing a dire threat, one which will require every one of us to be pulling in the same direction. If I think for one minute that there is even the slightest possibility of obstruction by you or your people, I'll throw you into a cell and let you rot until this thing blows over."

Devon stared at the man opposite before doing the one thing that neither of them expected. He burst out laughing.

"You think this is some kind of joke? You think the special relationship the General enjoys with the PM will somehow stop me from doing what I know to be right?"

"Forgive me," Devon interrupted. "It's just that your little outburst reminded me so much of the General. That's exactly the way he would have reacted to my stonewalling, and I can see why you two would have gotten on. In many ways, you are both cut from the same cloth."

Ramsden relaxed. "So, you admit you have been stonewalling?"

"Only insofar as the bigger picture is concerned. In respect of this particular operation I have been ordered by the General to work closely with you and the other heads to make sure we nullify this threat. You have my word that we will not hold back on anything."

"That's more like it. Now run me through what you've got so far."

Devon outlined the events of the past five days, starting with the discovery of the assassin list in Austria and ending with the early-morning arrest of Sir Norman Melrose. He was careful to leave out details of the surveillance mechanisms used but did disclose the agency's involvement in the deaths of the assassins."

Ramsden acknowledged the report. "I'm grateful for your honesty. I knew there was something fishy about the way the Germans took credit for killing a known terrorist in Frankfurt, not to mention the unexplained death of an international assassin in Edinburgh last evening."

Devon was impressed by the breadth of Ramsden's knowledge. He made a mental note to never underestimate the man.

"Anything else?" Ramsden enquired.

Devon reached into his jacket to retrieve his iPhone. "Forgot to turn this back on. I'm waiting to hear how our sketch artist got on with Melrose."

If Ramsden was curious about why Melrose was in the custody of *LonWash* instead of being handed over immediately to Scotland Yard, he didn't show it. He waited for Devon to let his phone run through its start-up sequence.

"Here it is. I have an e-Fit photo of the man who Melrose says blackmailed him into betraying our agency. We will of course forward this to you and other agencies for immediate circulation. Perhaps you could get someone to co-ordinate running this through all the facial recognition databases?" He handed the phone for Ramsden to look at the picture.

"Good Lord!"

"Devon sat up straight. "What is it?"

Ramsden emitted a short whistle. "No need to bother with all that. I'd know this face anywhere. Used to be one of us." He turned the phone's screen back to Devon.

"This is none other than Carl Stratton.

Chapter 29

CONTAINER SHIP Captain Charlie Wilson paced the living room of his small apartment, his eyes red from a combination of sleep deprivation and frequent bursts of sobbing. He knew he was coming apart at the seams but struggled to find a way out of the crisis of conscience that had plunged him into the pits of despair over the past week. He looked down at an old Mark VI Webley revolver lying on the table and wondered if his father would have had the guts to do what he couldn't. The weapon had been used with distinction by Albert Wilson in World War Two action throughout a fierce campaign in Italy but had not been fired in anger since his demob in 1945.

Charlie had continued to clean and maintain the revolver out of respect for his father, never expecting to one day fill the cylinder again with the .455 cartridges that were stored in a locked drawer of a small writing bureau. At the weekend, Charlie had opened the gun's break-top mechanism, filled all six chambers, and held the barrel against the side of his head. His hand shook as his finger tightened on the trigger. He closed his eyes, steadied his breathing, and fell to his knees crying. He couldn't do it. Three further attempts over the next four days produced the same result.

He resigned himself to the fact that he hadn't the guts to commit suicide. The only way to keep his daughter safe was to keep his mouth shut. But that didn't sit too well with Charlie Wilson. Enough was enough. He had to do something, tell someone. He had to get this out of his system before it ate through to his very soul.

He knew when he was blackmailed into smuggling the small laptop battery units into the country that there was something sinister about them. At first, he had hoped they were nothing more than fancy containers for drugs or diamonds, but something had kept gnawing away at the back of his mind. What if the units contained some kind of chemical? He had heard about things like Ricin and what the effects of even small quantities could have if sent in the mail to unsuspecting people. No, Charlie was not having it. He would go to the police, tell them what he knew, and demand protection for his daughter and her family.

He locked the Webley back in the bureau, grabbed a bag containing his red laptop, and walked out the front door.

Twenty minutes later he was sitting in a small room on the third floor of the New Scotland Yard building in Broadway. It had taken some time to convince a reception officer of the importance of his visit, but he was finally taken to a lift and ushered into the room to await the attention of a Detective Inspector.

The rest of the afternoon became a blur for Charlie. He remembered the policeman appearing rather officious and bored at the outset of their meeting, but after leaving the office to check on something, his whole demeanour had changed quite dramatically on his return. Other people had crammed into the small room in the course of the day, and Charlie found himself having to respond to a barrage of questions, often fired at him simultaneously by different officers.

At around four o'clock, a tall man in a braided uniform opened the door and ordered everyone out. He took Charlie to a plush office on the top floor and assured him that his family had already been taken into protective custody. Charlie himself was to be detained for his own safety. The man, who introduced himself as the assistant commissioner in charge of anti-terrorism, asked Charlie for permission to conduct a thorough forensic check on his apartment in the hope of picking up traces of DNA from the uninvited guest who had held him at gunpoint and forced him into becoming a courier.

Without hesitation, Charlie handed over his keys.

Shortly after lunchtime that afternoon Manfred Stelling had walked around the corner of the building in which Charlie's flat was located. He failed to see the taxi moving out into the traffic stream, or the back of Charlie's head as he rested against the rear seat. Five minutes earlier and Charlie Wilson would have been a dead man.

Stelling had carefully picked the lock and let himself into the flat. He had spent over an hour ransacking the rooms but could find no sign of the red laptop. He knew from the warmish feel of one of the rings on a small kitchen cooker, that his prey was currently home on leave, rather than at sea, just as Carl Stratton told him would be the case. There was no way for Stelling to know how long Wilson had left the flat, but he had decided to settle in to wait.

Two hours later, Stelling had had enough. He rigged a small explosive device to the gas cooker, set a five-minute timer, and opened all the valves. Annoyed with himself for having missed the opportunity to kill the old seaman, Stelling slammed the door behind him and made his way back to his car, parked two streets away.

By the time a Scotland Yard forensic team van pulled into the street, the area was cluttered with Fire and Rescue trucks. There was no prospect of saving the building.

Melissa Foster thought nothing of the high-roof Ford Transit that pulled up outside the door of her Woodburn Road electronics shop shortly after midday.

The markings on the side panels clearly showed it was a private mail service, although she couldn't remember any outstanding stock deliveries. She was happy and content in her work, grateful for the independence afforded by an absent owner. Getting this job so close to home was her one stroke of good fortune in an otherwise dreary life, spent trying to make ends meet while providing constant care to her ailing mother. All in all, however, Melissa considered herself to be one of the lucky ones.

She smiled as the delivery man opened the door and walked in with a small brown parcel. He set in on the counter, asked her to sign for it, and handed her an envelope. The two exchanged pleasantries before the man exited the shop, leaving Melissa to wonder what it would be like to have someone such as him in her life. He looked the strong, athletic type, even if he carried with him a haughtiness that reminded her of Mr Darcy in *Pride and Prejudice*, her favourite book.

She grabbed a letter opener and slid it under the fold of the white A5 envelope. She recognised the letterhead of the holding company which owned her business. There was a brief three-line typed message, instructing her to hold the package unopened for collection on Friday by a representative of a mail-order computer supply business. She glanced at the box and read a label announcing: *This Side Up – Laptop Parts*.

Melissa reached out for a yellow Post-It notes block, tore off the top sheet, and scribbled a reminder message about Friday's collection. She thumped it against the box, before carrying it across the room to a small shelf. By the time she walked back to the counter, she had already forgotten about it.

It had never crossed Melissa Foster's mind to wonder why the package had not been delivered directly to the intended recipient.

Chapter 30

THE GULLIBILITY of people never ceased to amaze Carl Stratton. He watched through the shop window, shaking his head in bewilderment, as Melissa Foster stowed away the package. Did she really believe that her limited experiences should have landed her such a cushy number? Had she never stopped to consider that jobs in the real world had to be earned by putting in years of foot-slogging toil to justify being given full management of a business in a busy high street store? Probably not. She was undoubtedly one of those people who grew up believing in the Tooth Fairy and clinging to the notion that she would one day win the National Lottery.

He aimed the Transit away from the pavement and joined the flow of traffic heading into Central London, already dismissing the silly woman from his thoughts. Come Friday, she would have served her purpose.

Stratton took the opportunity to look around as the van sped down Woodburn Road. It was one of the busiest outer-limit regions of the city, with shops, office blocks and schools crammed into a few square miles, surrounded by the districts of Enfield, Hounslow, and Harrow. He had chosen well. A major explosion here would cripple the entire western side of the city. More importantly, it would divert attention away from his primary targets in the southeast.

But, he chided himself, he was looking too far ahead. He had just over two days to go, and there were things still to be done, starting with the removal of Sir Norman Melrose. Now, there was a man beneath contempt! Quite apart from his baseness in the pursuit of young boys, he had found the politician an altogether contemptible person, willing to sell out his soul and his country for his own self interests. It was because of people like Melrose that the Islamic world could no longer live in the shadows. The world needed to be cleansed of the filth and hypocrisy represented by these elitist fools. Melrose would die tonight.

He looked at the dashboard clock and estimated he would arrive in time to watch Melrose climb from his official Government car and disappear into the luxury of his riverside apartment. He did so most evenings at precisely seven o'clock. Stratton would wait for the security detail to leave for the evening, and then he would provide Melrose with a one-way ticket to hell. He relished the prospect of drawing the knife slowly across the bastard's white neck.

He nosed the Transit into a parking spot opposite the apartment entrance, noting he had five minutes to spare. He killed the engine and looked up the street, not quite believing what he was seeing. Stratton had been around too many corners not to realise that a pair of black, window-darkened Range Rovers, abandoned at the kerb fifty yards from his position, were security service vehicles.

Before he could marshal his thoughts, the door of the apartment building opened and three men stepped out, each carrying two sealed plastic bags. They walked to the rear of the vehicles and placed the sacks into the boot compartments. A fourth man emerged from the building and stood on the top step. He fished into his pocket, removed a packet, and lit a cigarette.

Stratton froze. He recognised the face of Peter Ramsden, now head of MI6, and one of the rising stars by the time Stratton had left the service. Their paths had rarely crossed, but he remembered Ramsden's reputation for being able to read intelligence tea leaves, and for his ability to plan the most intricate of operations.

It was obvious this was no social call. Stratton knew at once that Melrose had somehow been compromised. This changed everything, but his dark mood didn't last for long. He did not for one second downplay the significance of Ramsden being on his tail, but maybe, just maybe, he could use this to his advantage.

Felix Hoffmeier woke shortly after three o'clock. His bedroom was bathed in darkness, save for a sliver of light shining through a partly-closed curtain. He checked the red glow from the digital screen of a small alarm clock on a bedside cabinet, wondering why he had stirred in the middle of the night. A glass of brandy and a strong sedative usually meant he could depend on getting an uninterrupted eight-hour sleep. He snorted in annoyance, and rolled on his left side, pulling the quilt over his shoulders.

A minute passed before Hoffmeier realised he was not going to get back to sleep. It was not because he wasn't tired. It was because he sensed a presence in the room. He shot upright in the bed, staring into the gloom. Gradually, the figure of a man began to take shape.

"Welcome back to the land of the living," Herr Hoffmeier. "Now, I want you to carefully reach across and switch on your table lamp. If you do anything silly, I will be forced to kill you, and that would be a pity. I feel we should get to know each other first."

Alfie Cheadle was enjoying the moment, his first major assignment flying solo. He had left London in the Dassault shortly after a final teatime briefing with Devon and was wheels-down in the executive jet section of Vienna's international airport within two hours. After clearing an onboard cursory customs check, he had retrieved his Glock 19 from a hidden compartment, deplaned, and taxied across town. He spent several hours in an all-night restaurant before making his way on foot to Leopoldstadt, an attractive suburban retreat on the bank of the Danube. Breaking into Hoffmeier's house was a piece of cake, despite the impressive-looking array of burglar-alarm boxes dotted around the exterior.

"What is the meaning of this? What do you want?" A tremor in Hoffmeier's voice betrayed his attempt to appear relaxed and confident."

Cheadle was in no mood for small talk. "We need to talk about why you engaged a bunch of assassins to target the company I work for. I want to know every last detail about the operation, and I want you to point me in the direction of any others who were involved in this conspiracy."

Felix Hoffmeier had been around too many corners not to know when the game was up. It really didn't matter how these people had tracked him down. All that mattered was that he somehow extricated himself from the situation he now found himself in. He had known too many men like this one, men who would have no hesitation in pulling the trigger. He had to come clean and hope he could find some leverage that would mean saving his skin.

Hoffmeier held nothing back. He explained about his past and how this was used against him. He recounted the methods he had employed to recruit the assassins and revealed the laborious email trails that were followed on the instructions of a man he kept referring to as *Mutterficker,* a name that lost nothing in translation.

Cheadle delved into his pocket for his smartphone, pressed a few buttons, and showed the screen to Hoffmeier. "Is this your Mutterficker?"

"Ja, that is he," Hoffmeier responded as he gazed at the e-Fit image.

Cheadle motioned for Hoffmeier to climb out of the bed. He stood aside to let the German cross to the bedroom door. "I need you to go to your study, power up your laptop, and do precisely what I tell you."

Hoffmeier looked at the Gemtech suppressor

threaded into the barrel of the pistol. The hand that held it was rock-steady. "I will do whatever you ask."

Cheadle had already scoped out the house before interrupting Hoffmeier's sleep. He had spotted the laptop and had decided he would be taking it with him. You never knew what the *LonWash* tech boys could pull from a hard drive.

He ordered the German to write all passwords on a notepad, then watched as he powered up the machine. The launch screen was awash with folder icons, some familiar to Cheadle, but most displayed pictures and logos he had never seen before. He quizzed Hoffmeier for twenty minutes, demanding explanations for most of the programme functions, and ensuring any encryptions were removed.

He learned nothing new. Devon was right about it being nothing more than a dead end. But it was a dead end that had to be tied up. It was time to do just that.

Cheadle stepped away from the desk and aimed the Glock at the back of Hoffmeier's head. "I want the names of all your accomplices, and that means anyone who was involved in this operation. Don't make the mistake of holding anything back."

Hoffmeier was in no mood to protect his lifelong friends. "My partners were Jurgen Kappel and Dieter Neumann. It was they who planned all this and forced me to work with them. I begged them not to get involved, but they wouldn't listen."

Cheadle ignored the obvious attempt at blame-shifting and pointed his weapon at the notepad. "Write down all contact details for these men. I want to know every address where they might be found."

Hoffmeier scribbled furiously. When he finished, he tore off the top sheet and handed it to Cheadle. "There, I have done what you asked. There is no need for you to kill me. I am just an innocent businessman who was duped by two friends."

Cheadle's response was to aim the Glock at the

centre of Hoffmeier's forehead. "There is just one more thing. By our reckoning you set aside ten million Euros to pay the assassins. They won't be needing it, but we know of at least one widow who will." He fished in his pocket for a scrap of paper and set it on the desk. "You will transfer ten million to this numbered account and don't try to build in any fancy recall transaction."

Hoffmeier saw his way out. "Ja, that is only fair. I too have been a victim and I don't want any part of this blood money. This will make things right." His fingers attacked the keyboard, and suddenly pop-ups started appearing on the screen. After several minutes he leaned back in his seat. "There, it is done."

Cheadle ordered him to unplug the machine and stow it in its case. He slung the strap over his shoulder and backpedalled towards the door. "Do not turn around. Wait for five minutes after I leave."

"Ja, Ja."

Cheadle reached the door and pushed down on a brass handle, but he wasn't ready for leaving just yet. He shouted back across the room. "Turn around! You didn't really think you could buy us off."

Hoffmeier spun in the chair, his eyes wide with fright. His brain didn't have time to process the small flash that erupted from the suppressor. The hollow-point 9mm cartridge entered just above the centre of his forehead, expanded on impact, and turned parts of his frontal and parietal lobes into a gooey mess.

Chapter 31

THE HUNT FOR Carl Stratton was now six hours old. According to one of the most detailed forensic audits ever undertaken by the Bank of England, he was profiled as being in the top one hundred of the world's richest men, with interests in a variety of multi-national companies, all of which were squeaky clean. Although he had personal accounts in a dozen countries, nothing of concern could be found in the statements of transactions that were being poured over by a team of twenty analysts. Carl Stratton was either a man with nothing to hide, or one who knew how to bury things he didn't want to be found.

An examination of the records of the National Property Database and the Valuation Office Agency elicited no evidence of property, be it commercial, domestic, or industrial, held in Stratton's name. Nor was there any mention of his leasing premises, or paying UK taxes, or even holding a mobile phone contract. To all intents and purposes, he had left England shortly after resigning from MI6, and never returned.

For the most part, the investigations were led by MI5, Britain's internal security service, but it was left to MI6, the local equivalent of America's CIA, to chase down the most promising lead. The summary of Stratton's business activities showed he was headquartered in New York, with a penthouse apartment in Manhattan. A call to Homeland Security resulted in six agents racing to the address.

A bemused doorman was able to tell them that his former resident had left on a business trip. The names of all flight passengers travelling out of LaGuardia, Newark, and JFK within a four-hour window of Stratton leaving the apartment were checked. The search drew a blank. Next, it was decided to match passenger boarding photos against the e-Fit that had been jpegged from London. The facial recognition software took less than ten minutes to find a ninety-seven percent match. Stratton had used an alias.

The information was relayed back to Peter Ramsden at MI6. He sent a team to London Heathrow to scan arrival security footage, a job made easy by knowing the exact flight check-in time. Stratton was pinged on a number of cameras as he moved through Customs and baggage clearance areas. The watchers saw him meeting with a large bald man in the arrivals lounge and were able to switch to exterior camera footage to track the pair to the short-stay car park.

A pole-mounted camera at the exit barrier clearly showed the faces of the two men in a beige-coloured Daimler. What it also showed was the vehicle's registration plates.

Ramsden ordered one of his analysts to check the ANPR database, the automatic number plate recognition network, which detailed the exact real-time location of all registered vehicles. The name of Manfred Stelling filled the top of the computer screen. He was the registered owner with an address at Prince Albert Road. According to the ANPR webcam system, the vehicle was last picked up by a traffic camera close to that address.

By the time the analyst turned in his seat to hand a print-out to Ramsden, the room was already empty.

Stratton prided himself in never having lost his cool. No matter what was thrown at him, he had somehow always managed to turn it to his advantage. He didn't see any need to start changing now. The arrest of Melrose, coupled with the involvement of MI6, could not have been foreseen, but, hey, shit happens all the time. Deal with it. Move on.

And that's exactly what he was doing. The last of a number of boxes were sitting duct-taped on the bench in the basement. He had been methodical about what to take and what to leave, regretting that most of his firearm collection would have to stay behind. He took one last look around the room before walking towards the stairs and shouting over his shoulder at Stelling. "Take these up to the garage. I have a few other things to take care of."

Stelling looked uneasy. "Carl, I still don't see why we have to leave the house. Nobody knows about us here. We have everything we need here, and we still have to hole up until Friday.

Stratton stopped and turned. "I made a mistake in letting Melrose see my face. I never imagined his involvement would have been discovered so soon. One thing for certain is that the spineless bastard will be spilling his guts, and that will include, no doubt, doing what he can to help them put together a very credible image of my face."

"But you are a master of disguise. How can this be a problem?"

"Because," Stratton responded patiently, "knowing who I am and what I have done will lead my old cronies at MI6 to start unearthing whatever they can find about me. I've no doubt they've already arranged for my Manhattan apartment to be ransacked, in which case they will have been able to track my movements to London. This city is known throughout the world for having the greatest array of intrusive CCTV coverage per square foot. I can't risk the chance that we were picked up and followed to this location."

Realisation dawned on Stelling, and without another word he grabbed three cartons and walked purposefully past Stratton. He bounded the concrete steps two at a time, as if he expected the authorities to come crashing through the door at any moment.

Eight first-response vehicles converged on Prince Albert Road from three directions. They were led by an armoured vehicle belonging to SO19, the Metropolitan Police Counter Terrorism Command Unit. Seated on two benches inside the vehicle were six men and two women, dressed in typical SWAT gear, each cradling a lethal MP5 sub-machine pistol. They would be first through the doors.

An additional twenty men and women were crammed into four MI5 Range Rovers, with half that number in two MI6 vehicles. Bringing up the rear was a high-topped truck, specially adapted with two-inch interior lead lining. The people inside this vehicle were all dressed in Hazmat suits and would be called into action if specialist monitors detected any chemical signatures from within the target house.

There was nothing frantic or disorganised about the cavalcade. A chain of command had already been established and honed by countless exercises in places like the SAS centre at Sterling Lines on the outskirts of Hereford. Normally, a team from one of the SAS Sabre Squadrons would have been part of this kind of operation, but it was judged that time was of the essence. Nonetheless, a helicopter was already en route from Hereford.

Command was entrusted initially to the SWAT team leader. He would plan the assault, clear the building, and then stand-down his unit in favour of MI5. Until he signalled the transfer of command, all other personnel would hold at the perimeter to mitigate the risk of persons escaping the building and breaking the cordon.

The vehicles were held at an outer perimeter as an unmarked police car conducted a drive-by of the premises. A female officer in the passenger seat radioed in that the Daimler was still parked in front of the house.

As soon as he received the message, the SWAT

leader announced a go. The vehicle raced to the front wall, parking close so that the occupants could scramble onto the roof, step onto the wall, and leap into the garden beyond. It was decided that ramming the gate or exploding it off its hinges would provide too much of an early warning of their arrival. In operations such as these, every second was vital.

Four members of the team broke ranks and raced down either side of the house to prepare for a rear-door assault. Two of the front-garden squad took position either side of the mahogany door while the remaining pair fired a sustained burst of automatic fire at ground floor windows. When the windows shattered, the SWAT men each chucked in two fragmentation and stun grenades.

Without waiting for the blasts, the men at the door stood back and fired short, sixty-round-per-minute bursts at the area around the door locks. A large eight-inch circle erupted in toothpick fragments. The team leader put his shoulder to the door, which give way under his weight. All four men sprinted into the foyer, their weapons trained on empty halls and stairways.

The leader waited for the four-man team from the rear of the building. They too had encountered no opposition. He signalled for his men to break into pairs to begin a room-by-room clearance operation. Ten minutes later, they met back in the foyer. The house was well and truly deserted.

Carl Stratton watched the action unfold. He was five miles away, in a large warehouse, where his laptop was logged on to a live feed from his camera surveillance system at Prince Albert Road. His mood was anything but celebratory. Another fifteen minutes and he would have been snagged. Had he not decided to visit Melrose's house, he would not have known that a net was closing in. It was indeed a fortunate turn of events, one that made him wonder again at the ways of Allah.

He had been right to leave the Daimler. It had already been compromised, but now he worried if the mail delivery van he used to flee the scene might also have been picked up by traffic cameras. Good job he had insisted on Manfred procuring the nondescript back-up Clio family car. They would use this for the final transportation of the last two packages.

He busied himself by preparing the two bombs. Satisfied they were operational he carried the boxes across to the rear of the Clio.

He removed three prepaid cellphones from a third box. Each had a colour-coded sticker, across which was scribbled the number of its target receiving unit. The first call would be made at precisely twelve noon on Friday, followed fifteen-minutes later by the remaining two calls. He glanced at his wristwatch. A little more than thirty hours to go.

It was time to settle in. They had packed enough food and water to keep them going, and he would wait until the morning of the last day before donning an elaborate disguise.

Chapter 32

DEVON NUDGED the *LonWash* Range Rover up to the perimeter police barrier, flashed his security credentials, and was admitted through to a scene of pandemonium at Prince Albert Road. Security vehicles cluttered the street, and massive arc lights bathed the area in dancing shadows, as a constant stream of operatives entered and exited the large town house. It was three hours into a gloomy Thursday morning.

Devon's cyber team had spent what remained of the previous evening in a frenzy of activity, using all their backdoor entry systems to listen into the chatter from MI5, MI6, the Metropolitan Police Incident Room, and GCHQ. He had watched from the sidelines, fascinated by the unfolding events on both sides of the Atlantic, but resisted lifting the phone to request an update from Peter Ramsden.

The news that Stratton had been tracked down to an address in the northwest of the city finally galvanised him into action. He had hoped for an invite to join in the operation, but understood the logistics involved. There was no way, however, that he was about to sit this one out.

He had left the building shortly after the assault on the house began. With him in the car were Alan Doyle and Chelsea Horgan. He reasoned that he needed to be in the vicinity, intending to grab the first opportunity to visit the aftermath of the action. He had parked up less than two hundred yards from the outer perimeter, switched off the engine, and tried to remain patient.

The uneasy wait was broken by a mid-air sat-phone update from Cheadle, who provided the heartening news that Felix Hoffmeier had paid his dues for his part in the conspiracy against *LonWash*. The news that Hoffmeier had confirmed Stratton's lead role made Devon's blood boil another few degrees.

He had no sooner broken the connection with Cheadle than his phone buzzed for a second time. It was a familiar voice. "Mike, it's Peter Ramsden. I need you down at Prince Albert Road. We have had an incident involving our former colleague."

"I'm less than two minutes away."

Devon detected a chuckle on the other end of the line. "Why does that not surprise me?"

Doyle and Horgan were asked to remain in the foyer while Ramsden handed Devon a paper forensics suit. "We've found a concealed basement. Thought we'd take a quick rummage through before we let the Scenes of Crime boys lock it up for most of the day. We haven't time for the usual niceties."

Devon squirmed into the outfit and followed Ramsden into a large study and down a flight of concrete steps. There were already six other paper suits walking around the confined space. No-one bothered to make any introductions.

Cabinet doors and drawers were hanging open and a centre table was cluttered with small boxes and a bewildering array of paraphernalia, including an assortment of firearms and ammunition cartons. A tiled floor sparkled under the fluorescent lighting, and Devon noted the absence of dust on any of the bench surfaces.

"Looks like someone left in a hurry, but not before they swept the place clean."

"My thoughts exactly," Ramsden responded. "Our HAZMAT boys picked up nothing with their chemical detection equipment. According to them, an initial IMS sweep produced zero results, so either our friend is not using chemical agents or he has them stored off-site."

Devon knew about the handheld Ion Mobility Spectroscopy units that had become the go-to tool for detecting hazardous materials. He felt a surge of relief. He didn't mind admitting that chemical warfare scared him shitless. Looking around at the elaborate construction of the room, he had no doubt this was the centre of Stratton's operation. If there were no chemicals here, they wouldn't find them anywhere else.

"No," he told Ramsden. "We can strike a chemical bomb off our list. We're dealing with something conventional, although I doubt there'll be anything conventional about the way Stratton intends to use it. Whatever it is, I can't help thinking we don't have much time to find it."

Ramsden nodded in agreement. "We know that whatever it is was smuggled into the country in laptop battery containers. According to the ship's captain who surrendered himself yesterday, he made a total of six deliveries, but we have no way of knowing if other couriers were also used. Stratton could have acquired dozens of these battery units and has God knows how much destructive power at his fingertips."

Devon leaned an elbow on the centre table and seemed to be engrossed in thought. Finally, he spoke. "It seems to me that Stratton didn't just whistle up an order for the latest variant of Semtex. This has been too long in the planning for someone like him to leave a trail with the usual arms and explosives dealers. Is there a possibility of anything in his past career that will point us to a source? He must have had dealings with some pretty interesting individuals while he played out his Queen-and-country charade. Can you get your people to do a thorough backtrack?"

"No offence taken."

Devon shot him a puzzled look, before realising what he had said. "Sorry, I wasn't trying to tell you how to do your job. I was just thinking out loud."

Ramsden shrugged. "Don't sweat it. I've had a team working on this for the past six hours. We're going through every mission and every contact Stratton ever made while he worked for us. I've given instructions for dozens of redacted files to be cleaned up and every eyes-only dossier to be taken out of the vaults. If there's something to be found, we'll find it."

He held up his hand to stop Devon from speaking. "Before you say it, we are also looking into Manfred Stelling's background. We know that he came over the Wall sometime around 1985, but it is not yet clear how he ended up as a British citizen. Something tells me that Stratton played a part in his good fortune."

This time Devon couldn't be stopped from commenting. "You're hoping that somewhere along the line Stelling has been less circumspect than his boss about leaving a trail. Maybe he bought a piece of property or is renting a lock-up garage or has left a credit card trail we can follow?"

"I admit it's a long shot, but we have to chase down everything. We have also asked the Bank of England people to check back through all Stratton's companies to see if any of them has been involved in property deals, no matter how innocuous. Unfortunately, I'm told an exercise like that could take more than forty-eight hours. There are just too many shell businesses involved."

Devon was impressed, but before he could say anything a woman walked forward and whispered into Ramsden's ear. After a few minutes she walked away and Ramsden turned to Devon. "It seems like someone is looking in at what we're doing here. Our tech people say the CCTV camera system is being monitored remotely, although there is no way of tracing it back to the source. I've ordered the system to be shut down."

"Wait!" Devon put his hand on Ramsden's shoulder. "I have an idea"

Stratton recognised the tall man who was standing with Ramsden in the centre of the basement. The photos he had of Mike Devon didn't do him justice. Here was someone who radiated an air of menace, the sort of steely eyes and calm assurance that he himself used to show in his career days. When this was all over he would make a point of paying Devon a visit.

He watched the two men in animated conversation, not quite understanding why the chief operative of the clandestine *LonWash* agency was overtly snuggling up to MI6. Surely the whole existence of Devon's operation depended on keeping under the radar of the other spy agencies? Of course! It was a needs-must courtship, brought on by the realisation of all parties that they were powerless to stop him.

As he stared at the laptop screen, he cursed inwardly for not adding audio to the video stream. He would have liked to hear what they were saying. He noticed a young woman approach Ramsden and soon afterwards Devon left the basement. Two minutes later Devon returned to the room, holding a large white board. The board was turned towards one of the basement cameras.

It had writing scrawled across the surface. Stratton fumed as he read the message:

Hi Carl, hope you're enjoying the show.
Don't stay in one place too long.
I'm coming to get you!

Chapter 33

THE FORD MONDEO police pursuit car rolled through the deserted entrance of the rundown industrial complex. Its tyres bumped on a recessed semi-circular track that once carried an electronic gate, part of which leant against what remained of a sorry-looking guard hut. The combination of smashed windows and the removal of its roof had caused the shed to collapse inwards, hiding the scorch marks of a failed juvenile arson attack a long time in its past.

A wide concrete roadway stretched from the gate area towards a row of dilapidated warehouses, each standing forlornly against the brightening dawn sky. Patches of brown rust stains and scores of missing corrugated panels provided clear evidence of the abandonment of structures that once covered all manner of industrial manufacturing activity. The combined effects of a global recession and cheap imported goods had wiped out the laid-back optimism of the eighties and nineties.

WPC Janice Barlow nursed a Starbucks plastic-topped cup as her partner, Tony Mountford, aimed the car up the centre of the weed-covered road. The needle on the speedometer vibrated on the ten MPH mark, a far cry from its usual position while patrolling the busy motorways into London.

Barlow and Mountford had been pulled from traffic duties to join in the hunt for a mail delivery truck. It seemed every available police vehicle had been similarly commandeered into the service of one security agency or another. As usual, the cops on the ground weren't told much, other than the normal jargon-busting directives. Suspect is considered armed and dangerous. Approach with caution. Call for back-up.

Janice absentmindedly caressed an e-Fit, wondering if her superiors meant she should call for back-up before approaching with caution, or should she simply walk up to the suspect and ask him to wait until she radioed in a report. She smiled at the procedural contradictions.

"What's so funny?" Mountford asked.

"Nothing. Let's get this over with. I'm due off shift in an hour."

The car passed the first four derelicts, all minus their doors, the gaps providing a look into empty shells. The doors of the fifth building were intact.

"Pull over. I'll check this out."

Barlow climbed out of the vehicle before it came to a rest. She walked to a small wicker gate and pushed down on a recessed handle. The door was locked. She stood back, eyed the frontage, and started to walk to the side of the structure.

Mountford leapt from the car. "Janice, wait. Get back in the car and we'll do a drive-round."

"Don't be such a wimp, Tony," she teased.

By the time Mountford reached into the car to switch off the engine, Barlow had already disappeared around the side of the building. There were no windows to look through so she fast-paced to the rear, her mind already conjuring up an image of slipping into a hot bath back at her two-room rental.

She turned the corner and walked straight into a large bald man. He seemed to reach out a hand towards her face, and she felt a small burning sensation on her neck. Instinctively, she lifted her palm to her uniform collar. It felt wet. She was aware she was going to faint but couldn't understand why. Her brain couldn't process information. It couldn't tell her that the bald man had drawn a sharp blade expertly from her left to right ears, severing the carotid arteries.

"No!" Stratton raced out the rear door in time to watch Stelling ease the policewoman's lifeless body onto the concrete. "What have you done?"

Stelling stared blankly at him. "There was no option. They have discovered our hideaway. We cannot let them report this."

The sound of footsteps drew Stratton's attention away from the corpse. He waited for the tall policeman to run into view, before lifting a silenced Beretta and firing a point-blank round into a startled face. Mountford collapsed in a heap on top of his colleague.

Stratton kicked out in frustration at the side of the building. "This is all we need. We have to get the fuck outta here. This place has been compromised. I don't mind admitting, Manfred, that things are not exactly going according to plan."

He knew it was an understatement. His two prime locations were now a wash out, the mail van was probably picked up by CCTV at Prince Albert Road and was no longer a safe means of transportation, and to top it off his photo was undoubtedly in mass circulation throughout London. Normally, these were setbacks he could handle, but he knew the main reason for his anger was the smirking face of Mike Devon as he'd held the placard up to the camera.

He had to pull himself together, get back on mission, and see this through to the final conclusion. After that, he would deal with Devon. It had become personal.

His first thought was to pile the two corpses into the boot of the police vehicle and drive it to a new location, but he dismissed the notion out of hand. These vehicles had sat-nav and GPS tracking, which would allow their colleagues to trace their movements over a long period. Even if he smashed the sat-nav box and relocated the car, the authorities would eventually end up back here. At best he would save an hour or so, which was hardly important when stacked against the risk of being discovered driving a police vehicle in broad daylight.

He ordered Stelling to drag the bodies into the warehouse and prepare the back-up car for immediate evacuation. He ran through the building, opened the front doors, and drove the police vehicle into the large interior. Next, he crossed to the mail van, recovered the two remaining packages, and stored them in the back seat of the Clio.

Ten minutes later, after working quickly on disguises, they exited the industrial estate and headed into central London.

Twenty-two mail vans bearing the livery of the suspect vehicle had been stopped in the course of a five-hour period throughout the night. All were cleared as bonafide, leaving irate drivers to bemoan the wasted time on their busy delivery schedules.

By dawn, the first results of the e-Fit circulation began to filter in. There were more than forty confirmed sightings, although the officers in charge knew that by the time they filtered out the usual time-wasters, and the honest, though mistaken, members of the general public, they would be lucky to be left with anything of note. However, all leads had to be followed up.

The desk sergeant at Shepherd's Road police station had something else on his mind. One of his units was not responding to repeated check-in requests. The vehicle, which was signed out to Constables Janice Barlow and Tony Mountford, was showing up as a stationery dot on the internal tracking screen in the communications centre. The sergeant waited nervously for ten minutes before he hit the panic button.

The duty Inspector authorised the mobilisation of a Firearms Unit and placed a call to the SO19 incident room at New Scotland Yard. Within eight minutes more than two dozen police vehicles descended on the industrial estate.

The discovery of the bodies inside one of the warehouses led to a spike in police radio transmissions on a level never previously experienced.

Chapter 34

LIGHTS WERE blazing from every window as Devon approached the ramp for the basement garage of the *LonWash* headquarters. He marvelled at the stamina and dedication of his team, knowing he would have to ask them to dig deeper into their reserves. He couldn't remember the last time any of them had a proper sleep, something he had to put right if they were to stay on top of their game.

He exited the lift with Doyle and Halloran and glanced at the empty pizza boxes, water bottles, and Styrofoam coffee cups that were crammed into wastebins or simply discarded on every available worktop surface. Everyone was doing their best to keep fuelled and keep going.

He knew Tim Halloran and his cyber team were taking the brunt of the non-stop merry-go-round. As he walked towards his office he stopped and turned to Doyle. "Alan, put everyone on six-hour shifts, starting now. I know things appear to be coming to a head, but we need to keep fresh. At this stage one mistake, or one little detail being overlooked, could be catastrophic."

"Yeah, well just see you practice what you preach."

"Don't worry," Devon shot back, "I'm heading for the couch now. Wake me in six hours." He looked at a wall clock. It was five o'clock in the morning.

Inside the office he kicked off his combat boots and collapsed onto a couch that was barely long enough to accommodate his six-foot-plus frame. He was asleep within two minutes.

"Mike, Mike. Wake up."

He came alert instantly and gazed up at Doyle. "Can't a guy get a rest around here?"

"Believe it or not, you've been out of it for five hours. Something big has come up. They've found the mail truck and two dead police officers."

Devon sprang to the floor. "When did this happen?"

"Not too long ago. Somehow two uniforms stumbled across Stratton's bolthole, but needless to say the bastard has taken off again."

Devon listened intently as Doyle provided a full report. There was no need to interrupt with questions. He knew Doyle's capacity for assembling all the salient facts in the right order. If there were questions, Doyle would have got the answers before disturbing him.

"Do you want to go to the scene?"

Devon considered the options. "No, I'm sick chasing Stratton's shadow. Let MI6 and the rest do the donkey work. It's time we came at this a different way."

"What are you thinking?"

"That's just it, Alan. I'm not sure. I need to think through a few things. I'm going to grab a shower and a coffee before a team briefing in twenty minutes." He lifted his boots, snatched a holdall from behind his desk, and headed outside to take a lift to the top floor.

He dialled the shower unit to the hottest setting he could bear and let the needles of water work their massaging magic. He clamped his eyes shut and forced his mind to assemble everything they had learned to date.

Unusually, at this stage in a major hunt, they knew exactly who they were after. He didn't doubt for a moment that Stratton was the top of the tree. There was no-one above him, but just why a former secret service agent should turn on his country was still anybody's guess. The answer would lie somewhere in Stratton's past, and it was up to Peter Ramsden to find it. Until then it didn't much matter. The truth would come out eventually, but right now it didn't seem important.

They also knew that whatever he was planning involved at least one bomb, or a series of bombs in London. That's why Stratton was here. He needed to see the results of his actions. Hell, he needed to be the one to press the switch. They still didn't know the potential lethal force at Stratton's disposal. Those laptop battery units could house all manner of scary bomb materials, although nuclear or chemical ingredients could be ruled out. The zero readings at the house in Prince Albert Road were conclusive in that respect. Again, it didn't seem matter how much damage could be caused. The problem was to stop it happening. Plan for the worst, hope for the best.

The method of delivering the lethal payloads was obviously the mail delivery van, which had been left discarded at the warehouse. Stratton was now minus his two primary vehicles, the van, and the Daimler, so what was he using now? That thought brought him to another conclusion. The size of the battery units suggested that the bomb or bombs could be assembled into one or more relatively small packages. From his discussions with Ramsden it was clear that only about twenty or thirty battery units could have been smuggled into the country, meaning that any commercial vehicle or small car or motorcycle could be used for transportation.

Whatever he now had at his disposal would have been already in place at the warehouse. He didn't just walk out of there carrying bombs under his arms. Again, he decided, he would leave that problem to the main agencies. They could trawl traffic cams and mount roadstop operations, without him to worry about wasting his own resources.

The involvement of Manfred Stelling intrigued Devon. According to Ramsden, Stratton had helped him flee from East Germany. God knows what the pair had gotten up to in the intervening years! It appeared obvious that Stelling had co-ordinated things in

London while Stratton was ensconced in New York, but what part would he play in the end game? Would they be together for the final act or acts? Or could it be each would have his own target? On the balance of probabilities, it would make sense for them to split up and maximise the chances of at least one of them achieving his objective.

That meant there were at least two bombs.

The shower room was filled with steam, not that Devon would have noticed. He continued to stand under the invigorating spray, his eyes closed, and his thoughts dancing from one step to the next.

He was heartened by the fact that so many things had gone wrong for Stratton. Had he himself not stumbled across the assassin list in Austria, his agency might not have been fully prepared to deal with the threat. The killers had been eliminated, with only one left standing, which meant they were able to turn their attention back to the real menace.

The General's unearthing of the traitor Melrose was the most telling blow. The e-Fit provided by Melrose led them directly to Stratton and from there to the house in Prince Albert Road. He smiled at the memory of holding up the message to the camera. It might have seemed a somewhat childish gesture, but it would have given Stratton something else to think about.

And what of the fire at the home of the man who had smuggled in at least part of the consignment of laptop batteries? Devon didn't doubt for a moment that it was an attempt to silence the courier, but how would Stratton have reacted to discovering that old Charlie Wilson had escaped his clutches?

Another thought struck him. If Stratton had gone after the courier, then he had also surely made a try for Melrose. Why deal with one loose end but leave another dangling in the wind? If he had gone after Melrose, then once again he had lucked out.

The mistakes were piling up.

Stratton and his sidekick now had to find a third location for their operational base. The longer they were out in the open, the better the chances of finding them. Was there one more crucial mistake to be made?

Despite the plus points, Devon was forced to admit to one massive downside. His target was still on the loose, and he was not the type to allow himself to be cornered. Stratton would be at his most dangerous if he believed the net was closing in too fast. He would have no hesitation in bringing his plans forward, and he would do so without fear for his own freedom or safety.

Devon stood a few minutes longer while planning his next moves. There was another Achilles heel to be found, another mistake to be uncovered.

And suddenly he knew where to start looking.

He stepped out of the shower, waved his arms in a vain attempt to disperse the steam, and dressed quickly in a clean t-shirt and a fresh pair of jeans.

Chapter 35

DEVON RAN PAST the briefing room, ignoring the glances of his assembled team, and shouldered open the nearest office door. He reached for the telephone console and asked the switchboard operator to patch him into Peter Ramsden's private number at Vauxhall Cross. His fingers beat an impatient rhythm on the desktop while he waited for the static to clear, hoping that Ramsden was available.

The silence stretched for more than a minute before a response came through. "I take it you heard about the death of the two police officers? I half-expected to see you turn up at the scene."

"No, it's not about that," Devon said. "Has there been any luck in tracing Stratton after he fled the scene?"

The disappointment was clear in Ramsden's response. "The Met have every available body scanning camera footage within five miles of the location, but I'm not holding out much hope. The industrial area is pretty isolated, and the nearest CCTV coverage doesn't kick in until a mile away. They could have gone in any direction, in any vehicle. Chances of getting a hit are virtually non-existent."

"Just what I figured. How are the police responding to the deaths of two of their own?"

"There are a lot of angry people demanding answers. The whole thing is getting very jurisdictional, with a number of top brass muscling in on the security side of things. The PM has called another COBRA meeting for tomorrow morning, and I'm just hoping we can sort out the mess before then."

Devon let the news sink in. "Have you given any thought about how to prevent a possible bomb detonation? Should we be looking at closing down cellphone towers and radio frequencies, or even introducing a no-fly zone for all private and non-commercial flights over the city?"

"It's on COBRA's agenda, but everyone recognises that you can't just choke the life out of one of the world's busiest financial markets. If we could narrow the threat down to a specific time-window then maybe there would be support for a blanket on communications. At the moment I just don't see it happening."

Devon changed tack. "How's the search going into possible property deals by the shell companies Stratton was involved with?"

"Nothing much to report there either, I'm afraid. It is being co-ordinated by the Metropolitan Police, but to tell you the truth I think it was stepped down after the discovery at the warehouse. The feeling is that since a back-up location was found, it's unlikely anything else will surface."

Devon paused to gather his thoughts. "We need to look at this again from a new angle. Stratton now obviously needs a third base. Maybe he had already procured one as part of his advance planning...."

"Doesn't make sense that he would lie low in an abandoned warehouse if he had another property at his disposal."

Devon ignored the interruption. "Maybe an additional property was never intended for a base of operations, but the site for the detonation of an explosion. It could be that he acquired some building or other which is close enough to his target to provide what he wants if he simply blows it to kingdom come."

Ramsden whistled down the line. "It's a bit of a stretch, but I've got to admit it's something we can't ignore. The problem remains that it is still going to take some time to strip away the layers involved in the operations of all the companies in which Stratton appears to have interests. However, I'll get them to put a full team back onto the search."

"There may be a shortcut," Devon told him. "What if we start with what we know? We know Stratton acquired the property at Prince Albert Road. It was not done in his name, but it was done on his behalf. Get them to trace that specific purchase. That should tie the financial side of things down to at least one company, but we can drill down still further by looking at other middlemen who would have been involved in such a transaction. What about an estate agency, or a purchasing brokerage, or a solicitor? Find one of those in the Prince Albert Road deal and we might learn if they were involved in other similar deals."

"I agree that could provide us with a bit of traction. Any other bright ideas?"

Devon had other avenues to explore, but he needed to flesh them out before sharing his thoughts with Ramsden. It was not that he didn't trust the MI6 man. He believed simply that each of the agencies needed to concentrate on individual tasks, rather than spread their resources too thinly. "No, nothing else comes to mind."

"Okay, Mike. I'm grateful for the heads up. Let me know if you come across anything else."

"Just so you remember. That's a two-way street. Keep in touch."

It took little more than five minutes for Devon to run through his conversation with Ramsden. He looked at the faces around the room, stopping to wink at Alfie Cheadle who had just returned from his trip to Austria, and looked like the cat that got the cream. The rest of the team seemed a lot less vibrant, judging by the dark shadows under unslept eyes, and the crumpled state of shirts and sweaters. Some of these people had been on the go for thirty-six hours, but there was still determination on their faces and fire in their bellies.

"We could have backtracked the property deal a lot faster than those two-fingered keyboard operators they have over at New Scotland Yard." Tim Halloran's face was a mixture of annoyance and devilment.

"I don't doubt it for a moment, Tim, but I needed to throw them some crumbs. Besides, I have something a lot more difficult for your team to tackle."

"Fire away, boss."

Devon smiled at the man's capacity for work. "Once again I'm going to ask you guys to change direction. Up to now we've been listening into cyber chatter, or dismantling firewalls, or cracking codes, or doing whatever it is you guys do to make sure we know everything that's going on out there. It's time to step back and let the other agencies earn their corn. We're going to have to trust that they will."

He waited for questions, but none came. "The way I see it is that if the property angle turns up a lead, then well and good. But what if it doesn't? How about we look at searching for the unusual? What about ignoring Stratton and his companies and looking at *all* property deals, say over the past year? Is there any way we can insert filters to help us narrow down transactions that were completed in circumstances that merit a closer look? Something that was rushed through? Something that attracted an over-the-odds price? Something that, I don't know, just got done in a way that ought to raise an eyebrow?"

Halloran slumped back in his seat. "Boy, you really don't believe in doing things the easy way. Have you any idea how many property deals are done in London every year? You are looking at trawling through countless thousands of transactions, and that's gonna need more than just two or three primary filters."

Devon responded. "How about if we ignore the house market? I think we're looking strictly for commercial property, and more likely it will be property that is inner-city based. I think we can concentrate on storage space, lock-up garages, and small wholesale and retail units."

He looked at Halloran for a reaction. "Tim?"

"It's beginning to sound more doable. I guess there's no point asking what kind of timescale we're under?"

Devon frowned. "Yesterday is probably too late."

Halloran pushed back his chair and stood up. "Yesterday it is then."

"Before you go, there's just one more thing." Devon regretted having to add to the workload, but he didn't have a choice. "Can you get one of your team to work separately on tracking down all the London retail outlets for a specific range of red laptops?"

"And the hits keep coming," Halloran muttered as he left the room.

Devin turned his attention to Cheadle. "Great job in Austria, Alfie. It was a nice touch to get Hoffmeier to transfer ten million into our operating account. I'll see to it that Clare Carpenter gets a sizeable share to help her get on with her life, not that it will go any way close to compensating for her loss."

Cheadle beamed. "There's something else I learned from Herr Hoffmeier before he departed for his wings. He gave up the names of two accomplices, Jurgen Kappel and Dieter Neumann. What do you want to do about them?"

"Nothing for now," Devon told him. "Don't worry, we'll get around to dealing with them when the time is right."

Chapter 36

AN ELECTRONIC door beep signalled the arrival of a new customer and drew Melissa Foster's attention away from a fashion catalogue that was spread on the counter below her. It was the first interruption of a boring morning.

She watched as a man closed the door behind him, noting the navy blue business suit, white shirt, and Paisley tie. Thick, black-rimmed glasses sat on a bulbous nose, and his beard stubble looked as if it had been groomed to match the length of the black and white buzz-cut surrounding his head. Melissa noticed details such as these, particularly when it came to sizing up men.

She smiled as her visitor approached the counter and hoisted a leather briefcase onto the surface. "Good morning. I take it you are Miss Foster?"

"Yes, yes, I am," Melissa stuttered, not quite understanding how this stranger knew her name.

Carl Stratton returned the smile, buoyed by the realisation that this woman couldn't see through his disguise. It was less than twenty-four hours since he had last spoken to her, and had watched from the mail van as she stored away the parcel intended to end her life and those of dozens of other people unfortunate to be in the vicinity of Woodburn Road when he triggered the explosion.

Now things had changed. He needed somewhere to lie low. The electronics shop, with its unused first-floor storage rooms, was as good as place as any. His first thought had been to kill the woman and stow her body, to be found among the carnage sometime after noon on Friday. However, there was bound to be a husband, or boyfriend, or sister, or mother out there somewhere. If a missing person's alert were raised when she failed to come home from work, this was the first place the police would come looking.

A more subtle approach was required.

"Miss Foster, I represent the owners of this business. I'm sorry to tell you that we are selling up and that your services will no longer be needed."

She gasped. "Oh my God, what will I do?"

Stratton smiled benignly. "Please don't fret. We have made arrangements for a very handsome severance packet. You will receive two hundred thousand pounds in lieu of your outstanding service. The paperwork will be completed within the next week, but for now I am authorised to make you an interim cash payment of ten thousand pounds."

He opened the suitcase and withdrew a brown envelope which he pushed across the counter. "I can tell you confidentially that we received an offer to sell the premises as part of a major redevelopment of this area. It was an offer we could not refuse, but I must warn you that you are to say nothing about this."

"I don't understand."

"It's really rather simple. Negotiations are at a delicate stage and we don't want to start rumours until everything has been settled. Tell your friends that you are on holiday, but do not mention this sale to anyone. This is extremely important. Remember, your final settlement depends on your discretion."

Stratton wanted to be sure the woman would not draw undue attention to the property. One look at her demeanour told him that she would do just about anything to protect the pay-off that had been dangled in front of her. He asked her for her keys, watched as she gathered her personal belongings, and then escorted her to the door.

She stepped outside the shop and looked around. "You know, this place could really do with being redeveloped."

Stratton smiled. "Trust me, it will be barely

recognisable."

Devon looked through the fifty magnification binoculars from his front-seat vantage point less than a hundred yards to the east of the building. The downstairs retail unit was in darkness, hardly surprising at six-thirty on a winter's evening. All shops in this particular area had closed for the day.

However, the target building differed in one respect from the others around it. It was the only one showing an upper floor awash with lights, and the shadows of people walking around the interior could be clearly seen from the outside, despite the severe opaque glazing designed to ensure privacy for whatever activity was taking place. Devon was pretty sure it was not something as innocent as a pre-Christmas stock-take.

He had picked out the address from a list of twenty-eight property transactions supplied by Halloran's analysts who had raised a flag against each of them, for one reason or another. Devon's initial scan took him barely halfway down the list before he stopped to read the short note against one entry. According to what the analysts could find, this terraced retail and office block had gone on the market for offers in the region of four hundred thousand pounds. The deal was closed within a week for a final selling price of just over one million. The unusual speed of the sale, combined with the inflated price, could be explained away by any number of reasons, including something as simple as long-term speculation on the part of the buyer.

What stood out, however, was that the deal seemed to have gone through various companies, including one based in New York, in what looked an obvious attempt to mask the identity of the purchaser.

Devon reckoned it was as good a starting point as any.

Doyle, Cheadle, and Horgan sat with him in the car. Before leaving the office, they had pulled down Google Earth pictures of the area and agreed on a two-point entry. The on-site inspection confirmed that a solid brown door beside the shop was a separate entrance to the upstairs part of the building.

Doyle and Horgan exited the vehicle and made their way to the rear of the building. It was thought probable that there was a separate fire escape for the upper part of the property, but this needed to be confirmed.

Two minutes later Doyle's voice cut through Devon's earpiece. "There's a set of aluminium steps leading to a first floor exit door. We're good to go."

"Copy. On my mark, a go is confirmed three minutes from .....now." Devon pressed the timer on his wristwatch.

A second car rolled quietly into a parking spot directly behind Devon's Range Rover. He glanced over his shoulder and spoke into his throat mic. "We move now. Take your positions."

The agency's two new boys, Terry Hunt and Jim Cross, were tasked with keeping watch on the rear of the building on the off-chance anyone attempted to escape through the shop, after Doyle and Horgan affected an upper floor entry. The other two occupants of the second car, Bob Mortimer and Bill Carlisle, would stand station at the shop front.

Devon and Cheadle climbed out of the car, crossed the street, and walked quickly to the brown door. There were no exterior cameras covering the property, probably because it didn't pay to advertise the need for in-your-face security precautions. However, this subtlety didn't extend to the door, which looked to be a solid chunk of mahogany reinforced by a steel plate and fastened by three mortice locks, evenly spaced from top to bottom.

Devon dipped into his tool belt, extracted a packet

of C4 explosive, and shaped a charge around each of the three locks. He inserted a one-inch aluminium rod into the moulds, brought together the trailing wires, and looped them into a single strand, which was inserted in a square timer. He checked his watch, set the dial for ten seconds, and stepped twenty yards to the side of the building.

The explosion was little more than three simultaneous pops, resembling the sound of champagne bottles losing their corks. The loudest noise was the door shearing off its hinges and cracking against the inner wall.

Devon jumped through the opening closely followed by Cheadle. He removed a stun grenade canister from his belt, tossed it up to the top landing, and dropped to his belly on the stairwell. The charge detonated after five seconds, sending a shockwave bouncing off every available surface.

Three seconds after the explosion Devon and Cheadle were on their feet and bounding up the stairs. They reached the landing in time to hear two flash-bangs from the rear of the building.

Doyle and Horgan had dispensed with the rear exit door in the same fashion. As soon as it collapsed, Doyle threw two stun grenades into a hallway, and turned away from the blinding light and thunderous roar. He waited five seconds before clambering over the busted door and peering into a room clouded in white dust.

A figure stumbled into the hallway ten yards to his left. He was a large man, stripped to the waist and wearing a nose-and-mouth mask, which had provided no protection for his eyes. He was using the backs of his hands to knead his sockets and was oblivious to Doyle's presence. He continued to stay oblivious, thanks to a wicked karate chop to the back of his neck. He collapsed unconscious to the floor.

Farther up the hall Doyle saw a second man bolt in the opposite direction. He stopped abruptly, flung his hands in the air, and back-pedalled down the corridor.

Devon appeared through the white gloom.

Five minutes later the *LonWash* foursome completed a full sweep of the property and declared it safe. Devon checked their two zip-tied captives, cursing at the discovery that neither was Stratton or his sidekick Stelling.

They had got the wrong building!

The search of the upper floor had uncovered a major drug-assembly operation. Bricks of heroin were stacked high on makeshift shelving and two rooms contained benches that were used for breaking down the product, mixing it with baking powder, and reconstituting it into small two-inch plastic packets ready for selling on the streets. Devon conservatively estimated the worth of the haul at over twenty million.

He looked glumly at Doyle. "Looks like we've been left with egg on our face. And before you give me that *No-Shit-Sherlock* look we can at least take some comfort from the fact that we are on the right track with our list of shady property deals."

"Yeah," Doyle agreed, "but we still have another twenty-seven to run down. We're going to have to share this out among some of the other agencies. There's no way we're going to be able to get through this."

Devon thought for a moment. "First things first. Contact the office and get this called in as an anonymous tip about a drugs war. At least we'll brighten up the day for the Met's Drug Squad. Before we head back, let's break into four pairs and each check another two properties while we still have the night as our friend. If we come up empty, then we'll have to pass the list to Counter Terrorist Unit."

Chapter 37

IT WAS SIX-THIRTY on Friday morning by the time the full team reassembled in the *LonWash* boardroom. One look at weary faces told the story of a wasted night. Five of the searched properties were vacant, two appeared little more than storage areas for used furniture, and the one remaining building was a bedsit where four teenage occupants were trying unsuccessfully to recover from a riotous party. They scarcely appeared to even notice their unwelcome intruders.

"We're banging our heads against a brick wall." Doyle looked at Devon for confirmation.

"No argument here, Alan. Part of me is saying we should keep going, that there's something here. Maybe we just got unlucky and we'll find what we're looking for if we keep plugging away, but the other part of me is shouting out to quit while we're ahead. If we do keep on this track it will take us days to run down the other addresses. And that's time we just don't have."

"So, what's the alternative?" Doyle asked. "Do we hand over the list and look at things from another angle?"

Devon couldn't hide his frustration. "That's just it. I'm fresh out of ideas. I really thought this property search would take us to Stratton's door. The sonofabitch could be hiding anywhere. I'm open to any and all suggestions."

Silence descended on the room. Everyone looked at each other, but nobody spoke. The mood was broken by the noise of the door opening, or more precisely, the noise of the door being almost flung off its hinges. Tim Halloran stepped into the room wearing a grin that ran counter to the sombre stares of his colleagues.

"Wait one!" he shouted with typical exuberance.

"You're gonna want to see this."

Devon's eyes flared into life. "Tell me you've found where Stratton is holing up."

Halloran was momentarily thrown by the comment. "Sorry, not my department. I've just run through the check on establishments selling the red laptops. Turns out there are only five outlets in London."

"Oh Christ," Doyle moaned. "Not more doors to bang on."

"I don't think you understand. I happened to be mulling over the list when it dawned on me that I should cross-reference it against our other list...."

"And?"

"And, bingo!" One of the outlets is also one of the properties that we flagged up as a dubious transaction. It's an electronics shop on the Woodburn Road."

It was rare for Stratton to feel so agitated before a mission. Usually a cool-headed operator, he found himself unable to quieten down the growing list of doubts that had racked his thoughts for the past twelve hours. He had never known so many things to go pear-shaped in such a short space of time, and the realisation had left him wondering what was around the corner.

His normal routine of grabbing a few hours' sleep before the start of an action phase had given way to a night spent pacing the small upstairs storage room whilst glancing continuously at his watch and willing the hour hand to move faster.

Finally, he was ready. He lifted a large shoulder-strapped backpack and began carefully to fill it with an array of items sitting on a rickety table. First into the bag was a tablet computer, which was wired to a joystick console that resembled an Xbox component, and looked for all the world like a child's play toy. It was anything but.

Next, he caressed the battery-bomb package into position, ensuring it was held rigid by wadding in a number of spare t-shirts. The package was wrapped in Christmas paper and would hardly rate a second glance at this time of the year. Heightened security measures in place around the city meant he couldn't discount the possibility of a random stop-and-search by fidgety police patrols.

The last item to be inserted was a workman's high-visibility jacket bearing two parallel strips of yellow fluorescent piping, the kind of change of clothing that would dramatically alter his appearance in the event of a pursuit.

He zipped up the bag and turned to the other items on the table. A fifteen-round Beretta, already threaded with a silencer, was pushed into the waistband of his trousers at the bottom of his back, and two spare magazines were stuffed into the pockets of a dark blue anorak. He then lifted a Tonto combat knife, sporting a nine-inch blade, and strapped to the inside of his left leg.

Only three items remained on the table. He checked the printed numbers attached to the mobile phones and grabbed two of the sets, which disappeared into the pockets of his trousers. The third phone was left sitting where it was.

He stood back from the table and glanced at Stelling. "This is it, my friend. You know what to do?"

"Please no speeches, Carl. We've had a good run, and it is fitting it should end this way. It has been a pleasure. I'll see you on the other side."

Stratton looked like he was about to embrace his long-term friend but seemed to think better of it. He simply nodded, hoisted the backpack on his shoulder, and walked down the stairwell to the front door.

Outside, he looked at his watch. It was exactly six forty-five. He pulled on a black beanie hat and walked purposefully up the Woodburn Road. Just another workman ready for an early shift in a city that was already coming alive.

Manfred Stelling peered through a pulled-back corner of the lace curtain and watched his mentor disappear from sight at the end of the road. He fought back a tear at the realisation it would be the last time he would see him. He owed him much, and now it was time to repay the debt.

Stelling had often wondered what life would have served up to him if he had not crossed paths with Stratton. He was sure of one thing. It would not have been as full of the adventure, excitement, and riches that he had enjoyed since the day they made their escape over the Wall. He had relished every moment of the past thirty years, but now it was coming to an end. He could think of no better way of letting the final curtain fall.

He had stopped his invasive cancer treatment several months ago. According to the doctors he would have less than six months. It was then he had decided that his part in the bombing campaign would be his final act on this earth. He would simply drive the vehicle as close to his target as he could get before dialling in the preset mobile number.

He walked past the phone sitting on the table and crossed the room to lift his package from atop an old wooden crate propped up in the corner of the room. He cradled the parcel in both hands as he strode towards a set of stairs that led to the ground floor shop. There was just enough light from a row of outside street fluorescents to allow him to pick his way to the rear of the building where he deactivated an external roller shutter, opened the shop door, and stepped out onto a service road that fed the cluster of retail units.

Directly opposite was a block of lock-up garages.

He headed to one that had the number seventeen painted in white lettering across an up-and-over door. It was not aligned with the shop rear but stood about fifty yards to his right. He set the package on the ground, fumbled for a set of keys, and released the garage door mechanism to reveal the parked Clio. He unlatched the car boot, lifted the package, and slid it into the small compartment.

He was so engrossed in his task that he failed to hear the sound of a vehicle as it rolled into the northern entrance of the roadway.

Chapter 38

DEVON FACED A DILEMMA. He knew with certainty that the Woodburn Road property was where he would find Stratton. The appearance of the address on two separate lists could not add up to anything else. It was what it was – a major break that needed to be handled with the utmost caution because where Stratton was, so too were his bombs.

There was no question of blasting down doors to force an entry into the lair of a man who would not hesitate to throw a detonation switch at the first sign of danger. If he had learned one thing it was that Stratton would wipe out himself, Devon's team, and a fair chunk of this part of London before he would allow himself to be taken.

The area was surrounded by residential properties, many of which would be devastated by the power of the horrendous blast Stratton could unleash. Homes would have to be quietly evacuated and streets would have to be closed to traffic before any action could be contemplated. The only way an operation of that magnitude could be undertaken was by bringing in the combined weight of all the anti-terror agencies.

He also had to consider the spotlight that would fall on *LonWash* if they were to be caught in the middle of a botched operation. His team were supposed to operate in the shadows, not out in the open where they would be fair game for the sort of political backlash that would roll like a tsunami right up to the front door of Number 10 Downing Street. The PM would have no choice but to close down the entire *LonWash* operation. Hell, all of them, including the General, would be lucky to escape lengthy prison terms.

In the end, it was an easy decision to make. As his two-car convoy set off across the city, he hit the speed-dial on his sat phone. Although Peter Ramsden headed up MI6, an agency that was tasked with dealing only with security matters outside the UK, he was Devon's main point of contact and therefore the only available link to the other agencies. It would be easier for Ramsden to explain what was happening and to mobilise the appropriate security response.

The call went through in a matter of seconds.

Devon wasted no time with a preamble. "Peter, we've located Stratton. You're going to need a full red-alert status with a complete shutdown of the area, a bomb disposal team, the boys from SO19, the SAS, and anyone else you can think of. This could get real nasty."

"Wow! Tell me what you've got."

Devon gave the address and explained how they had tracked it down. "I know it's not a locked-on guarantee that Stratton is actually there, but it's too big a pointer for us to ignore. We're out of options here."

"I agree. Stay on the line while I make a few calls."

Five minutes later, Ramsden spoke again. "Things are on the move. Where are you now?"

"We're just arriving at the scene."

"Mike, you know you can't be part of this? You have to pull out and leave this to the official agencies."

"Don't worry, I figured as much. We're just going to keep a watching brief until the big boys arrive. That's going to take a while, and we can't risk Stratton deciding to leave. However, we don't want to be mistaken for the bad guys. Tell everyone we're part of your surveillance operation. We're in two G-registered black Range Rovers at either end of the road. We'll disappear as soon as help arrives."

"Make sure you do," Ramsden replied. "There's one more thing."

"What's that?"

There was unusual warmth to Ramsden's voice. "Just wanted to say great job. I'll owe you a drink when this is all over."

Devon thought about cautioning against celebrations but decided against it. Instead he ended the call and watched as his driver, Alfie Cheadle, switched off the Range Rover lights and freewheeled onto a service road at the rear of the row of shops.

He looked down what was little more than a one-vehicle laneway, its surface badly potholed and dimly-lit by a single lamppost bulb midway along its length. Litter was strewn everywhere, blown it seemed from the serried ranks of dented litter bins that stood sentry every twenty yards or so, their lids pointed up as though in mock salute.

Devon looked across at Cheadle. "I'm going to take a quick recce. Let me know when Doyle and his team are in position at the southern end of the road. I'll be back in less than five minutes."

He got out of the vehicle, taking care to squeeze the door noiselessly behind him. He walked slowly, keeping to the shadows as he counted off the shop units. When he arrived at number seventeen, he noticed the roller shut was curled up into its casing, the only one that was not secured. Even more curious was the fact that the inner door to the rear of the electronics shop was showing an opening of three or four inches. Either someone had got careless, or they had left in a hurry.

He cursed at the thought of missing Stratton. Without hesitation, he withdrew his Sig Sauer, toed open the bottom of the door, and stepped inside.

Manfred Stelling was about to exit the garage when he detected movement to his right. He looked up the road to watch a black-clad figure standing outside the shop and taking an unusual interest in the wedged-open door.

When Stelling saw the man withdrawing a weapon and walking into the shop he broke into a cold sweat.

His first thought was that somehow they had been rumbled, although he couldn't understand how that was possible. Maybe the bitch who had been paid off with a smile instead of a bullet had developed a loose tongue. No, he reasoned, she had looked too greedy to want to risk promised severance pay.

His next thought hit him like a punch to the solar plexus. "My God, the mobile phone!"

The realisation that he had left the detonation unit on top of the table galvanised Stelling into action. If this was a takedown by the security services, he would have to get to that phone. Nothing mattered more than triggering the bomb!

He reached back into the car boot, retrieved the package, and set off at a run towards the rear of the shop. When he detonated the device, he wanted it to be at the front of the building where it would do the most damage.

He stormed through the open entrance and set the package down on the nearest bench he could find. He would return for it later when he had dealt with the intruder. He dug into a coat pocket and withdrew a Beretta, before carefully picking his way through the ground floor storage area towards the internal stairway.

When he turned the corner to peer up the ten-step flight, he could see the man already near the top. He couldn't miss from here. He lined up a head shot and fired.

Devon had stopped on several occasions to get his bearings and listen for any sign of activity. The silence was unnerving. Somewhere in the distance he could hear the monotonous beat of a clock and occasionally the muted crack of a floorboard, not enough to signal a footstep, but that odd sort of settling sound that wood makes in in a deserted building.

He found the opening to a stairway and began a slow ascent, careful to place his feet on the outer edges where there would be less risk of disturbing loose floorboards. He had almost reached the top when his ear was assaulted by a loud burst of static.

"Mike, on your six, on your six!" Cheadle had watched from the car in amazement as a large man appeared out of nowhere and followed Devon into the building. He knew he had waited longer than he should to break radio silence but prayed his shouted warning into the throat mic would not be too late.

Devon instinctively rolled to his left and tried to bring his gun to bear on whatever threat was lurking behind. He had barely time to register a blur of movement before he experienced a sharp pain across the side of his head and things started to go black. Before he passed out, his finger contracted on the Sig's trigger.

Moments later the haze lifted. He could feel a burning sensation across the top of his ear and warm liquid was flowing down his cheek and neck. He tried to move his legs, but they refused to function.

He waited a few seconds before trying gingerly to lift the upper part of his body. Ignoring a wave of nausea, he looked down to see a bald man lying across his knees. At least he wasn't paralysed! He kicked out and watched the man flop over onto his back. It was Manfred Stelling.

Devon looked at three blood-filled holes in Stelling's chest. He could only wonder at how he had climbed the stairs after taking a devastating burst of nine-millimetre Parabellums.

He pushed the thought from his mind. One down, one to go. Where the fuck was Stratton?

He looked around for his Sig and found it on a lower step. It must have slipped from his grasp when he passed out. He wrapped his hand gratefully around the butt and began climbing, aware the lightheadedness he felt was restricting him from operating at not much better than fifty percent capacity. He would need a lot more than this if he ran into Stratton.

"Mike, Mike, you okay? I heard shots." It was Cheadle's voice.

"Yes, I'm good. Hold the outside perimeter. Stelling is down. I'm on the top floor, but so far no sign of Stratton."

Crouching on one knee Devon peered around the corner to look at a single large room. It was sparsely furnished, with no obvious place for a man to hide. He stood up and moved slowly across threadbare carpet, sweeping his gun in a two-fisted traverse of the entire area. There was no-one here. He moved to the window and looked across the lights of the London dawn. "Where are you Carl?" he murmured

A sudden noise drew his attention back to the room. He had to blink to make sure he was not imagining what he was seeing. The image was like something out of a zombie horror movie.

A blood-soaked Manfred Stelling shuffled into view. His right hand, still holding a Beretta, was flopped at his side, while his left arm wavered at shoulder height as if he were trying to swat a fly. He could barely put one foot in front of the other, and a low wailing sound caused a froth of bubbles to erupt at the corner of his mouth.

Devon watched bemused as Stelling continued his ponderous advance. This was a dead man walking, but the message somehow hadn't yet got through to his brain.

Then Devon noticed Stelling's fixated stare. The eyes were glued to the top of a table less than three feet away. There was nothing unusual about the table, except.... except that there was a mobile phone sitting on it!

Stelling made a lunge for the table, his hand reaching out to grasp the phone. In that instant Devon knew it had to be the detonator. Perhaps all it needed was the merest touch of any button.

It was all over in a blur. Devon raised the Sig and fired a double-tap through Stelling's forehead. The big man smashed lifelessly into the table, sending the phone spinning into the air.

Devon caught it one-handed, before sinking to the floor and falling into another bout of unconsciousness.

Chapter 39

THE SIXTY-SEATER river cruiser was not much to look at. Unlike many of her fibreglass contemporaries the *Maid of Inishfree* was fashioned out of good Somerset oak and was as hardy a seagoing vessel as anything around her in the berthing wharf close to Westminster Bridge. But as she bobbed sedately at her mooring, she showed clear signs of neglect in a garish yellow-and-black paint job, which had flaked badly on all sides and complemented a polka-dot pattern of the worst kind of dark-stained rust on her rivets.

The interior was no less appealing. Rows of bench seating were covered in patched-up brown leather, cracked and stained by countless passengers with no thought for her wellbeing. It had been a long time since anyone had applied sandpaper or varnish to the once ornate decking surrounds, never mind that any thought had ever been given to regular treatments of warm, soapy water.

Despite her shortcomings she was popular with tourists, her rigid canopy cover with open sides providing a perfect view of the many tourist attractions the Thames had to offer. In addition to her cruise schedule, the *Maid* also provided a river transfer shuttle for landmarks such as the Millennium Dome and the former Royal Naval College at Greenwich. She was an instantly recognisable part of daily river life.

What the old girl lacked in grace and charm above the waterline, she had her compensation below decks where two Volvo Penta D4 engines could propel her up to thirty knots, well in excess of the eight-knot limit imposed on most stretches of the main tidal waterway.

The engines were recent additions, having been fitted under the directions of Carl Stratton shortly after the boat was purchased. They were linked to a sophisticated computer-control panel, which provided real-time diagnostics capable of adjusting oil and diesel flows and ensuring the strict regulation of speed.

Unknown to the Captain, the computer could be accessed remotely. Once activated, the fully integrated wireless-controlled system would effectively become an auto pilot, at the whim of an operator who could dictate steerage, speed, and direction. The Captain would not even be able to turn the engine shutdown switch.

Shortly after seven-thirty Stratton stepped onto the deserted deck. A morning gloom hung over the misted waters as he easily bypassed the cabin lock and descended to the boat's lower viewing compartment. He moved forward to the bow, lifted a small square wooden grate, and carefully lowered his package into a rope-storage box.

Twenty minutes later he was sitting at a window table of a greasy-spoon cafeteria, tucking into a full English breakfast. He had another four hours to kill.

Devon awoke to a blinding light and a familiar voice.

The light was a pencil-torch shining directly into his left eye. It was held by a white-coated man who was using his thumb and forefinger to press back the eyelid.

The voice belonged to Alan Doyle. "Nice to have you back in the land of the living. You gave us quite a scare."

The haze slowly lifted to allow Devon to focus on the faces around him. His head throbbed and he reached up to feel a bandage pressing against his scalp.

The white-coated man spoke. "Take it easy, Mr Devon. You've suffered quite a bit of trauma and you need to lie still. We've given you a blood transfusion and you have six stitches inserted to close a two-inch wound that gouged a nasty rut along your left parietal ridge. There shouldn't be any lasting damage, but I would like to run a scan just to be sure."

"Where am I? What time is it? What's happening?"

Doyle eased the doctor out of the way and bent forward. "Relax, Mike. You're in the back of an ambulance. We've been moved outside the cordon, thanks to the good offices of Peter Ramsden. You've been unconscious for just over an hour and have missed all the fun. You're not going to believe this, but they found two bombs during an initial sweep of the electronics shop. You're a bloody hero mate."

"Have the bombs been defused?"

"Yes. First reports suggest that had they detonated we would have been kissing goodbye to about a half-mile radius of buildings. Pretty powerful stuff by all accounts."

Devon sat up and swung his legs off the ambulance gurney. "I need to speak to Ramsden. Something doesn't add up here."

As if on cue the back door of the ambulance opened and Ramsden stepped in. "How's the patient?"

Devon ignored the query. "Peter, I need you to tell me everything that's happening."

"The long and short of it is that thanks to you we now have two bombs that won't be causing death and mayhem. Your man Cheadle noticed Stelling carry a package into the rear of the shop and we found it in a store after the briefest of searches. We thought that was it until one of the bomb squad members found a second device wedged into a shelf at the front of the premises....."

Devon cut in. "You do realise there is at least one more bomb to be accounted for. Stratton didn't just walk out of there empty handed. He's already en route to his target. We have to find him."

Ramsden nodded agreement. "Here's what we have. A CCTV picked up a man matching Stratton's general build climbing into a taxi at the top of Woodburn Road. We're trying to trace the driver to get a drop-off location to help with a follow-up scan of all available traffic and buildings cameras. It will be like looking for a needle in a haystack but given time we might get lucky."

"We're running out of time!"

"Don't you think I know that? If Stratton gets wind that this place is a bust, he's likely to step up his timetable and detonate immediately. Christ, we could get news of an explosion any minute now."

Devon dropped his eyes to the floor and stared at a spot for more than a minute. "We have to buy time. There's no way Stratton can know what's happening here unless...."

"Unless what?" Ramsden snapped.

Devon smiled. "The way I figure it, the bomb at the front of the building was meant to be detonated here. The one that Stelling carried into the shop must have been intended for transit to another location. Nothing else makes any sense."

"I forgot to tell you," Ramsden said, "we found a crude diagram in the pocket of Stelling's trousers. It was a scribbled linear map of part of London, with an X placed in the middle of a car park at Saint Margaret's Church, close to the rear of the House of Commons. We think he was preparing to drive there when you showed up, although we're not sure why he carried the bomb back from the garage into the shop."

"That's easy," Devon beamed. "He was trying to reach the detonator phone and wanted to bring the whole place down with him."

Doyle stepped in between the two. "Guys, let's not get off track here. Didn't someone mention about buying us some time?"

"Yes," Devon responded. "The only way we can make Stratton believe things are still okay is that we provide him with an explosion. By now, he's across town somewhere and has a second mobile to trigger the device located at the front of the shop. We can't disappoint him."

"That's madness," Ramsden snorted. "We have no way of knowing when he will activate the timer."

"Of course we do," Devon beamed. "We have the receiver mobile phone. As soon as it's pinged, we can trigger a safe explosion of our own, something with enough noise and smoke to make Stratton believe the little shop has gone up. I'm guessing here, but there's no headline value in this location other than to create a diversion away from his primary targets. He'll have to allow a window to draw security resources to the Woodburn Road. There's your bought time."

"Brilliant!" Ramsden was already jumping from the ambulance as Devon turned to Doyle.

"Alan, help me outta here. We've got to get moving..."

"Whoa, Mike, you heard what the doc said. You need to take it easy. Let Ramsden and the Met run down Stratton. You've already done more than your fair share."

Devon ignored him and rose unsteadily to his feet. "There's no way we can rely on cameras picking out Stratton. We have to figure out where he's going, and we have to get there ahead of him. Tell our analysts to recheck the purchase of the Woodburn Road property. See if anything else pops up among deals done by the same company. There's got to be one more location for us to find."

Chapter 40

FOUR HOURS. Two hundred and forty minutes. Fourteen thousand and four hundred seconds. And Carl Stratton had to endure every one of them.

Move here, walk there. Try to look inconspicuous. Avoid security cameras, stay off the streets, browse through department stores, visit one restaurant after another. There's only so much coffee the body can take.

But the waiting was now over.

The Victoria Embankment was busy with the customary assortment of office workers, sightseers, and general commuter foot traffic shuffling backwards and forwards in the endless motion of city life.

No-one took any notice of Stratton as he reclined on a bench and stared at the mobile phone nestling in his left hand. According to the Nokia's backlit analogue clock, it was precisely eleven-forty-five. He double-checked with his wristwatch. Both timepieces were in agreement.

He tore off the piece of paper with the preset number. He wouldn't need it. The number was already encoded in a speed-dial sequence. Printing out the full ten digits was merely a precaution in the event of a device failure. He knew he could quickly get to a public phone inside one of the many hotels dotted around the area.

He took one last glance around, as if expecting someone to stop what he was about to do. The sea of apathetic faces told him there would be no heroic last-ditch cavalry charge riding in to save the day.

His right index finger moved over the keypad. He tapped the number two button twice and pressed enter.

There was no going back.

Three seconds elapsed.

Nothing.

Five seconds.

Nothing

Seven seconds.

Nothing.

Then he saw it. A large plume of dense black smoke, spiked by red and yellow flames, shot up over the north-western rooftops, five miles from where he was sitting. It took another second for the sound to reach him. It was an ear-splitting, thunderous roar that rolled across the landscape, blotting out the usual myriad of city noises, and turning countless thousands of heads in shock and bewilderment.

People seemed to freeze on the spot. Some held their hands to their mouths to cover their amazement. Others simply pointed. Strangers began to converse, seeking answers from each other about what they were witnessing.

Stratton rose from the bench and walked away in the opposite direction, ignoring attempts by frightened people to engage him in speculation.

No-one seemed to notice that he was the only person on the Embankment who wore a smile as wide as the fast-moving Thames running alongside the cluttered pathway.

Two bomb squad officers shared a rickety table in a deserted car park on the Woodburn Road. Sitting in front of one of them was a two-inch moulded plastic receiver wired to a portable electrical meter, its single arm resting on the twelve o'clock position. In front of the other officer was a black metal box with a button glowing red in the centre of the console.

Both men had spent the last hour staring at their respective units.

Directly in their line of sight, almost two hundred yards away, was a twenty-foot high chimney structure, made of large concrete rings commandeered from a roadworks site where they were waiting to be installed as sewerage tunnels. Instead of lying end-to-end, the rings were stacked on top of each other to create a funnel for the shaped charges that were crammed into the base unit.

The materials were a mix of explosive and pyrotechnic components. They had worked for most of the morning to get the right blend of propellants, adding layers of gunpowder, aluminium hydroxide, magnesium, and flash powder to create an exothermic chemical reaction that would emit smoke gas, flame and sound capable of mimicking a powerful conventional explosion. The base was packed with hard foam and steel plates to direct the blast upwards through the funnel and into the London sky.

The best judgement was that anyone hearing and seeing the result from more than a mile away should be fooled into believing they were witnessing a catastrophic event.

The theory was sound, but the hardened bomb squad officers knew the dangers too well. The hoped-for spectacle could prove nothing more than a damp squib. Then again, despite the precautions, the detonation could shatter the chimney, sending fragments of concrete hurtling over a large area. They had done the best they could. Now it was a matter of waiting and praying.

A sharp buzzing sound blared from the receiver unit and the needle jumped off its static position.

"We've got a signal!"

The second officer calmly reached across to the metal box and pressed the red button. An electrical impulse shot down the double-insulated line of wires and disappeared into a hole at the bottom of the chimney.

It took barely a second before a muted whoosh barrelled out from the top of the chimney, followed by a decibel-busting soundwave that shook the ground for hundreds of yards. Waves of flames and smoke shot high into the air, blotting out the faint morning sunlight and causing a thousand pairs of eyes to look heavenwards.

The officer tore his gaze away from the pall to examine the funnel structure. It was intact, save for thin wisps of smoke squeezing through the gaps where the concrete rings were stacked on top of each other.

The two men at the table looked at each other for a moment. Then they raised their hands to connect with a high-five slap that was as much a gesture of relief as it was a celebration.

Sirens screamed from more than twenty emergency vehicles attempting to manoeuvre through choked inner city streets on their way to the distant disturbance. Ambulances, fire and rescue tenders, police cars, and high-topped security trucks were forced to take to footpaths as they barged their way through the growing gridlock.

Stratton took in the sights and sounds as he walked towards the grounds of the St Thomas Hospital on the Westminster Bridge Road. It was a typical hospital site, crammed with a hotpotch of buildings accommodating various external specialist wards, an Accident and Emergency Department, office complexes, and an assortment of staff and public car parks. He walked past the main building entrance, crossed a small well-manicured lawn, and made his way to the rear of the site, following the outstretched arms of a dozen pointed signs.

A building on his left was announced in six-inch lettering as the central laundry facility, behind which he knew was a smaller building that served as the hospital morgue. A small pathway ran alongside the bleak, grey-stoned edifice and took him to a boundary fence fronted by a row of six-foot-high bushes.

He took a quick glance around to make sure there were no prying eyes before pushing his way through the thicket.

He smiled at the vista that opened in front of him. Manfred Stelling had done well when he selected this vantage point for him during a reconnaissance visit earlier in the year.

The Thames stretched before him, its waters speckled by the reflection of the tall Palace of Westminster building sitting serenely on the opposite bank. The river lapped against the outer wall of the iconic building, a curious mixture of Gothic architecture and modern add-on buildings that spanned over 300 yards and sat within an eight-acre site. He knew from his research that there were eleven-hundred rooms, three miles of passageways and one hundred staircases scattered around the interior, all looked down on by more than eight-thousand works of art, the oldest of which are thirteen statues of medieval kings. It was a site that contained the House of Commons and the House of Lords and attracted more than a million visitors every year.

Stratton was aware that regular sightseers are not allowed direct access to waterside views of the landmark. One of the many security measures in place around one of London's most heavily-protected areas was a river exclusion zone, in this case the Lambeth Reach Zone, which prohibited vessels entering within seventy metres of the northern bank between Westminster Bridge and Lambeth Bridge. The only craft to be seen in this area are patrol boats operated by the Port of London Authority and the Met's Marine Police Unit.

Stratton gazed across at four of these vessels as they weaved aimlessly up and down the precluded stretch of waterway. They would not pose a threat to his plan.

He looked to his right at the imposing façade of

Westminster Bridge, barely two hundred yards from where he now hunkered on a grass bank. There was a lot more activity on that stretch of waterway, and somewhere among the colourful assortment of river traffic was the *Maid of Inishfree*. It was time to bring her into play.

He removed the laptop from his briefcase, set it across his knees, and attached the joystick console.

He had less than fifteen minutes before initiating his final act.

Chapter 41

DEVON HAD TO ADMIT the frantic show of emergency response vehicles was pretty impressive. The outward and visible signs were there for all to see, except for those who might have been afforded a closer look. For the most part, the convoy that raced towards Woodburn Road were older, out-of-service vehicles with only a driver and passenger aboard, each under instruction to put on as big a display of attention-getting as they could muster.

All main frontline resources were held in reserve. Leave was cancelled, personnel were called back in from holidays, and in every borough men and women stood ready to respond to whatever the next few hours might throw at them.

More than three-thousand uniformed and plainclothed police officers mingled in tube stations and bus depots, or simply walked a forlorn beat in hope of snatching a glimpse of their quarry. The centre of London was being blanketed, if only because there was nothing much else that could be done.

Devon's head throbbed despite a heavy dosage of Paracetamol tablets. He grabbed a black woollen sports hat to hide his bandaged scalp as he sat in the Range Rover passenger seat looking glumly over the crowds milling around Trafalgar Square. It was as good a place to be as any. At least it was central, and Devon was convinced the last throw of Stratton's dice would be somewhere in this two-mile radius that housed the city's best-known landmarks.

"Anything yet?"

Alan Doyle shared the rear seat with Chelsea Horgan. He looked up to catch a glimpse of Alfie Cheadle staring at him from the driver's overhanging mirror. "Not since the last time you asked me twenty seconds ago."

Devon pivoted in his seat. "If we don't catch a break soon, we'll end up sitting here like a bunch of idiots while that fucker blows half of our capital to kingdom come. Somebody must have noticed something by now."

"Mike, everyone's busting their balls, but we're dealing with one clever bastard who's not simply going to amble up to a security checkpoint and announce his intentions. There's nothing much we can do until we get some decent information from somewhere out there. We've got to trust the Met boys to do their job."

Devon sank back into the seat. "Is there any significance in the location we got for Stelling's target? If he intended to be in the vicinity of St Margaret's Church, then it's obvious he was going for a detonation as close as possible to the Palace of Westminster. Does that tell us Stratton will go for a location at the other end of the city, something that would produce a widespread destructive area?"

"Hard to tell," Doyle responded. "We could second-guess ourselves all day and still not come close to knowing. The only thing we can be sure of is that the Woodburn Road attack was meant to be a diversion to pull us away from the rest of the city. Unfortunately, that leaves a lot of areas he could choose for a supplementary blast."

"No." Devon said emphatically. "Stratton will be in charge of the main event. This is his baby, and there's no way he'll play a secondary role. Whatever he's going after will be a far more significant target than Westminster."

Doyle threw his hands up in despair. "Take your pick. Buckingham Palace, the Tower of London, Oxford Street during Christmas shopping. The list is endless."

"What if we're looking at this the wrong way?" All eyes turned to Horgan. She paused before continuing. "What if the Palace of Westminster is the only target?

What if it's a two-pronged attack? Seems to me that if you put two bombs within the same location you will be minus one big palace at the end of the day."

"I'm not convinced about the logic," Devon told her. "People like Stratton go in for divide-and-conquer strategies that dictate not putting all your eggs in one basket. If a target is compromised there should always be a fallback location, somewhere far enough away to allow for a follow-up action."

"Yeah, but......"

Horgan's response was cut short by the sharp buzz of Devon's sat phone. He looked at Tim Halloran's name on the screen and hit the speaker button.

"What is it, Tim?"

"We might have something on that property search. We haven't come up with any new buildings, but there's an item here that might interest you."

"Shoot."

"Well, it turns out the same company that bought the Woodburn Road premises was also involved in the purchase of a river cruiser in the same month. The money was funnelled through the same bank in the Caymans, and the same brokerage firm was used to tie up the deal within a matter of days."

Devon bolted upright. "Where is this cruiser operating from?"

"She has a long-standing berth at the Dinsdale Wharf on the Thames. Not much to look at by all accounts, but somebody paid a lot of money for her."

"What's her name and where is she now?"

"Goes under the title of *Maid of Inishfree*. I'll contact the Port of London Authority to bring her up on their satellite-location screens."

Devon ordered Halloran to give top priority to finding the vessel and was about to end the call when he thought of something else. ""Tim, do we know if this cruiser has river access close to the Palace of Westminster?"

"Well, there are restrictions about getting too near to the Palace, but yeah, that's the general area where she plies her trade."

Three sets of eyes turned to stare incredulously at Horgan.

Peter Ramsden was not having a good day. Despite acting as a conduit for the information flow from *LonWash* to the other agencies he had found himself frozen out by the hierarchal system of responsibilities that had seen a lot of territorial infighting over the past few hours. The Metropolitan Police had made it perfectly clear who was in charge. Everyone else, including Ramsden, was told to butt out.

He could see their point, but it rankled, nonetheless. The dangers of too many cooks in the kitchen were all too obvious, although he had hoped at the very least to be kept informed. For the past hour there was nothing, just a helpless phase of staring out through the fourth-floor window of the MI6 headquarters at Vauxhall Cross on the Albert Embankment.

Sure, he got a lot of kudos for relaying valuable intelligence, thanks to Devon, but he wanted more than a spectator view. He had managed to keep the *LonWash* involvement under the radar, but he wondered how long that would last, particularly given Devon's habit of continually popping up when least expected. How had the service ever let someone of Mike Devon's calibre slip through the net?

The thought was still in his mind when the desk telephone buzzed. "Mike, don't tell me you're still running around chasing ghosts?"

"I think we've found him."

"What!"

Devon detailed the discovery of the river cruiser purchase and urged Ramsden to set every available vessel on an interception course for the *Maid of Inishfree*. "It looks like he's going for a water assault on the frontage of the Palace of Westminster."

"But there's an exclusion zone in place. He'll not get within a half-mile of the area."

"Do you not think he's thought about that? He'll have something up his sleeve, although for the life of me I can't yet work out what he intends to do."

"Tell me," Ramsden said, "do you believe he's operating from on board the cruiser?"

"No way of knowing, but my gut tells me it will be a remote detonation like the other two bombs we found this morning....."

Ramsden interrupted. "That means he has to have an accomplice steering the cruiser into position. Who do you get these days for a suicide mission?"

"My thoughts exactly," Devon told him. "Take your pick from any one of a number of jihadist warriors. We can't worry about that now. How are we with the cellphone blockage of the area?"

Ramsden cleared his throat. "I'm going to give you this the way it was told to me. All cellphones masts in the greater London area were shut down as of five minutes ago. On top of this all radio signals operating on the standard three kilohertz to three-hundred gigahertz wavelengths have been taken off the grid, along with as many computer wireless transmitters as can be accessed."

"That ought to do it."

"No," Ramsden told him forcibly. "We still have satellite communications to worry about. The GCHQ boys are up to their necks in retasking or bombarding dishes with as much junk as they can find to overload the systems, but nothing is guaranteed. Even with all these measures we're still left with the possibility of something else being used. Basically, all that's required is a transmitter and receiver, both of which can be made in your bedroom if you have enough savvy about how these things work. Hell, you don't even need a wavelength or a phone or a satellite to bounce a signal from one to the other. These days you can do it via computer to computer."

Devon's voice couldn't disguise his anger. "Are you saying we can't stop a signal getting through?"

"What I'm saying is that they've done the best they can do. The bottom line is that despite the blockages it takes very little for even a weak pulse to find its way from the transmitter to the receiver. Any sort of connection will complete the circuit and trigger the device."

Chapter 42

CAPTAIN STEVE MARTIN eased the *Maid of Inishfree* away from the South Bank and out into his allotted channel, mindful to keep his speed down to three knots on this, the busiest leisure stretch of the Thames. He was carrying a full complement of sixty tourists, eager to leave behind the London Eye and continue on the last leg of their cruise to the Southbank Centre under the Hungerford Bridge.

Martin frowned as the boat's bow began a slow turn to port, something that shouldn't be happening with his hands set firmly on the ship's wheel. He attempted to make an adjustment, but the wheel was locked solid. He pulled frantically on the mahogany frame, which refused to budge, and outside the window he could see his vessel continuing a sharp turn.

Horns blared around him as the *Maid* completed a one-eighty. He fought to wrestle back control, thinking that something must have jammed in the rudder's electro-hydraulic drive. He reached his right hand forward to the dashboard console and pushed a button to disengage the engines. Nothing happened.

The pitch of the engines began to rise, and with it the speedometer reading climbed. The needle moved to five knots, then seven, then ten. And it kept rising. The cruiser was now in mid-channel ploughing towards Westminster Bridge, with the London Aquarium building disappearing from his portside window.

His passengers must have sensed something was wrong. He could hear the babble of voices, and then a scream from a woman standing immediately outside his bridge compartment. He looked ahead and gaped in amazement as two Marine Police fastboats closed together to form a barricade directly under the bridge's central span. He was headed straight for them.

A man in uniform was standing on the prow of one of the boats, screaming into a megaphone and waving his left arm in a frantic stop motion. The noise of the *Maid's* engines prevented Martin from hearing what was being yelled. He glanced again at the speedometer. The needle was now almost touching the fifteen-knot notch.

The combination of speed and the sturdy wooden construction of the *Maid of Inishfree* meant there could be only one outcome. The sharp oak bow ploughed headlong into the police craft, sending them spinning away, their fibreglass hulls spider-cracked by the force of the collision. The *Maid* shuddered slightly before breaking free under the bridge and into the clear waters ahead.

Martin noticed two other boats racing towards him. He could make out the shape of a uniformed man leaning on the bridge of the first vessel. He was pointing something. Martin couldn't make it out, but it was clear it was not a megaphone this time. As it loomed closer, the old captain could see the distinctive shape of a rifle barrel.

There was still a gap of eighty yards when the Maid began to turn to starboard. Martin realised with horror that she was heading directly for the centre of the Palace of Westminster building.

The reading now showed twenty knots!

Stratton had a grandstand view as he toggled the arm of the steering console with his right hand. At the same time his left index finger moved a dial on the laptop's touchscreen, increasing the speed of the hapless cruiser, which was now under his absolute control. Within a matter of minutes he would crash the boat against the building.

His timing was almost impeccable.

A glance at his watch told him it was two minutes

before noon. He pictured Manfred Stelling walking from the car park at St Margaret's Church behind the Palace of Westminster. He knew Stelling would attempt to get as close to the rear of the buildings as possible before detonating his bomb. As agreed, they would both enter the cellphone signal at precisely twelve o'clock.

Even from this range, Stratton knew he couldn't take his chances of survival for granted. The concussive wave from across the river would tear into the hospital buildings, sending glass and brickwork hurtling in all directions.

As soon as he initiated the firing sequence, he would rush behind the sturdy morgue building, lie flat against its base, and hope for the best.

What will be, will be. His fate rested with Allah.

The *Maid of Inishfree* was now less than fifty yards from the Palace buildings. Suddenly she came to a shuddering halt, her stern lifting in a froth of water. He could see people being thrown into the water from her decks, the noise of their screams mingling with the piercing screech of dying engines and the crack of timbers. The water continued to churn into a muddy whirlpool before the engines finally died and the boat bobbled helplessly in the maelstrom.

All sorts of thoughts raced through Stratton's mind. Had the boat hit an underwater mine? Nonsense! Had someone fired an RPG into her? No, he would have seen the flash. What then?

The realisation of what must have happened made him smile. Obviously, the cruiser had run against some kind of below-water barrage or boom, intended for just this type of eventuality. It should have occurred to him that the buildings would have some sort of river protection in place, but in the end it didn't matter. The boat was close enough for his purpose.

He discarded the laptop and fished in his pocket for the mobile phone. He scrambled back through the bushes and made his way to the morgue while he tapped the buttons on the phone. As he rounded the corner of the building, he pressed number three twice and hit enter.

Five seconds later panic set in. Nothing had happened! He stared at the phone, noticing for the first time that the small icon for service availability was not blinking as it should be doing. There was no reception. He entered the speed-dial sequence again. Still nothing!

He needed to get to a landline. Maybe the receiver would accept an alternative-routed signal.

Chapter 43

THE TERRIFIED LOOK on the face that began to take shape in the lens of the Hensoldt binoculars told Devon everything he needed to know - the man behind the wheel of the *Maid of Inishfree* was most definitely not Carl Stratton. Even allowing for a make-up artist's skill and imagination, the base blueprint of this figure was all wrong. The head was about twice the size of Stratton's and disappeared into square shoulders, seemingly without the need of a neck to hold it in place. The shock of unkempt white hair, which covered the face and plunged headlong into a sharp point somewhere about the waistline, looked too outrageous to be anything other than natural.

Something else was also apparent. Judging by the pained facial contortions and the frantic arm-wrestling contest with the ship's wheel, the man in the small bridge compartment was not in control of his vessel!

It took Devon only a few seconds to process what he was seeing. Somehow Stratton was piloting the boat from a remote location. Not too remote, Devon reasoned. He had to be somewhere in close proximity, a vantage point from where he could directly affect what was happening out there on the Thames.

Five minutes earlier, Devon's Range Rover had roared onto Westminster Bridge in time to watch the cruiser start its sharp U-turn. He had grabbed the binoculars, leapt from the vehicle, and leaned against the stone parapet, frantically adjusting the telephoto lens to magnify the small window area sitting amidships on a two-meter platform above the deck.

He was about to start a sweep of the shore in search of Stratton when he saw the two marine boats take up a blockade position directly below where he was standing. The river cruiser nonchalantly elbowed them aside and tore under the bridge. Devon raced to the other side to watch it reappear in clear water.

When the boat made a sharp turn to starboard Devon gasped in horror at what was now in front of it. Jesus, he's attacking the Palace of Westminster!

He tore his eyes away from the *Maid* to scrutinise the opposite bank. The only building of note was the St Thomas Hospital, a six-storey glass and brick edifice that hugged the river's perimeter and provided an ideal vantage point for anyone wanting to monitor what was happening.

Devon hoisted the binoculars and began a slow sweep of the building, starting at a rooftop veranda and traversing the full extent of the frontage.

Left to right.

Right to left.

Down a level.

Left to right again.

Sunlight glinting off the glass made it impossible to distinguish shapes. In frustration, he lowered the glasses to ground level and began a perimeter sweep along the tree-lined fence. Nothing was out of place.

He was halfway through a second sweep of the fence when he spotted movement. He trained the binoculars at a shadowy spot between two thorn bushes. Yes, there was someone there!

A crashing noise on the river made Devon turn away from the shoreline. He saw the *Maid* thrashing and disgorging passengers and knew she had hit some kind of barricade. He forced himself to ignore her plight and focussed again on the disturbance within the treeline.

He was just in time to see a man emerge from the thicket and run towards the maze of buildings dotted around the interior of the site. There was only a fleeting sidefaced glimpse of the fugitive, but it was all Devon needed.

The black beanie and the addition of thick-rimmed

glasses couldn't disguise the way the man carried himself, moving in long easy strides with a singularity of purpose.

The running man was Carl Stratton!

Stratton retraced his path back through the outside buildings and headed straight for the main hospital entrance. He dashed into the foyer and strode up to a long receptionist counter where more than a dozen people manned telephones or were engrossed in images from computer screens. To his left was a busy waiting area for patients, many of whom were straddling chairs and holding on to crutches, no doubt awaiting their turn for a visit to the fracture clinic.

A young woman in her early twenties glanced up as Stratton banged his fist on the countertop. "Can I help you, sir?"

"I need an outside line and I need it now!" he yelled.

"I'm sorry, sir, you can't just barge in here and......."

Stratton's hand disappeared into his jacket. The woman blanched when she saw the snub-nosed Beretta pointing directly at her forehead. Stratton snarled at her. "Give me the fucking phone."

The general buzz around the room fell silent as heads turned to watch the commotion. The woman began sobbing as she pushed a handset onto the counter, the plastic base beating a tattoo from her shaking hands.

A security guard approached and put his hand on Stratton's shoulder. The man didn't have a chance to utter a challenge. Stratton swept the gun barrel mercilessly across the guard's cheek, the forward sight-ridge raking a trail of blood from his ear to the tip of his chin. The hapless victim staggered backwards and collapsed unconscious onto the tiled floor.

Screams punctuated the air and people began running for the exits. One man forgot about his crutches and hobbled painfully in a slow foot-encased drag away from the danger.

Stratton ignored the rumpus, pulled out the scribbled mobile-number note, and began attacking the desktop telephone buttons. He waited patiently for the system to accept the sequence and produce the familiar dialling tone bleeps, the final number announced by the sound of what appeared to be a connection.

His anticipation of a thunderous roar across the Thames was destroyed by a tinny voice: *"It has not been possible to connect your call. Please try again later."*

He hurled the telephone into a huddle of hospital workers cowering behind the counter and turned to gaze in fury through the main front window. People were running and limping up the four-hundred-yard stretch of road leading to a gated entrance where an ambulance had just swept into the driveway. Behind its flashing lights he could see two black Range Rovers roar to a sideways stop, providing an effective barricade to any other vehicles entering or leaving the site.

He knew exactly what was happening. As if to confirm his worst fears, eight people leapt from the vehicles and took up defensive positions behind parked cars. Two of the group stepped out and advanced down the driveway.

Stratton's eyes widened in shock. The tall figure at the front was Mike Devon!

There was no time to process the hows and whys. He could stand there for hours trying to figure out what had led them to him so quickly. In the end it didn't matter. What mattered was getting to hell out of here.

He lifted the Beretta, unscrewed the noise-suppressor, and fired three times into the ceiling. He wanted the shots to be heard, he needed to create pandemonium. He turned to the remaining staff members. "Everyone out!"

It started as a nervous trickle, but quickly developed into a full-blown stampede for the exit door. Some people slipped and fell, others banged into the glass frontage, sending shards of glass tumbling to the floor. It was mob rule, survival of the fittest.

Stratton tucked the pistol into his waistband and pulled his sweater over the butt. Then he removed his hat, coat, and spectacles, before crossing quickly to lift a pair of discarded crutches. He moved with such speed that he easily caught up with the mass of bodies still struggling through the exit.

Chapter 44

THE SOUND OF GUNFIRE flooded Devon with mixed emotions. While he was grateful for confirmation that Stratton was still in the vicinity, the risk he posed to the public was not something to be overlooked for a second. Maybe it would be best to simply bottle him up and let SO19 or the SAS take it from here.

The sight of people running from the building changed the dynamics. Devon recognised it for what it was – a diversionary tactic, the creation of pandemonium to mask an escape attempt. He knew Stratton had no intention of staying behind.

It had taken Devon less than four minutes to whistle up his second team and get both vehicles back across the bridge to the hospital entrance. He ordered Mortimer, Carlisle, Hunt and Cross to remain outside the gates while he joined Doyle, Horgan, and Cheadle inside the compound. He watched the first of the crowd emerge from the entrance and reached a decision. "I'm going down there. The rest of you, stay put."

He had just made a few strides before realising that Doyle was walking beside him. "Don't you ever take orders?"

"Why should you have all the fun?"

Devon's intended reply was cut short by a three-round burst from within the hospital building as another group of people burst out through the main doors. "He's making a run for it! He'll try to hide himself among the crowd."

Doyle turned back to his team at the entrance. "Check everyone going through your cordon. Nobody gets past without a full screening."

People flew past Devon in all directions. He swept his eyes frantically from face to face but was constantly bumped and barged by the onrush of terrified bodies.

He tried to look ahead, but his view was blocked.

The ambulance, which had earlier pulled up to the left of the entrance, was now moving off again, the driver no doubt sensing this was not a place to be setting down his patient. The back door swung open as it accelerated away from the chaos.

Something about the scene was not quite right!

Stratton did his best to hunker down on the crutches and look helpless as he squeezed through the doorway. He spotted the ambulance parked to his right at the kerbside, the driver already standing on the footpath wondering what the commotion was all about. He was about to find out.

"There's a madman in there with a gun. You'd better drive this ambulance away from here as fast as you can." Stratton tried to inject his voice with as much urgency and command as he could muster.

As soon as the man climbed back into the cab, Stratton pulled on the back door and waited for the swivel step to fold into place. Not daring to lift his head towards the driveway he threw himself into the interior, rising quickly to dash past a startled nurse and an elderly woman strapped to a gurney. He pulled back a small divider window and thrust the barrel of the Beretta through the gap and into the back of the driver's neck.

"Find me another exit road out of here."

"There....there isn't one," the man stammered.

Stratton pressed the gun deeper into the driver's flesh. "You'll have to do better than that if you want to live a bit longer."

"Wait! We could go through the staff car park on the east side, but we need a pass."

Stratton smiled. "You let me worry about the pass."

The blanket shutdown of communications had left everyone fumbling in the dark for information. Even the fully-integrated Metropolitan Police radio network, which operated off its own satellite-dish towers, had to be taken offline as a precaution against providing an unwitting platform for carrying a signal to the bomb. The blackout appeared to be working, but at what cost to managing the vast resources deployed in the hunt for the bomber?

Two armed SO19 officers en route to Westminster Bridge had no way of knowing what was happening when their armoured vehicle encountered a rush of bodies running away from the entrance to St Thomas Hospital. The policemen were sure of only one thing. They had stumbled into the path of their quarry - and they were not about to let him escape.

The driver stomped on the centre pedal and yanked the handbrake to slew the police car to a sideways stop across the road. His passenger leapt out, cradling an MP5, his thumb disengaging the safety switch as he ran against the tide of fleeing civilians.

One woman screamed at him. "There's someone back there shooting at us!"

Less than a hundred yards ahead he could see a black Range Rover parked across the hospital entrance. A man dressed in black was just rising from behind the cover of the vehicle, holding what appeared to be an automatic pistol in a two-handed grip. The man turned to look directly at the SO19 officer whose eyes were fixed firmly on watching the weapon sweep towards his position.

All the training and combat simulations in the world amount to little when someone is finally confronted with their first potentially-lethal situation. The policeman ignored the shake in his hands and tried to remember the proper procedure. Identify yourself before engaging. Be sure of a clear line of fire. Check for potential risks on the through-path of any rounds discharged towards a suspect. Engage only as a last resort.

It was all happening too fast. The gunman was beginning to walk forward, closing the distance between them while still holding his weapon. The SO19 man sighted along the barrel, moved his index finger into the trigger well, and began a final squeeze.

At the last moment he remembered to shout a warning. "Armed police! Stop or I will fire."

The last of his words were lost by the noise of a three-round burst he fired.

Bill Carlisle had watched the police vehicle screech to a halt, grateful for much-needed back-up to help deal with the throng of civilians to be screened and processed as they exited the hospital. The big *LonWash* operative was not comfortable with crowd control, preferring to remain crouched behind his car as his colleagues attempted to stem the flow of bodies running out into the main road.

He rose to walk towards a policeman who had exited the patrol car and watched bemused as the man aimed an MP5 in his direction. The face resting on the pistol butt looked to be that of a young man in his early twenties with a wide-eyed stare that showed a mixture of shock and uncertainty.

Didn't the young fool realise the dangers of being bumped by the bodies barging past him? When this was over, he would have to get some of these youngsters into a training camp and teach them the correct way to deal with what his old SAS instructors had described as a "potential urban clusterfuck."

As the space between him and the SO19 officer began to clear, Carlisle looked in horror as the man closed his right eye. He was sighting on him!

"Stop!" His frantic shout seemed to evaporate into

nothingness. He thought he could see a discharge of smoke from the barrel of the weapon but knew that wasn't possible. At this short distance, a bullet would have reached him long before his brain could register the fine details.

He felt two sledgehammer blows to his chest, then a searing pain in his neck. He experienced an odd sensation of clouds spinning and whirling maniacally above him. He watched as they changed hue from blue to red before someone pulled a big black screen across the sky.

Chapter 45

THE AMBULANCE disappeared around a sharp bend, the swinging back door slamming hard against the side of a building. The driver fought the steering wheel, narrowly avoiding an oncoming estate car, before straightening the vehicle to tear off into the distance.

Devon was in full sprint, determined to keep sight of the black-and-yellow high top, but knowing that it was becoming a futile chase. His head felt as if a dozen workmen were going to work on him with pneumatic drills that were peeling away at his energy and sapping the strength from his legs.

He shouted over his shoulder, knowing that Doyle was not far behind. "Alan, get back to the entrance and bring one of the Range Rovers down here. Get someone to find out if there's another road exit from the site and see if we can plug the gap before the bastard breaks free."

Several minutes later he heard gunfire from somewhere to his rear. Had he miscalculated? Was Stratton still back in the hospital building? He shrugged off the thought and kept pounding on the tarmac.

He turned the corner where the ambulance had clipped the building. Far ahead he could see its brakelights as it disappeared around yet another corner and was lost to sight. He stopped to suck in some much-needed air, his hands resting on his knees as he tried to push a wave of nausea to one side.

He wasn't sure how long he remained like that. A screech of tyres brought him back to the moment and he lifted his eyes to see Doyle, sitting grim-faced behind the wheel of the Rover. He sprinted around to the passenger side and climbed in. "What, no witty remark about being out of shape?"

Doyle flung the car into gear and accelerated away before speaking. "Bad news, Mike. Bill Carlisle is down. Don't know if he's going to make it."

"How? Is Stratton still back there?"

"You're never going to believe it. He was shot by the fucking Metropolitan Police. Some rookie mistook him for our terrorist. This whole place is getting too cluttered and nobody knows who the fuck is doing what. Maybe we should just stand all our people down."

Devon kicked out at the vehicle dashboard. "It's too late for that. If we don't nail Stratton now there's no telling what he can still do. Put your foot down and catch up with that ambulance."

Chelsea Horgan had been the first to react to Bill Carlisle's shooting. She pulled out her CIA badge, held it above her head and raced towards the SO19 policeman. "Stop shooting. We're on your side. Lower you weapon."

The young officer was still trying to process her words when his colleague ran up behind him and gently nudged his arms down to his side. Satisfied the danger was over, Horgan rushed to Carlisle and bent down to stare at the blood pooling below his upturned head. She could hear the air rasping in the man's throat.

She unfastened her protective waistcoat, tore off her cardigan, and pressed the material firmly against a wicked-looking neck wound. It was only then she noticed two spent rounds sticking up through the fabric of Carlisle's bulletproof vest. Thank heavens for small mercies, she thought.

Without looking up she began to bark orders. "Someone get down to the hospital and whistle up an emergency team. Get a gurney up here and tell someone to get a theatre ready for an emergency operation."

She continued to press on the makeshift bandage and began whispering into Carlisle's ear. "Stay with us Bill. We're already at the hospital. What more could you want?" Despite her attempts to lighten the mood, her heart sunk as she watched Carlisle's eyes glaze over. She squeezed his arm. "Stay with us, damn you!"

She became aware of someone kneeling beside her and turned to look into Alan Doyle's anxious face. "What's happening? I thought you guys were in pursuit of Stratton?"

Doyle gently touched her hand. "We're still in the picture, but we need to get mobile again."

"I'm not letting go of this compress until the medical team arrives. You do what you have to but be careful."

Doyle rose and addressed the rest of the team. "I'm taking one of the vehicles into the hospital site. Cheadle, you and Mortimer grab the other one and head off in that direction," he said pointing to his right. "There's bound to be another entrance or exit farther down the road. See if you can head off an ambulance attempting to make use of it. We think Stratton's on board."

Chaos reigned on the Thames as the driveshaft on the *Maid of Inishfree* sheared off its central mounting and choked the engines with a backwash of exhaust fumes. The propellers stopped thrashing the water and an eerie silence descended, save for the odd sobs and screams of some of the terrified passengers.

Four heavily-armed marine policemen boarded the vessel and manhandled the innocent captain to the deck of his ship. He was clubbed on the back of his right ear and zip-tied at the arms and feet before two pairs of hands tore at his clothing in an attempt to recover any weapons or bomb-arming devices. The officers were not to know he was not the terrorist.

The same treatment was meted out to the cowering passengers. Until the police could be sure of their innocence, everyone was treated as if they posed an immediate and serious threat. Far from objecting to what was happening, the tourists seemed to catch the mood of the uniformed boarders and succumbed meekly to what they were ordered to do.

Six people had been flung from the vessel on its immediate impact with the protection barrier. Five marine divers in full scuba gear were already in the water attempting to bring them to safety, but the fast-flowing tidal stream was working hard against their efforts. Four people were already hauled into a circling recovery boat, a fifth would be saved within a matter of ten minutes.

The last passenger to be accounted for was a sixty-year woman who had been celebrating her wedding anniversary with a visit to London from New York. Her body would be recovered two miles downstream, but not for another twelve hours.

The marine policemen were not sure how to proceed. Eventually, the senior officer, an inspector with seven years' experience, decided to evacuate everyone from the *Maid of Inishfree*. If there was a bomb hidden somewhere on the cruiser, he reasoned he needed to clear the way for a bomb disposal team. The thing was there was no bomb disposal team – and he had no way of knowing if one was on the way.

A flotilla of small Marine Police boats began to ferry the passengers to the South Bank where the inspector had arranged a holding enclosure to contain everyone until a full screening process could be completed. He was not about to let a terrorist, masquerading as a tourist, simply walk away from the scene.

The exercise was completed within thirty minutes of the initial crash.

The inspector and two other officers now stood on

the deserted deck of the *Maid*. His next decision was to take the cruiser in tow, drag her to the centre of the river, and prepare her for scuttling in the event that a bomb disposal team didn't show up anytime soon. He would rather face the consequences of clogging the Thames rather than risk a detonation that could cause untold damage to the Palace of Westminster.

He ordered two extra anchors to be attached to the stricken vessel, knowing that the tides would help her to fight hard against her restraints. As soon as he stepped back on to dry land, he ordered the immediate closure of all roads and buildings in the area. Satisfied he had done as much as he could, he retired gratefully behind the cordon he had created, content to let someone higher up the chain decide what to do next.

He was surprised to be approached within minutes by the group leader of a Royal Navy bomb disposal squad that had arrived from Plymouth and had apparently been ordered into action over an hour previously. He arranged for the three-man team to be ferried out to the cruiser and waited for less than thirty minutes before they declared the area safe.

The crisis on the Thames was over.

Chapter 46

A NARROW ALUMINIUM pole covered in yellow fluorescent paint stretched across the entrance to the car park. As far as barriers were concerned it might as well have been a solid brick wall to the driver of the ambulance.

He hit the brakes hard, sending his back-compartment passengers crashing forward. The elderly woman in the gurney was thrown upwards but restrained by the leather straps folded across the bed. The other two occupants were not so fortunate. The nurse was flung against Stratton whose forehead slammed into the metal divider, causing a gash to open across his forehead.

He rubbed a smear of blood with the back of his hand and cursed. Then he pushed the barrel of the Beretta violently into the back of the driver's head. "You fucking idiot! What do you think you're doing?"

The man stammered. "I can't go any farther. There's a barricade in front of us."

Stratton couldn't believe what he was hearing. "Leave the engine running and get out. Do it now or I'll splatter your brains across the windshield."

As soon as the man reached for the door handle Stratton turned to the back of the ambulance. He flung open the rear door, jumped to the ground and raced to the front of the vehicle where the driver was standing sheepishly beside the opened door. Stratton walked forward, lifted the pistol, and clubbed him mercilessly several times on top of the head.

The man fell to the ground and Stratton used his body to step up into the cab. He placed the Beretta on his lap, meshed the gearstick, and depressed the accelerator to the floor. The ambulance shot forward, snapping the pole like a twig, and broke clear into a central driveway running between rows of neatly-parked cars.

A silver Mercedes, inching out of a side bay, was sent spinning by a jarring impact with the front offside of the ambulance as Stratton peered ahead for an exit onto the main road. He followed a sweep of white arrows painted on the road surface and several hundred yards ahead he could see another yellow pole reaching its arm across the road. Just a few more seconds and he would be clear.

He gripped the wheel tightly in anticipation of cracking against the pole, but as it turned out, that was not his main concern. A black Range Rover had suddenly swept into view across the entrance.

He kept his foot on the accelerator, smashed past the pole, and careered into the side of the *LonWash* vehicle.

Alfie Cheadle had spotted the ambulance as he sped up the main road outside the hospital grounds. Without hesitation he jerked the wheel sideways, bumped across a central reservation, narrowly missing the first of an oncoming stream of cars, and braked to a halt across the car park exit. His driver compartment took the full brunt of the impact, the sudden jolt whiplashing his head viciously to the left before he was caught on the seatbelt restraint. The violent rocking of the Rover tossed him back to the right, his head striking the plate-glass window with such force that it cracked and starred. Cheadle slumped unconscious.

Beside him, Bob Mortimer was quicker to react to the impending crash. As soon as their vehicle slid to a halt, he pushed open the passenger door and dived out onto the ground, rolling several times before he checked his momentum and ran back towards the cover of the front wheel arch.

The impact deployed the driver's airbag on the ambulance, but Stratton had already opened his door and jumped clear. He came quickly to his knees, with the pistol aimed directly at a space in front of the Rover's passenger-side windscreen. Before he had left the ambulance, he had seen Mortimer roll free and guessed what he would do next.

A second later Mortimer's head appeared; the eyes directed about two feet from Stratton's position. It was reasonable for Mortimer to assume the ambulance driver would still be behind the wheel. It was an assumption that would cost him his life.

Stratton fired twice, both rounds entering Mortimer's face just below his right eye.

Devon saw the execution as his vehicle slid round the final corner of the car park. He hit the passenger window's automatic button and leaned out to draw a bead on Stratton. There was a gap of less than fifty yards.

He shouted at Alan Doyle behind the wheel. "Aim straight for him and keep it steady."

Devon's arms swung wildly as he tried to steady them against the motion of the vehicle. The gun sight jumped from ground to sky and back again before he could centre it on Stratton, who was now standing and taking aim at the onrushing Range Rover.

"Watch out, Mike!"

The words had no sooner left Doyle's lips than a burst of automatic fire raked across his windscreen, the impact doing little more than dislodge a handful of chipped shards from the toughened polycarbonate surface.

Devon blotted out the danger and forced his mind into a Zen-like trance. Everything around him seemed to blur into a slow-motion haze that created a private tunnel between him and Stratton. It was almost as if everything was coming to a grinding stop, his arms suspended rock-steady, allowing the gunsight to rest unwaveringly in the centre of Stratton's chest.

Just as he squeezed the trigger, he became aware of the screeching sound of brakes as Doyle hit the pedal. The Range Rover slewed to the right, the tunnel disappeared, and for a moment Devon lost sight of Stratton.

He blinked in dismay as his bullets stitched a harmless line across the top of the tarmacked surface, a good ten feet from where Stratton was now running towards the car park exit. He watched him hand-vault across the other *LonWash* vehicle and heard a blare of horns as he ran out into the main road.

Devon cursed, threw open the door and set off in pursuit. He felt a spike of adrenaline flushing into his blood stream, delivering a burst of energy to tired legs and propelling him forward with the thrust of a one-hundred metre sprinter leaving the starting blocks. He knew it was not the thrill or excitement of the chase; it was a cold, ruthless determination not to let Stratton escape. One way or another, he would put an end to the madness of the past week.

He slowed to look at Cheadle slumped across the seat of his vehicle and prayed it was nothing more than impact trauma. He fought an urge to rip open the door and check for vital signs but knew he couldn't stop the pursuit. When he rounded the front of the barricaded Rover and saw what was left of Mortimer's face, his anger erupted in a blood-curdling scream.

Two hundred yards ahead he could see Stratton running down the centre of the busy street, waving his weapon at startled motorists. He knew if Stratton grabbed a taxi or commandeered a vehicle, he could disappear into the inner city lunchtime traffic. If that happened, the chances of picking up his trail again would be remote.

Doyle ran up behind him. "What are we waiting for?"

Devon flung an arm across the big man's chest in a gesture of restraint. "No, you stay here and see what you can do for Cheadle. I can take this bastard on my own."

Chapter 47

THE LAMBETH PALACE Road was beginning to clog with traffic, typical of a Friday afternoon on one of London's main tourist routes. It snaked along the South Bank of the Thames, sweeping in front of the main access to the historic Lambeth Palace, home to the Archbishop of Canterbury, the senior cleric of the Church of England, and onwards past the entrance to St Thomas Hospital and beyond to Westminster Bridge.

Stratton knew the location afforded a number of opportunities to melt into the background, not least by using the cover of an extensive garden area immediately adjacent to the large Lambeth Palace building. His first thought was to track through the garden and work his way back to Waterloo train station, barely two hundred yards from the rear perimeter.

He immediately dismissed the notion, reasoning there was bound to be increased security at one of the city's main passenger terminals. He decided instead to head for the Kensington area where he could hail a taxi, get himself across town, and regroup as far away from this area as possible. All he needed to do was find a large department store, make a number of purchases, and spend thirty minutes in its toilet area to transform his appearance. By nightfall he would be well away from London and heading for any one of a number of European destinations.

He sprinted from the road to the footpath leading past a small queue of tourists outside the palace gates. He slowed to a walk and glanced behind, his plans suddenly flying out the window at the sight of Mike Devon bounding down the central reservation. Another two minutes and the bastard would be onto him!

Stratton picked up his pace, scanning frantically ahead for an unwitting motorist parking a car or even hoping for the off-chance of a discarded bicycle - anything that would help him get the hell out of here. There was nothing.

He ran past the railed-off garden and saw a row of bars and restaurants directly ahead. He decided his best chance was to duck into one of the buildings and take a rear exit that was bound to lead to the vast sprawl of Kensington. There was no time to think further ahead. He crashed through the first door, ignored the startled looks, and raised the Beretta, firing two shots into a plasterboard ceiling.

He turned the gun on a startled woman behind the bar. "Where's the back door?"

She tried to speak, but the words wouldn't come. Instead she lifted her arm to point to an archway.

Stratton pushed his way past a row of tables, sending glasses and bottles flying as he fought to clear a path. Behind, he could hear the patrons scrambling for the front door.

Devon reached the end of the railings just in time to see Stratton run through a pub doorway. He heard the shots as he approached the entrance and was impeded as frightened people spilled out onto the pavement. He was forced to wait in mounting impatience until the last person flew past before taking a deep breath and stepping into the interior.

He held the Sig Sauer rock-steady in his right hand and began a slow sweep with his eyes. A woman was standing rigid with her hand pointed to the right, her eyes glazed over in shock. She bore all the symptoms of going into a catatonic trance.

Devon walked towards her, leant across the counter and slapped her firmly on the cheek. Her eyes refocused and her arm dropped to her side. "Best if you leave now, Miss," Devon told her.

He watched as she walked unsteadily towards the door and disappeared into the street. He turned his attention back to the archway where she had been pointing and noticed a small hallway that led to a push-bar security door. A small glimmer of light could be seen down one side where the door had failed to close automatically.

Devon moved carefully, checking into a recessed drinks alcove before lifting his foot and slamming the security door open. A walled yard stretched ahead of him, the place cluttered with stacks of empty beer crates and wheeled dustbins. A slight movement to his right caught his attention and he looked up to see Stratton atop a ten-foot wall, his knees bent as he prepared to launch himself to the other side.

Before Devon had a chance to aim his weapon, Stratton hurled himself off the wall and was gone from sight.

A mound of crates sprawled against the wall provided a makeshift ladder from the yard. Devon holstered his weapon and ran forward, planting his right foot on the edge of the bottom container and scaling up the rickety structure. The top crate slipped under his weight, but he had already grabbed for the top of the wall and was hanging on when the mound disappeared below him.

Straining every sinew, he fought his way to the top, hooked his right leg over the wall, and pulled himself into a sitting position. Instantly, he saw Stratton running along a grass verge at the back of the row of buildings, heading for a small footbridge that crossed a confusion of rail tracks stretching into the distance.

Devon dropped to the ground and took up the chase.

He reached a flight of concrete steps leading to the bridge in time see Stratton's head dip out of sight on the far side. He summoned up an additional reserve of energy and tore across the bridge at breakneck speed, his boots drumming a hollow beat on the wooden planks.

A second set of steps led down from the bridge to a pathway that arrowed directly towards a row of dilapidated sheds. Judging by a mountain of discarded wooden sleepers and two abandoned carriages lying forlornly outside the open doorways, the units were used as some sort of a service area for the nearby railyards. Stratton disappeared into the first opening.

From his vantage point Devon paused a moment longer, taking in the scene to the side and rear of the building, and decided to approach the area by skirting the sheds, using the sleepers as cover to get to the rear of the site unnoticed.

He ran as if his life depended on it and slid to a halt behind a low concrete wall overlooking a small rear exit door, less than twenty yards away. He retrieved his Sig, leaned across the wall, and aimed at the doorway.

Stratton's head appeared a few seconds later.

Devon fired twice, chipping shards of wood from the door frame and forcing Stratton back inside the shed.

A glance to his left told Devon he could now cover both ends of the building. Finally, he had his man trapped!

Chapter 48

THE INTERIOR OF the shed was strewn with the detritus of a railway chop-shop. Stratton noticed two carriage axel bases tossed haphazardly against piles of rotten wood, rusted and twisted sections of track and a mound of outdated tieplates and dogspike fasteners. One corner of the building was covered by a sloping hill of crushed stone that was once used as underbed ballast but was now clogged with dust and patches of dried cement. The air was rank with the smell of creosote and decay.

Stratton moved away from the rear door and found a small peep-hole that provided a view of Devon's position. He watched as his pursuer's eyes darted left and right - and that could only mean one thing. Devon had a bead on both doors. He needed to find an alternative exit.

He crossed to the far end of the shed but could find no openings. The timber-framed walls looked sturdy, although the chances were he could dislodge enough struts to climb through into the next unit. Even if Devon heard the sound of his efforts it would give him an edge. The big man would have to come out from behind his cover to pursue him – and that might just provide a more level playing field.

He stood back and aimed a kick at the wooden wall. To his horror it refused to budge. The solid timbers were reinforced at intervals by iron cross-girders which prevented any movement or flexibility in the structure. Apart from using a sledgehammer – and where do you find a sledgehammer when you need one? – there was no way of breaking through.

He made his way back to the other side, knowing time was not on his side. The longer Devon kept him pinned down the greater the chances of support arriving on the scene.

He wondered briefly if he could use his knife to widen the peep-hole enough to push his gun barrel through the gap. He dismissed the thought immediately, realising that even if he completed the task without Devon seeing him, he would be firing blindly with little hope of doing any real damage.

He was running out of options.

He had one last card to play. It was a long-shot, but he believed it might work. He walked back to the rear door, careful to stay inside the framework, and yelled a challenge.

"How about we settle this like men?"

There was a pause before a response came echoing back. "What exactly have you in mind?"

Stratton smiled. The idiot was taking the bait. "It's really rather simple. I toss out my weapon, step outside and we find out who's the better man."

From his vantage point Devon couldn't help but admire the gall of the man. He knew he could take Stratton but guessed there would be more to it than a simple case of unarmed combat. "Tell me, Carl, why should I give you a chance when you didn't offer the same courtesy to Dave Carpenter or Bob Mortimer or any of the other people who have come within your sick shadow. Why don't I just toss a few grenades over there and mop this up in time to go home and have supper with my wife?"

Stratton burst out laughing. "Come on, Devon. If you had grenades you would have used them by now. I'm betting this is so personal for you that you want to see the whites of my eyes when you kill me. Why deprive yourself of the pleasure?"

"Nothing doing. You've nowhere to go. I can afford to wait for back-up. You're right about one thing though and that's how much I'm looking forward to seeing you go down. I'll bet when the time comes, your eyes will betray you. I'll be looking into the frightened soul of a man who knows that what you tried to do has come to nothing. Allah will not be pleased with your feeble efforts. You can forget about having forty virgins waiting for you on the other side."

Stratton bristled at the taunt, but he fought to keep his emotions in check. "You know, Devon, if I were a betting man, I would say your reluctance to take me head-on has more to do with the fact that you're scared than because you think you hold all the aces. I'm conceding more than twenty years to you, but deep down you realise I'm the better man and it rankles that you won't be able to get the better of me. From where I stand, I've already won the fight."

Far from being stung by the words, Devon allowed himself a smile at the brazenness of the man. He reached a decision. "Okay, Carl, let's do it your way. Toss your weapon where I can see it and step out with your hands above your head."

Behind the cover of the doorway Stratton bent down to unclasp a Walther PPK from a strap around his right ankle. He tucked the weapon into the waistband at the base of his back, smoothed his jacket over it, and flung his Beretta out into the courtyard. Then he raised his arms and stepped out into the sunlight.

Devon ordered him to walk forward a few paces before he rose from behind the wall, his Sig aimed at Stratton's centre mass.

The two men glared at each other in silence for more than thirty seconds before Stratton broke the spell. "I'm taking a lot on faith here. What say you lose the Sig?"

Devon thought fleetingly about pulling the trigger. The man within his sights had come close to causing an untold number of deaths with his bombing campaign. He could not be allowed to live a second longer. But even as his finger squeezed down lightly on the trigger, he knew he couldn't do it.

He lowered the Sig and let it fall to the ground.

Alan Doyle felt a chilling sense of foreboding as he cradled Alfie Cheadle's head in the front of the crashed Range Rover. He was not unduly concerned about his young colleague, who was beginning to stir and trying to force himself away from the embrace. Doyle's thoughts were much farther away, somewhere down the Lambeth Palace Road where Devon was in reckless pursuit of one of the most dangerous opponents the agency had ever faced.

He didn't doubt for a moment his best friend could handle himself, or that he would allow Stratton to sucker him into a trap. Yet the feeling persisted. Something kept telling him this was a situation that would not end well. It was Devon who needed his help, not Cheadle.

He looked at the youngster and came to a decision. "You're gonna be okay but stay put and let someone take a look at that bump in your head. At the very least you've probably got concussion, so no heroics. Don't move from this seat until I get back."

Doyle clambered out of the vehicle, drew his Glock 19 to check for a chambered round, and bounded down the road in the direction Stratton and Devon had taken.

Ahead he could see a large crowd gathered on the pavement outside a row of pubs and made straight for them. He roughly grabbed the arm of a tall city gent, dressed in a three-piece pinstripe suit, and demanded to know what was happening.

"Some bloke ran in there," the man responded, pointing to the first door, "and began firing. Another guy with a gun arrived shortly afterwards and went inside after him."

Doyle sprinted for the door but was stopped by a woman sitting sobbing on a stone flower plinth. "I think they both went out the back door which is straight ahead when you go through the foyer."

Without hesitating, Doyle pulled open the door and stepped inside. He made his way carefully to the rear compound, noting the fallen stack of beer crates lying against the perimeter wall. He grabbed a wheeled dustbin, dragged it across the compound, and used it to scale the wall.

He looked both ways on the other side. To his left was nothing – just an open expanse of overgrown grass banks stretching for hundreds of yards along rail tracks leading to Waterloo station. The right side offered better options as an escape route, particularly a bridge that seemed to be the only way to cross to the distant area of Kensington.

Five minutes later he stopped to scan a spot with old sheds standing forlornly in an uneven row. His heart soared when he saw Devon step from behind a wall, his pistol aimed at a figure emerging from the rear of one of the buildings. It was Stratton, his legs spread apart in a defiant gesture, but his hands were hoisted in surrender.

Doyle was about to shout out to congratulate his boss when he saw Devon toss away his weapon. *Jeez, Mike, what are you doing?*

Chapter 49

STRATTON LOWERED his arms and smiled. At last he had his chance. He would dispense with this upstart and make a clean break, his mind already focussed on replenishing his stock of *Malponium 23* and returning someday to London to finish the job. Next time, he would make sure there would be no hiccups.

He stared at Devon, almost wishing he had time to see what the younger man was made of. He was forced to admit the *LonWash* operative was way better than he had expected – it was a misjudgement that had stymied him at virtually every turn, and one he would not repeat in the future. But now was not the time for grandstanding. It was time to move on.

Stratton made a show of gently removing his jacket. As his right arm cleared the sleeve, he moved it slightly behind him, his hand reaching out for the concealed Walther. If Devon detected the subtlety of the manoeuvre, there was nothing in his eyes to betray it.

Suddenly there was movement to his right. He turned to see the figure of Alan Doyle racing towards him, the black outline of a Glock held firmly at arm's length as he bore down on his position.

All three men seemed to want to speak at once. It was Stratton who shouted the first words. "I see you decided on getting some help. I might have known you didn't have the guts to face me in a fair fight."

Devon turned towards his friend. "Stand down, Alan. I've got this covered."

Doyle fumed. By now he was within twenty feet of Stratton, his gun pointing directly at the terrorist's head. "Fuck the macho bullshit, Mike. We came here to kill this fucker and that's what we're going to do."

Stratton's lips parted, but Doyle cut off his attempt to speak. "Not another word from you. Isn't it just typical that scumbags like are not prepared to play as fair....."

"I don't know what you're talking about," Stratton yelled back.

"Try this for size, asshole," Doyle said. "Your right hand is at a curious angle, almost as if you're trying to reach for a concealed weapon. So, here's the deal. In about two seconds from now I'm going to start shooting. You can use that time to try to draw your gun, or you can simply raise your arms and take what's coming to you like a man."

"What if I don't have a weapon?"

"Makes no difference. One way or another I'm going to kill you. I owe you for the lives of two good friends who deserve better than to watch from above as you get yourself some cushy cell with three square meals paid for by the very people you tried to blow off the face of the earth. It's not going to happen, Carl."

Devon nodded in appreciation of Doyle's words. As much as he wanted to play a primary role, he had to admit the big fella was making a decent job of putting Stratton firmly in his place.

Stratton switched glances between the two men, deciding immediately that the feral look on Doyle's face meant he would have to deal first with the ex-SAS man. He had read the dossier on Doyle. By any standard it made for some pretty impressive reading, including the time he had spent fighting the IRA alongside Devon. Talk about being between a rock and a hard place!

Stratton inhaled deeply, looked up at the bright blue London sky, and a newfound surge of resignation washed through him. What the hell? He had had a good life, one with few regrets. He thought about all the things he had accomplished, particularly his early days as a paid assassin for the British Government. It was a pity he would not be around to see this country brought to its knees, but others would come forward to take his place and finish his mission.

Finally, he thought about his mother and about Manfred Stelling, the only two people he had ever really cared for. He looked forward to seeing them again.

His hand moved in a blur of motion and he smiled as his fist wrapped around the butt of the Walther.

That was as far as he got.

Doyle opened fire, his first two bullets slamming into Stratton's forehead. A fist-sized exit hole appeared at the back of his head, his eyes already closed by a death spasm that sent the body backwards onto the concrete.

Doyle wasn't finished. He walked forward, firing continuously into the lifeless torso. By the time Devon sprinted to stop him, he had loosed off another five shots, all of which had found their target.

The two friends looked down in silence at what was left of Carl Stratton. Across the expanse of waste ground the blare of a dozen sirens could be heard rolling over the rooftops as the first of the response vehicles screeched to a halt on the Lambeth Palace Road and signalled a fitting end to London's high state of alert.

Devon put his arm around Doyle's shoulder. "I'm glad to see you, big man, although I had things covered."

Doyle snorted. "Yeah, you left yourself unarmed while that bastard was planning to fry your ass with a concealed weapon. What were you thinking about? That was the oldest trick in the book."

Devon stepped away, reached around to pull a Glock from behind his back, and waved it in Doyle's face. "You don't think two can play at that game?"

The two men burst out laughing and hugged each other in a tight embrace.

Chapter 50

THE MAN WHO stepped out of a taxi and made his way up a small flight of concrete steps to the door of an upmarket townhouse in Cheltenham didn't rate a second glance from the resident population. Dressed in a John Lewis three-quarter-length wool overcoat, buttoned over a Saville Row suit he looked a lot like the doctors, lawyers and successful businessmen who usually strode the pavement outside this crescent-shaped Victorian corner of real estate that was the domain of the mega rich.

If push came to shove, he could have measured his bank account against many of the property owners. Unlike them, however, he had accumulated his wealth during a life of crime, a career that was littered with dead bodies rather than underscored by successful business deals.

The same could be said of the man he was visiting, an underworld fixer who had grown fat, physically as well as figuratively, from the misery of others. They were a perfect match.

Dragan Boskovic swung a small attaché case in his right hand as he reached the landing on the top step. Before he had a chance to press a small amber-lit button recessed into the wall, an electronic beep sounded, and the door rolled noiselessly inward. A voice boomed from the interior of the house.

"Third door on your right at the end of the hallway."

Boskovic's leather-soled shoes made a sharp echoing sound on the parquet floor as he walked forward to pause in the open doorway. In one corner of the room he could see a large, florid-faced man wedged into an armchair that seemed to be straining under his immense weight. A small coffee table was littered with plates of leftover delicacies.

Boskovic thought briefly about telling the man to stay away from the chocolate biscuits and get some exercise. Instead he said simply: "Did you get everything I asked for?"

"It wasn't easy. This was a rush job which incurred more expenses than I'm used to. You do realise I have to protect my profit margins?"

"Yeah," Boskovic retorted drily. "I noticed your fee was larger than normal."

"Speaking of which?" The bushy eyebrows rose to emphasise the question.

Boskovic held out the attaché case and watched in amusement as his host swept a chubby arm across the coffee table, sending an array of crockery onto an expensive Persian rug. He grabbed at the case and used his thumbs to push two lock-bars. The lid sprang open to reveal neat stacks of twenty-pound notes crammed into the interior.

"I will do you the courtesy of not counting it." He closed the case and reached under a cushion to retrieve a small brown envelope. "The address is inside along with a key. The vehicle was purchased brand-new and has been modified to your specifications. Everything you asked for is neatly stored away in a box in the interior. The van is parked on level three in a multi-storey car park. We chose a spot away from the security cameras. I believe that concludes our business."

Boskovic grabbed the envelope, tucked it into his coat pocket, and turned without saying another word.

Thirty minutes later he squatted inside a Peugeot Bipper van and studied the contents of a large wooden box. He spent less than forty seconds reassembling the components of a lightweight Russian-made Dragunov SVD sniper rifle, finishing the assembly by screwing a six-inch telescopic sight into the barrel arm and sliding a pouch of ten 7.62mm cartridges into a rectangular magazine slot.

He changed quickly into workman's overalls, pulled back a divider partition, and clambered into the front compartment. He shoved the key into the ignition slot, his mind already focussed on what lay ahead.

Professional pride had brought him back to London. When the bomb he had planted in Mike Devon's house failed to do its job it was the first professional failure of his career. In his profession such things are not tolerated. The world of the assassin is a small marketplace, where reputations dictate fees and where there was no room for excuses. He needed to put things right.

Deep down he knew there was also a personal dimension to his decision. He had watched Devon through his binoculars shortly before booby-trapping the front door of his house. He had marked his target as a highly-capable individual, someone whose death would mean more than all the others that had gone before.

He turned the key, eased the van into the arrowed exit lane, and prepared for the short drive to Charterhouse Street, home of *LonWash Securities*.

Beer bottles clinked together as a dozen men raised a toast in a cubicle at one of London's fashionable pubs. The sombre mood of the funeral they had just attended - their second in two days - was lifted by the age-old soldiers' tradition of celebrating the life of fallen comrades.

General Sir John Sandford led the eulogies. Two weeks after his discharge from hospital he was back in full swing, determined to honour the men who had made the ultimate sacrifice in defence of their country. He stood proud and erect as he raised a half-filled whiskey glass towards the ceiling.

"Gentlemen," he began, "let's not forget that but for the efforts of Dave Carpenter and Bob Mortimer this city might well be a wasteland today. Heaven knows how many hundreds of families have been spared from grieving for loved ones. Those of us still standing are here because of the unselfish determination of two great warriors, men whose names must remain concealed from the public they served, but whose dedication and example will shine forever as a beacon for every man and woman who chooses to pick up a weapon and stand to post.

"These are men who make democracy what it is. History has taught us there are always heroes ready to step up to the plate. I'm reminded today of the words attributed to the eighteenth-century philosopher, Edmund Burke, who said: *The only thing necessary for the triumph of evil is that good men do nothing.*"

The General paused momentarily. "Evil did not triumph simply because we had men of courage prepared to do what was necessary. I give you Dave Carpenter and Bob Mortimer. I give you two good men."

When the toast was completed, Sandford remained on his feet waiting for the noise of celebration to settle down. "There are two more things I need to report. You will be glad to hear that Bill Carlisle is making a full recovery. Indeed, I had a deuce of a job keeping him away today, but he'll be back to work within a few weeks.

His words were greeted with another round of cheering. He signalled for quiet. "The second thing I have to tell you is that I met with the PM yesterday and he has asked me to convey his thanks and gratitude to all of you. Our role in the events of the past few weeks has naturally been airbrushed from official records, but the highest compliment that can be paid is that we have been given a green light, not to mention an increased budget, to continue doing what we do best."

Later, as the group spilled out onto the pavement, Devon and Doyle walked with Sandford towards his chauffeur-driven limousine. "Mind giving us a lift back to the office? There's something I need to discuss with you," Devon told him.

The men settled in the spacious rear interior of the Rolls-Royce Phantom, the General sitting opposite his two senior operatives. He waited until the car eased into the traffic flow before speaking. "Let's have it, Mike. I know there's something you need to get off your chest."

Devon had rehearsed the speech on a dozen occasions over the past few days but skipped his well-prepared preamble. "I'm not sure I want to continue. I've been doing this for a long time and I need a break. I have a wife and son to consider, two people who need me at home doing a regular job rather than running around the world risking my neck and putting their futures in jeopardy. I want a normal life and I think I've earned the right to have a crack at it."

The words came as little surprise to Sandford. He had known for some time of Devon's desire to be taken out of the firing line and had been preparing for the moment of truth. "Listen, my boy, I respect you too much to spin you a line of waffle. There's no argument that you *have* earned the right to do whatever is best for you and your family. I will not stand in the way of that happening."

"Thank you, sir, I appreciate your understanding."

Sandford leaned forward. "However, I do have a proposition for you. Take a month off, go visit your friend Claude in the South of France, and come back here to a different role within *LonWash*. Come back as my successor."

Devon stared wide-eyed at his boss. "Your successor? I don't understand."

"Let me explain. The PM wants me in a more central role within the COBRA anti-terrorist committee. I have to admit that being the co-ordinator for all the agencies is something that appeals to me. I will finally get the opportunity to put a few much-needed reforms into practice, as well as being able to watch out for the interests of *LonWash*. We could do good things between us."

Devon shook his head. "I'm no diplomat. I can't see myself running around acting as a buffer in the way you do, Sir. It wouldn't work."

"Nonsense!" The General's retort was louder than he intended. "You let me worry about all the political handholding and backslapping. That'll still be my job. Your job will be to see that *LonWash* is honed into a lean, mean fighting machine ready to face up to the new challenges coming over the horizon. Best of all, you get to do it on a nine-to-five basis and go home to your family every evening."

He switched his attention to Alan Doyle. "You will take over as senior operative in place of Mike."

Doyle shot forward in his seat. "With the greatest respect, sir, you're out of your mind. It's a total non-starter and there's nothing you can say that will change my mind."

Sandford smiled. "I thought maybe the prospect of working permanently alongside a certain red-haired ex-CIA agent was something you would relish."

Doyle's reply was almost incoherent. "Do you...are you...is this about Agent Horgan...she's back in America....we haven't seen her for two weeks...and...and what do you mean by ex-CIA?"

Sandford slapped Doyle's knee. "I spoke to Agent Horgan before she was recalled for a thorough debrief. Seems she likes it here and likes it even more when she's working with you. I've pulled a few strings and she's now a full card-carrying member of *LonWash Securities*, if you'll have her, of course. Her flight from Washington landed just over an hour ago."

Doyle looked across at Devon. Both had wide-eyed stares, each lost in his own thoughts about what had just happened. The interior of the Rolls-Royce was engulfed in silence for the last mile of the journey back to Charterhouse Street.

Chapter 51

CHELSEA HORGAN was grateful for the taxi driver mistakenly dropping her off at the lower end of Charterhouse Street. The half-mile walk would do her good. She needed to get her circulation rebooted after a seven-hour flight, but most of all, she needed time to rehearse what she was going to say to Alan Doyle.

She had experienced a whirlwind of mixed emotions over the past few weeks. The prospect of uprooting her life had caused a few sleepless nights until finally she had contacted General Sandford with an answer to his offer of a new job. The work being done by *LonWash* appealed to her sense of independence and the desire to be at the cutting edge of the fight against international terrorism. Unlike the Bureau, she would not be hamstrung by the paperwork and chain-of-command petty infighting that had characterised so many of her assignments. The constant glare of Congressional oversight was setting the Bureau back fifty years at a time when it needed to be at its operational peak.

The *LonWash* operation was a different kettle of fish. She admired the way the agency saw what had to be done and went full-tilt after it. It was a place that would challenge her full range of abilities, somewhere she believed she could actually make a difference. In the end it was a challenge she could not walk away from.

She had convinced herself it was for all those reasons she had decided to take the job. Deep down she knew the tipping point was Alan Doyle. He had gotten under her skin. Her time back in America had been empty without him. She was in love with him. There, she had finally admitted it.

She was pretty sure he felt the same way, but what

if he rejected her? What if actually working together led to a wedge being driven between them? Could their feelings for each other cause a mission to be compromised? Would the Agency frown on a relationship the same way the CIA did?

The only way she would know was by having a heart-to-heart with Doyle. She would look him straight in the face and tell him what was on her mind. She was trained to read reactions. She would spot a hesitation. She would know if there was future for them.

Her thoughts seemed to bear down on her as she walked along Charterhouse Street, pulling a wheeled suitcase behind her. She took no notice of a dark-blue Peugeot van parked at the kerbside less than four-hundred yards from the *LonWash* entrance ramp, although her attention was drawn to a familiar silver-coloured Rolls-Royce that was approaching from the opposite end of the road.

She watched as it purred to a stop and disgorged two instantly-recognisable figures. Her heart soared at the sight of Doyle, standing, as he always did, slightly on his left side, as if to hide his prosthetic right arm.

Dragan Boskovic came alert instantly at the sight of the Rolls-Royce. He moved onto his knees and rested his head against the side of the tripod-mounted Dragunov, his right eye sliding over the telescopic sight, already pointed through the vehicle's tinted rear window. It was a window that was not made of glass, but from a special compound of sugar, the sort used by movie special-effects teams. It would disintegrate on impact and cause no deviation to the intended trajectory of the bullet.

He was less than two hours into a vigil that he believed would probably stretch into days. This was a job for a patient man, and Boskovic prided himself on being the very essence of patience.

He knew he would have to go through this ritual

every time a vehicle came anywhere close to the *LonWash* building. It was better to be prepared than to miss a golden opportunity. If Devon was in any of the vehicles it would likely slow before making the turn into the ramped entrance. He would have less than a second to make the shot. It was all the time he would need.

His ammunition had been reconfigured to armour-piercing capability. The heavy-duty round would burrow through reinforced safety-glass and find its target.

He was ready for all eventualities, but not the one that now presented itself. He could scarcely believe his luck when the big car stopped at the entrance and his target stepped out alongside another man he didn't recognise. The target even waited there while he appeared to carry out a conversation with someone still in the vehicle. *This was too easy!*

The crosshairs inched across to Mike Devon's head. It was a full sideways view, with the axis of the scope's two lines resting neatly on Devon's left ear. All he needed to do was squeeze the trigger.

Horgan was about to wave her left arm to get Doyle's attention when she noticed the small movement of the Peugeot van. It was no more than a miniscule rocking motion, but it was enough to catch her attention. Someone was moving inside the vehicle!

Horgan was on the pavement directly midway along the van. She didn't know why her danger-radar had kicked in, only that something wasn't right. She stared ahead at Doyle and Devon, her emotions frazzled by indecision.

She wasn't carrying a weapon which had been surrendered to the CIA when she left the service. She did the only think she could think off. She hoisted her suitcase, stepped around to the rear of the vehicle, and slammed it hard against the window. At the same time she screamed at the top of her voice. "Get down!"

The suitcase flew through the window as if it wasn't there. She could see the outline of a man crouched over a sniper rifle, which took the full force of her case and rocked on its tripod. The gunman fell back, but not before he squeezed the trigger and filled the air with a staccato crack that echoed off the buildings.

Boskovic knew the bullet had missed the target. Even before he had sent it on its way, the eyepiece jerked upwards and he felt the impact of something heavy slamming against the side of his head. The last squeeze on the trigger was a convulsive reflex rather than a carefully-designed act of professionalism.

He looked up to see a redheaded woman standing outside the shattered window. He had no way of knowing who she was or why she had decided to do what she did. A murderous scowl twisted his face and he rose to disconnect the rifle from the tripod. The bitch would pay for her interference!

He pushed open the rear door and jumped into the street cradling the Dragunov, his arms swivelling for a sight of the redhead who had ducked to the side of the vehicle.

His anger was so intense that he failed to register the approaching sound of pounding feet. The woman was all that mattered. He found her running to the front of the van, her back presenting an easy target as she scrambled for safety.

Devon and Doyle needed little time to grasp what was happening. They heard the scream and watched in amazement as Horgan hurled her case into the back of the van. They ignored the rifle report and were already running by the time Boskovic leapt from the rear of the vehicle.

Realising the danger Horgan had put herself in, Doyle ran like a man possessed. He was still a hundred yards away when he saw the gunman track Horgan to the side of the van. It was too far to be sure of an accurate shot, but he needed to do something. He raised his Glock and began firing wildly in the gunman's direction, more in the hope of distracting him than in taking him down.

He watched helplessly as the gunman ignored the rounds whizzing around him and brought his weapon to bear on the front of the vehicle. He was aware of Devon brushing past him at full tilt before stopping thirty yards ahead to steady his Sig.

A single shot rang out.

The gunman appeared to freeze in position. Then Doyle saw the big rifle fall to the ground. The man crumpled sideways against the van before sliding to the pavement. *Jeez, Devon had made the shot!*

The two men bolted towards the vehicle, Devon stopping to make sure the gunman was dead. An exit wound dead centre of the forehead told him he was.

Doyle ran past to find Horgan sprawled across the bonnet. She looked up and smiled. He grabbed her in his arms and kissed her. She pulled away and looked into his eyes. "I remember once hearing someone say in a movie that relationships that start under intense circumstances never last."

"Yep," Doyle responded with a smile, "but here's the good news. Sandra Bullock was not a redhead and I'm no Keanu Reeves. I think our relationship will stand up to whatever's thrown at it."

"Oh, so we *do* have a relationship?"

"We most certainly do."

Devon found them in a passionate embrace but pretended not to notice. "Our friend back there is Dragan Boskovic, the last of the assassins to be accounted for. Guess that means I'm leaving you with a clean slate.

"Hold on a minute," Doyle said as he disentangled himself from Horgan. "Does this mean you're definitely going to leave the agency?"

"No, it means I'm heading to France for a holiday. I'll leave you to clean up this mess and get things shipshape by the time I return. I can promise you I'll be more hands-on than the General was, so make sure there's no slacking."

Doyle frowned. "I don't remember agreeing to take over as chief bottlewasher."

Devon looked at him, then at Horgan. "Yeah, you did that about five seconds after it was offered to you. It just needed a good-looking former CIA operative to make you realise it."

"So, when did *you* decide to take up the General's offer?"

Devon laughed. "The moment I knew you were suckered in I couldn't just walk away. Someone has to keep an eye on you."

Doyle shrugged his shoulders in mock resignation. "So, nothing changes. I still have to take orders from you?"

"Perish the thought! I may make a few suggestions from time to time, but you're on your own when it comes to operational matters. Look on the bright side; your team is much better than the one I had!"

Devon watched in amusement as Doyle processed the remark. "Here's my first suggestion. Despite what I said earlier, we don't yet have a clean slate. Track down Jurgen Kappel and Dieter Neumann and see they pay for their part in this whole sorry mess."

"You can bank on it."

He patted Doyle on the shoulder, turned and walked away, his mind already drifting to visions of a holiday in the South of France.